I0645275

ELLE

···

KAITLIN PUCCIO

Bent Frame Publishing
NEW YORK, NY

Copyright © 2015 by Kaitlin Puccio.

All rights reserved. No part of this publication may be reproduced, distributed, or transmitted in any form or by any means, including photocopying, recording, or other electronic or mechanical methods, without the prior written permission of the Publisher, except in the case of brief quotations embodied in critical reviews and certain other non-commercial uses permitted by copyright law.

Publisher's Note: This is a work of fiction. Names, characters, places, and incidents are a product of the author's imagination. Any resemblance to actual people, living or dead, or to businesses, companies, events, institutions, or locales, is purely coincidental.

www.bentframepublishing.com

Elle/ Kaitlin Puccio.
ISBN 978-0-9964329-6-2
Library of Congress Control Number 2020949778

For Elle and Lui

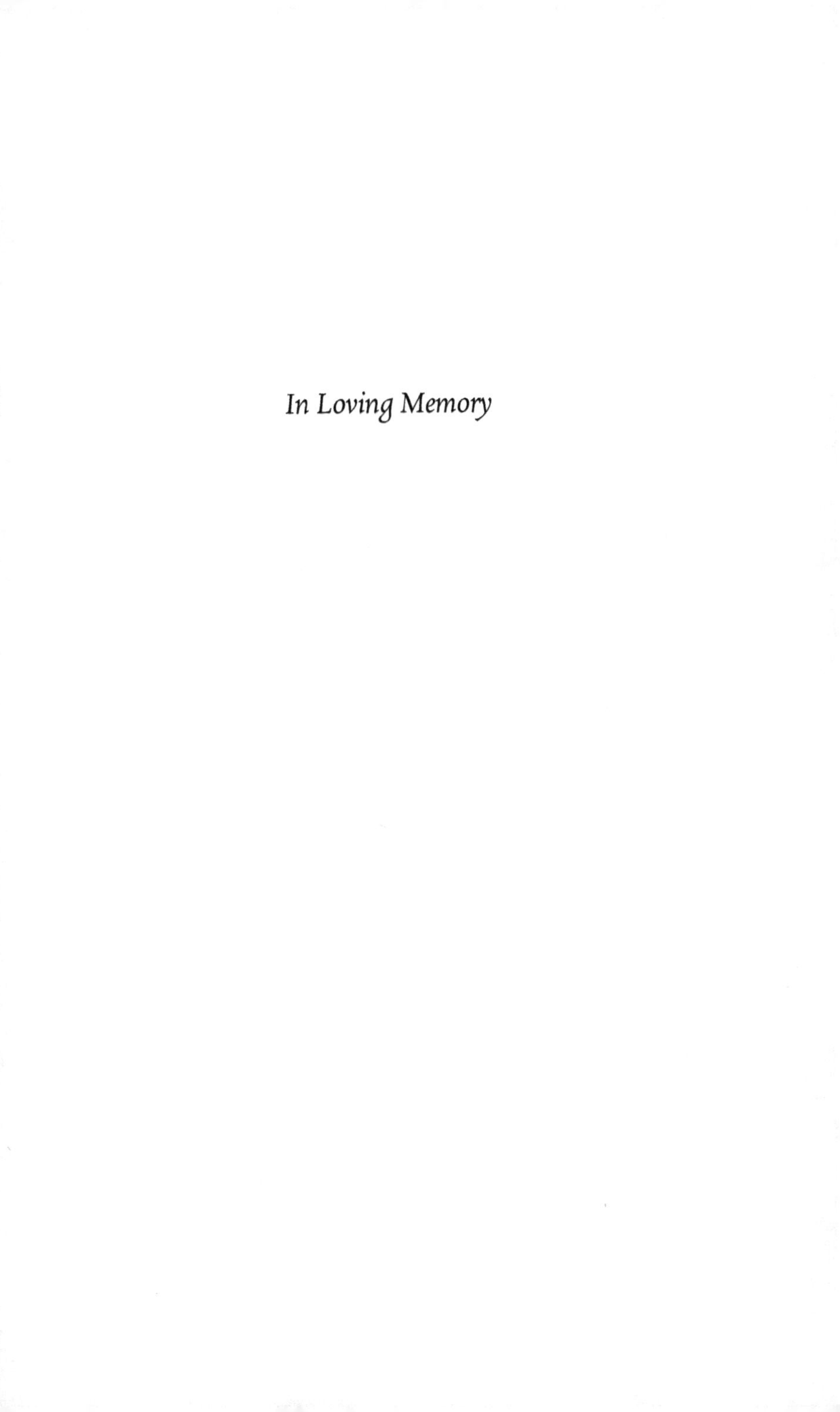
In Loving Memory

....

The wooden bench where he sat was rotting away as quickly as the autumn. Lee observed. He wondered how he looked from behind, his head sunken in his wide, coated shoulders. An empty figure staring at the swing set across the hardened field. Cars curved behind him, their exploratory headlights peering in through the slits of the closed shades of ground-floor apartments. The audible wave of displaced air silhouetted Lee and cascaded into the sleeping park, then retreated, curling low around his ankles with a steaming hiss.

Ahead, a bundled child giggled in time with the patterned grunts of the swing. She passed in and out of Lee's focus as the pendulum—as he saw it—hurried her dutifully through the trough. It didn't matter whether she was moving forward or backward. She looked the same. At any point she looked the same. It was the progression from one point to another that told her direction. But she was frozen at infinite points between points. Forward, or backward. Lee couldn't tell.

On the outskirts of the park he sat balancing along the line between the darkening park and the street. An undefined limbo between two definites. Lights flicked on around him, one by one. Dusk. He thought nothing of it. He thought instead of his legs, numb from hours atop the frozen bench. Twelve years before and years before that Lee would have peeled them away from the rimy bench and walked himself toward warmth. He would have taken himself just around the corner to the small coffee shop where he was often the only patron, that only had counters at which to stand instead of tables and chairs. Or to the library next to his lab where the heat was so abundant that it was suffocating. Perhaps he would have strolled a little farther into the museum café, which he would have forgotten closed early on Sundays, redirecting him to the warmth of his own home.

His wife Allie—simple, lovely Allie—would have cookies or muffins keeping warm in the oven. She hated to cook, but baked something new every week.

The oven hot behind her, she would sit at the kitchen table with a novel and a pen, preparing for her lecture at university the following day. A small fire would be nearly dying in the next room. Hot tea with milk would be waiting for him to come home, even though he preferred his tea black. He never said anything. Allie would always put milk out, just in case. Plus, she would argue, the milk creamer came with the set.

He would have.

But now. He wouldn't move now. The thought of standing was overwhelming enough. Sunday evenings were not meant for such labor. He would stand when it required no effort. And so he sat.

The child on the swings had endless lungs for laughter. With every push from her young mother she soared higher, her mittens gripping the rusted chains that squeaked out disregarded pleas to be left alone. Lee frowned. The discord was most unwelcome.

Through the chains of the swing set he spotted two figures in the distance. The descending night obscured their features. Though their shapes were only black cutouts against the trees, Lee recognized his elderly but able neighbor, Walter, walking adoringly with his much younger companion. Elle. She clung to his arm and strolled beside him, a dutiful smile painted across her face. Lee stilled his breath, not blinking lest he miss a moment. His frigid legs started to burn as the blood pumped faster through each vessel in his body. Each pulse he noticed. Each one burned.

Elle approached, her sinewy arms wrapped around Walter's. They took long, slow steps together. Elle's slender legs moved as one. As if there were no right and left, but only a single limb cut in half, an invisible connector between them rolling her energy seamlessly from one half to the other.

An unnatural pairing, thought Lee as he watched Walter step synchronously with Elle. He wondered if Walter thought the same.

Elle looked up, near enough to catch Lee watching her through the swings. She stared back at him.

His eyes were in line with hers but were unfocused, as if strings run through from the back of his head connected the center of his pupils with Elle's, and his irises were lolling lifelessly on top of them. Resisting the urge to wave, Elle acknowledged him curiously with a slight tilt of her pretty head, then smiled once again at Walter as they strode past out of the confines of the park.

She wondered—hoped—if Lee had known that she would be there. But no. If he had, he wouldn't have gone himself. She glanced quickly back at Lee, catching a pitiable expression on his face that was a combination of emotions she couldn't quite place.

Lee attempted a smile too late and with great effort. He knew as he watched Elle walk away that the expression he had produced was closer to a wince than a smile. The cracking of the dry skin in the wrong places on his face told him as much. He was despondent.

A single leaf tiptoed past his feet with a slight breeze. He saw that the swing set had been abandoned without his noticing. It swung loosely back and forth, relieved, its chains hanging limply. His eyes scanned the park and settled their gaze on the mother and the child with endless lungs walking toward the gate. The child laughed still as it bounded forth. When they were gone he would be alone, sitting on the outside of the blackening park.

The night had rushed in quickly but stealthily, fooling his eyes into thinking that they could still see. He looked out at the flat, desolate land before him, the hard pavement of the playground, the solid wintry dirt instead of grass.

He felt the cold.

Despite protests from both the bench and his bones, he stood. The steady waters of his limbo, disrupted. For a moment he did not move, allowing the stillness of the dividing line between the park and the street to settle back into its place. After warmth filled his legs he started walking in the opposite direction of Walter and Elle, hearing the pattern of the swing, nearly still after the abandonment of the child, grow quieter as he entered town.

....

TWO

The wind picked up quickly when the night had fully settled in. Lee cut through the small, lively, cobblestone streets to the quieter side of town where he lived. He approached his block, a large cul-de-sac lined with identical, unattached brownstones standing at evenly placed points around the loop. Each had a third-floor terrace that sat atop the rounded bay window of the second floor, and a staircase that led to the raised front door. The roundness of the houses coupled with the curvature of the street itself gave Lee the impression of living in a fishbowl. A dead end where there were no straight lines and watchful eyes around every bend.

It was a cozy block despite its great size, with streetlamps and benches and small, even, branchy trees that never seemed to grow or die. Lee kept his hands in his pockets, muting his movements as he slinked down his block. His head was buried in the upturned collar of his trench, his eyes cast down as he passed Elle's house only a few doors from his own. Without lifting his head, he glanced sideways and saw a slight break in the blinds.

Elle.

His heart leapt but he stifled his movements, which became suddenly uncoordinated. He wanted to walk faster, to be out of sight behind the closed door of his own home, but his legs had become stiff under her gaze. He felt like he wasn't moving at all, as if a slow paralysis were creeping upward from his feet and blooming throughout his entire body. He forced his legs to take the last few steps toward his house, jammed the key into the lock and slipped briskly inside, having just barely opened the door wide enough to fit.

THREE

....

Peeking out from inside her dimly lit but inviting home, Elle watched Lee pass by. His movements were too heavy for a man only in his fifties. His brow was knitted tightly together, his eyes smoldered even against the dark sky. She breathed carefully as if he could hear her from outside where he walked.

He glanced quickly up at her without moving his head. She let the blinds go. They snapped back together softly, having only been separated an inch. For too long after, she stood motionless in front of the window fearing that she had been seen. Could he see her shadow projected onto the blinds? She should have kept the lights off.

When she was sure that Lee had passed, and even after minutes of standing behind the closed blinds being quite sure that he had, she lifted her arm and twisted the blinds hard to be sure that they were fully shut. She was both relieved and saddened that Lee had passed without incident. It was the way it was to be.

FOUR

....

Lee still felt Elle's eyes watching him, even after he was inside. He noticed, as he always did, not any single scent that he could pinpoint, but a decided lack of aroma emanating from his empty oven. There were no muffins. No lit wood in the fireplace burning off the smell of cold, no hot tea waiting for him. No wife. The absence of the aromas, of the warmth from the fire, alerted his senses. He noticed the absence of sensory stimuli as often as he noticed its presence. It was involuntary. But he had become accustomed to soaking in the features of absence as if it were palpable.

Unlike the curves of the brownstone's exterior, the interior was all straight lines. Everything was meticulously placed. There were no colors. No pets, no plants. No signs that the house was in use.

No wife.

Straight ahead, the four chairs around the square kitchen table were aligned precisely across from each other. It was an open, eat-in kitchen. Two concepts that Allie used to argue were mutually exclusive. Can you be "in" something that's open? That has no walls around to create the space which, when entered, could be called "in"?

To the left, directly across from the fireplace on the far wall, sat the couch in the living room. The back of it acted as a partition, the fourth wall, creating a closed square of a room. To the right, the staircase. Measured and placed so that it stood at an equal distance from the couch as the couch from the fireplace. Such specificity created a symmetry that Lee required of his surroundings. He didn't notice it, but if it had been done improperly—if the fireplace had not been centered between the two windows on the far wall—he would notice it every day. Every inch it was off would throw him. Of his own balance he would be uncertain. The tilt of the floor underneath his feet he would question. He wouldn't know why, or where his unease in space had originated, but he would feel it. His body before his mind would perceive the imbalance, and he would become acutely aware of his surroundings at all times, of his ruffled equilibrium, unable to focus on his work.

His work required focus.

The open layout of the downstairs felt large and empty to Lee. He walked up the polished wooden stairs into his study, not bothering to turn on any lights. The stairs hadn't moved. He had walked up and down them countless times before. His body knew where they were in relation to the front door. How many bottom steps there were before he would reach the platform, where he would turn right and walk up three more steps to the second floor. He didn't need lights.

His study was stacked with papers, textbooks, half-empty coffee mugs—but never near the books. He liked the idea of coffee more than the coffee itself. He tended to set it down and forget about it as it cooled, immersed in his work.

The garbage can was overfilled, but only with papers. Crumpled sheets balanced on top in an impossible heap.

Lee shut the door behind him. He always shut the door behind him. The open, empty house on the other side made him feel uncomfortable. Vulnerable. He felt most at ease in a small room with no windows and only one door. His study had windows, but he didn't mind. He knew those windows.

He shuffled toward his desk in the dark and clicked on the small table lamp. The room yellowed. His desk sat between the door and the windows on the far adjacent wall. It faced into the room, the chair placed so that nothing could fit behind it. He sat. From it he could see the entire room. The door. The windows. It wasn't a large room, but his chair sat in the only place in the room from which he could see the room entirely. The desk was large for his study and looked larger because it wasn't against a wall. Never would he have put it against a wall, his back to the open room. He had once considered putting it on the opposite wall, so that he would face the door instead. But, he realized, if someone were to open that door, he would need for it to open more than halfway before he could see who it was from that angle. With his desk next to the door, at the slightest crack he could look to the right and see a face. Sitting that close to the door made him uneasy sometimes. Sometimes he thought it might be best to sit at the farthest point from the door. But that was why he kept it closed. A closed door quelled his irrational thoughts and allowed him to focus on his work.

His work demanded a closed door.

Before him was a mess of papers. It wasn't a mess, really. He knew what every paper was and every paper had its place, even if that place was not in any specific pile or stack.

His mind was idle, his hands stinging from being taken out of the cold. He thought once again of the horrific wince with which he had returned Elle's nod, and shifted shamefully in his chair. What she must think!

His fingers grasped the corner of a page buried beneath a notebook. He knew what page it was, had stared at it many times before. Memorized it. And yet, he looked again. A large, horizontal photograph showing Elle surrounded by a group of scientists. His scientists. He tried not to, but spotted himself in the photograph immediately, looking lost with his halfway-smile alongside the rest of the beaming team. Without thinking, the same words popped into his head as always. *There's me.* What a curious statement it was. Wasn't it an intrinsic part of being a "me" to be "here" rather than "there"?

Indeed, "there" he had been only a year ago, the first sign of the grimace he could barely muster in response to Elle's smile stretching its wings before the lens. He should have been elated. It had been a remarkable success, a brilliant creation. But he hadn't felt the lightness of elation in over a decade, and would only know how to greet it with discomfort if it were to encroach now. There she stood only a year ago in the middle of them all, with her long dark hair and blood-filled lips: their first Artificial Intelligence.

At the time, Cordova Laboratories was already researching plans to create sophisticated artificial intelligence systems that would act as companions to the elderly. They would be able to converse just as humans would converse, processing what was said to them and formulating a response. Curl their fingers as a human would curl her fingers. They would present as if they were living humans. Their capabilities would make them ideal for older widows and widowers who still had life left in them, who could still take care of themselves and be present in the world, but were fading away, disappearing into loneliness, simply becoming bodies in the world waiting to decay.

They'd had the funding and had already been working on the technology years before Lee brought his idea to Frank.

Frank had been a good friend of Lee's since they met at university while pursuing their PhDs. It was a top, modern school in a densely populated country town that boasted the most sought-after researchers in England. Though it offered more than studies in science and technology, that was the main draw of the school.

The outskirts of the campus were surrounded by life, but its sprawling lawns and gothic architecture often made Lee feel a separation, both of time and place, between the school and the surrounding town. There was rarely a need or desire to leave campus, though perhaps that was because there was rarely time to spare.

Frank and Lee began working together at Cordova Laboratories as researchers. It wasn't an uncommon trajectory for graduates of their prestigious program. Though they were both awarded a PhD in the same year, Frank was five years younger than Lee, a hard worker who had completed his pre-university studies in unnatural time.

Within a few years Lee had worked his way to the top, his unconventional approach catching the eye of the lab's founder and head, Albert Cordova. It had long been expected that the aging head of the lab would step down, and when he finally did, Lee seamlessly took his place, maintaining the name but overhauling the entire inner structure to allow for even greater innovation, wider freedom to question, and means to find answers. The lab thrived, quickly turning into the most advanced research lab in the country. Soon after Lee assumed his new role, with Frank behind him, they were ready to design and test a prototype of the AI system. And they had the perfect test subject. Walter.

Walter had been married to his wife, Minnie, for sixty-two years. They were inseparable, having never spent more than two nights apart in all their years together. They had no children, and never meant to. They had both been healthy, active, and mentally sharp until much later than most people maintained control of their own minds. But all at once Minnie started to fade, and died six weeks later.

But Walter hadn't faded at all. He was devastated by Minnie's absence, and lost his will to live. Shortly after her death, with his body slowly shutting down from purely wishing it to be so, he was hospitalized. He was there for nearly a month, the nurses fighting to keep him alive, his will fighting to let him die. But he lived, was released from the hospital, and was escorted back to his empty home. There he stayed, struck with incomprehensible grief, with no friends, no family, and no Minnie.

Though they lived only a few houses from each other, Lee had never interacted with Walter. He learned of Walter's ordeal by overhearing two neighbors discussing it in the privacy of the great outdoors.

It didn't surprise him that it was already a conversation piece. The neighborhood had always been loud with whispers. He immediately told Frank, who agreed. Walter was in need of a companion.

As the designer, Lee had created blueprints for their prototype. Her detailed anatomy, the connections in her head that she would follow during a conversation, the way the moisture in her eyes would interact with gravity. Frank and Lee would monitor her closely, observing her being in the world, her interactions, how she processed in the absence of stimuli when she was alone. They needed to integrate her into society and approve her proper functioning before bringing the idea public as saleable. Only Walter, who had agreed to participate in the test in spite of his skepticism, would know that Elle was an AI.

It wasn't long ago that they had approached Walter with the idea. It had been some time after Minnie passed, and Lee had been keeping an eye on Walter. He didn't go out much. When he did, he was polite. He didn't seem bitter, or sad. He didn't seem to be much of anything. Just another someone passing through, waiting for his passage to pass.

It often made Lee consider his own mortality. How it seemed more devastating that he would one day die himself, and when he did he would be somehow more eternally apart from Allie than he was already. He supposed that because he was still alive and still carried the memory of her, they were in some way less separated. As if their eternal separation hadn't yet started. He knew it had, of course. Allie had no memories of him. She was in her own darkness, forever apart from all things living, all things dead, all things.

Lee dreamt sometimes that the act of burying the dead caused them torment, but they were silenced by the living's perception of their loss of consciousness. They could no longer communicate in a way that could be understood by the living, so the dead would keep being buried, tormented, as the living wept. He imagined it being as if they were buried alive. They would appear to be dead according to the usual, scientific standards, but would be very much alive in their own minds, trapped in a dark, lonely cell, large enough only to be suffocating. They would never be released. Not after those who had buried them died, not after humanity died, not after the world imploded would they be released. There would be no one to hear them, no one to save them. Trapped in their own private, solitary hell.

Perhaps it was that way for everyone. A hell of their own. Lee thought about how silly it was to even think of death as darkness, or as heaven, or as anything at all. There would be no way for the living to ever know. Perhaps the way society imagined death was completely wrong, and the way the dead were treated was simply torturous to them in their death, and everyone who walked the earth still would soon meet the same fate. They would know how they would be treated. The same way they treated the dead before them. And they wouldn't be able to stop it. There was no escape.

He thought of Walter's attempt to end his life. To end the torture of a life without Minnie. How could he be so sure that death was better?

He wanted to ask him. "Walter," he would say. "You tried to kill yourself." Walter would protest. He had done no such thing. He had simply tried to let himself die. "But why would you do that? How do you know that death would be better? What if it's much, much worse? Or even, what if it's exactly the same?"

Walter would look at him. His words would have disturbed Walter. He wouldn't know what to do with them. Wouldn't be sure anymore that he wanted to die, but would be certain that he couldn't go on living. It was hopeless, trying to decide between life and death when not knowing what death is. Like choosing between two cages to stick one's hand into, one piled with spiders, or rats, or whatever would be the worst thing of all to the person to whom that hand belonged, and the other covered with a sheet. It could be filled with sleeping kittens, but it could be filled with things much, much worse than spiders or rats. Things that can't even be imagined. A gamble, it would be.

No doubt, some would choose the cage with the sheet. Only they would know what lay in wait inside. Only they would know if spiders and rats would have been much more pleasant, but there would be no way out once they reached inside. They would choose to walk the path to the unknown rather than face the unpleasantness before them, and there would be no way back. The world as they had known it would disintegrate behind them. They might look back and say, "This is a mistake," but there would be nothing they could do. Like a man jumping from a bridge who thinks just this as his feet lift from the ground. It is done. Eternally done. And as he thinks of his life, and wishes for it more desperately than he had wished for his death, he would sail through the air, having no one to blame for plunging him into the unfathomable darkness below but himself. Seconds only between his feet lifting off the bridge and his unknown eternity.

But Lee didn't ask Walter. The thought of it alone drove him mad, his mind going in circles as he tried to make sense of the idea of eternal, inescapable torture. Death was a gift to the living. A release from the torments of life, of consciousness. But there was no escape for the dead. No end to pain. No death after death.

He thought of these things often when he was alone in the lab poking around aimlessly, content as long as he was not in his house. And it often made him want to flee, to flee his own skin, to run away from the unlimited potential of death. Perhaps, he thought, life was given as a way to elicit trust that death would be just as bearable. Or perhaps in some cases it was something to run away from, to run toward death willingly. A trick, either way.

He remembered looking at Walter and noticing how very aged he looked. How strange it was that humans, living, conscious creatures so advanced, could simply crack away, age and crumble like a felled leaf simply because years pass by. Years, which are only made up of days. How days could make men wither after reaching a certain peak after a mere twenty or thirty years. Was it an advancement along the zero on a timeline, or a decline on a line graph?

But he had said none of this to Walter. He simply said, "Thank you for coming in to speak with us. I know how hard it's been."

Walter had looked at him as if he wanted to argue, as if Lee didn't know how hard it had been. But Walter knew that Lee had lost Allie, and he kept silent.

Lee continued. "It might take some time to get used to, but we think it will, frankly, improve your quality of life."

"Ha! Science, medicine—that's what's kept me alive when all I've wanted to do is slip away. Improve my quality of life?"

"But you're willing to try," Lee said, checking to make sure that Walter wasn't backing out.

"If doctors are going to keep me alive, scientists might as well keep me company."

Lee detected a hint of excitement in Walter's tone. Not only was it quite a thing to be a part of, but he would have someone to talk to who could talk back, someone to sit with who wouldn't leave after her shift ended, someone, anyone, who would exist for the purpose of making him not alone, who would be there unconditionally.

"We're excited to have you on board," Lee had said, sticking out his hand to shake Walter's. He felt the paper-thin skin hanging loosely over his fingers. Those would be his hands one day, he thought as he let go.

By then, Allie would have been dead for more than half his life.

Lee squinted at the photograph on his desk, fixated on Elle, letting his thoughts fade. Her eyes looked dark. Her upper lip boasted a defining freckle just above it, her milky cheekbones, high and fleshy. The whole team looked younger, excited and optimistic, only a year ago. He put the photograph down on top of a stack of papers and started arranging the items on his desk. It would clear the clutter in his mind. He picked up a pen and placed it meticulously, label-side out, next to an assemblage of other pens. The papers remained in stacks.

For hours he sat. Clouds lolled across the sky. He stared at his walls, his window, then back at his walls. His eyes adjusted to the lowering darkness and he could see the outline of the many books on the wall of shelves across from his desk. It had become too dark to read their names, his little desk lamp illuminating only a bud of a circle around him. As he had sat hours before on the park bench, he sat in his desk chair. Still, hollow.

He recognized a row of books belonging not to him. Allie's, classic literature, tucked away amidst Lee's heavy science texts. They gave depth to his collection.

Without them his books would all feel the same. Words, bound together with numbers.

When he had first shown Frank the blueprints of Elle, Frank didn't recognize her. It was no surprise. At that point Lee had drawn only an outline, but he knew exactly the image he wanted to create. He wouldn't forget it. He would never forget it. It was the only image that was always in his mind. The image of his beloved late wife. Allie. Allie. With her long dark hair, her deep blue eyes, her tiny frame that housed the entire greatness of her being. How he had wished for so long to lay eyes on her smooth skin, to have her eyes look back at him just once more.

He sifted through more papers. Detailed drawings of the human anatomy, notebooks full of designs for each section of her body, long, illegible strings of handwritten notes. The complete designs for Elle. Allie, quantified.

The bulb in his lamp blew abruptly, and he stopped shuffling papers. He sat at his desk frozen with the papers in his hands for several seconds. The interruption was an unwelcome occurrence. It jarred his thoughts and drew his attention to his surroundings. He put the papers down in front of him and sat back, sinking into the total darkness of the room. He didn't replace the bulb.

The night grew old. Lee remained in the unlit study, the moon revealing only outlines of things around him. He observed them at length. The spines of his books all looked either black or white in the dark, which he knew was not the case. The mesh wires of his garbage can showed themselves to be only a black mass on the floor. The squat shape of his mugs, their glowing white handles all facing left.

It occurred to him that he had no sense of the time, and it irked him that he was so reliant on timekeepers on his wall, his wrist, his counters. Could minutes really express all that encompasses the passage of time? He distrusted the man who decided what time the clocks would read in the whole west of Europe. Perhaps his message had arrived a minute later than the time he had stated it was. Who was to decide but the sun, now sunken low, out of sight, appearing in the west to keep time?

What a magnificent many things occurred between the sun and the earth every day. An incessant loop of day to night. The west rolling toward the east. It seemed somewhat backward to Lee that the west would move east. He recalled thinking as a child that the pages of a book should flip the other way, since the movement from left to right seemed most natural to him. He read words from left to right, and then turned the page from right to left. It seemed to disrupt the natural direction, as it seemed now to him that west moving toward the east was unnatural. But when he considered it, when he imagined east moving toward west, he couldn't stop it from collapsing in on itself as it moved, of the east diving into the west and spiraling itself inward, the west at the tail of the spiral being pulled farther east with each spin. Regardless of the dive east took into west, west indeed moved east. But which provided the energy for the motion? It was the initiation of west's movement that perplexed him. Should east pull west, or should west push east?

He began to toy with a pen, then replaced it where it belonged. His ears felt wide in the silence. His eyes had adjusted to the dark, but were unsatisfied. He waited, quieting his mind so that his eyes could see without obstacle.

How curious that time was so connected to direction. Indeed, to space. Letter by letter, the words seeped into his head. He became conscious of them, and scowled at his rudimentary musings. Those of a child, or at least of someone very much unlike him. He did not only know, but accepted the laws, the theories, the numbers, the philosophy. But in spite of that, as he sat in the dark with no books, no mentors, a man with only his mind, the sublime nature of space and time mystified him as it had before he knew that there existed a science to explore such things.

The darkness in the room felt suddenly thick and oppressive. His thoughts emptied into the void around him and were held inside a tightly capped bottle alongside light and sound.

An unwelcome brightness was unleashed into the darkness when Lee turned on his computer. It overwhelmed his face, but, from his perspective, stayed close instead of distributing throughout the room. The light from the screen and the heat from his body concentrated in a small area of his spacious house. He began typing.

His fingers sounded loud against the keys. Or, more accurately, the keys sounded loud against the plastic.

Tap tap tap.

He thought of Elle and Walter in the park again, of how unnatural they had looked together. Did Walter indeed share his thoughts and find it unnatural whenever he caught a glimpse of Elle at his side? He pictured her by his own side and was disturbed by how unnatural even that seemed. But then, Elle appeared twelve years younger than Allie would be now. He had remembered himself younger when Allie was that young. Would Walter have found it unnatural if he didn't know what she was?

Whether Walter knew or not wouldn't change the objective unnaturalness of it. Elle was an AI. She was inherently unnatural, and by consequence, so were her interactions in the world. Though he knew it was true, it wasn't as Lee observed. He saw Elle being in the world as naturally as anyone else. Her conversations were easy, her movements were smooth. She was quite ordinary in society. It was precisely that which made her extraordinary.

Compounding her remarkability in Lee's mind was the fact that she displayed so accurately, as Allie would have displayed. While the lab had the technology to create an AI with its own "personality" and train of thought, recreating those of someone who had once lived was difficult on another level. But Lee had been determined. If it was possible to recreate Allie's physical exterior, it was possible to recreate her physical interior. And thus it was possible to recreate her mentality. Elle would respond in conversation as Allie would respond. She would react to stimuli as Allie would react. She would feel as Allie felt, as much as feeling was quantifiable. As Lee, and almost everyone he knew, believed that all feelings and thoughts and emotions were the product of physical connections made in the brain, he could make Elle truly feel, as Allie would have truly felt, by producing the right physical connections.

It had been tedious work, precise and systematic. There was no room for design at that stage, there was only what needed to be. A right connection and a wrong connection. All that had to be done was make the right initial connections. To set Elle up with an identical physical structure to Allie. And she would once again be in the world, standing before Lee, her love for him not having missed a day.

Lee was adamant. But Frank had reservations. He had told Lee, "Of course it is possible." And of course it was. But it bordered on things that Frank didn't want to be involved in. He expressed these thoughts to Lee, focusing his argument on the ethics, but keeping quiet his concern for what it would do to Lee. How his mind would process Allie walking the earth once more, knowing against all physical evidence that she had died many years before.

Tap tap tap.

He thought again of west and east. The west had not yet discovered the technology that boiled discreetly under the roof of Cordova Laboratories. A decided change in the direction of advancement over the past decades. Lee wondered if, after the success of the trial and the release of the systems into society, his American roots would be a source of pride for the west, or if technology from the east moving west would feel unnatural, as if moving backward instead of advancing solely because of the way the world turns.

It didn't much matter. What was real, what he knew, was what was present. He knew that he was sitting behind his desk in the dark, and that was all there really was.

He redirected his mind, pulling it back into focus. His fingers typed without instruction, bypassing his consciousness and recording his observations about Elle that he had stored in a mental file for analysis.

The words poured endlessly from his cold fingertips. They were still cold indeed, despite being indoors. There was a chill in his house, and he noticed that the window was cracked open slightly. He couldn't remember doing it, but didn't move to close it. He thought if it hadn't been cold in his house it would have felt cold anyway from the stillness of the air around him.

Elle Elle Elle.

He had only been working for a short time before something outside his window caught his attention. Red lights flashed, probing indiscriminately into the windows of the cul-de-sac. Medics. A lump of panic threatened Lee's throat, but he swallowed it down as an irrational, involuntary reaction to the color red pulsing at a startling speed. The lights were in what could have been a position outside Elle's house.

He had no reason to think that it was Elle who was in distress. But what if she was? What would they try to do to her, thinking they could fix her? The thought disturbed him, but he tried to regain control of his calm.

He leaned over in his chair to get a better view out the window and saw Elle sitting on the steps as medics walked past into her house. His mind slowed. Elle was fine. But they were going into her house. Lee watched until the medics came back out carrying what he knew was a body on a stretcher. Covered. He ran through the possible scenarios in his head. Perhaps it was an intruder who had come to an unfortunate end. It was strange of him to hope so. But the odds of it being Walter were too great to ignore. A more than untimely occurrence.

Elle moved to the side as the medics carried the body under her nose. She watched them lift the stretcher, push it back into the ambulance, and continued to watch as they shut the doors. They drove away, the flashing lights extinguished, and she stood alone on her doorstep in the sudden dark.

The front door of her house was wide open, urging her to walk back inside. She didn't. Instead she looked up at Lee's house, straight into the window where his figure stood peering back at her. Wind rippled through her nightgown and stretched itself up to Lee's curtains, making the very journey she wished to make at that moment. She looked back in the direction of the ambulance, willing herself to see Walter's outline walking back toward her out of the darkness, it all having been a mistake. She stood shivering, stunned. The ground beneath her bare feet did not feel cold.

Lee observed. He wished, as he so often did, that he could go to her. With great restraint he stayed back, hovering like a protective hawk, recalling Frank's warning about remaining objective. It pained him greatly to watch Elle standing out in the cold, helpless and confused. It seemed inhumane to watch, perverse, even, that he would stand back when she was in need.

But what if he did go to her? It had been so long since they had spoken, so abruptly it had stopped. And then there was the grimace that he had given her earlier that evening in the park. He touched his face reactively, feeling the phantom lines of the grimace mold together on his skin. That it so affected him was perhaps even more undesirable than the grimace itself. That their physical distance had little effect on his struggle to remain objective.

He had developed a jealousy of Walter early in the trial. Until Walter, Elle had been completely Lee's. His design, his creation. His. He tried to remind himself that Elle was just an AI, but he believed it less and less the more he watched her. As she tilted her head back to laugh, as she held it to one side when listening to someone speak. He hadn't thought of her as an AI when he designed her. Never thought of her as an "it." The closer he came to completing her, the more desperately he longed to finally see her walk. To be.

It was frightening, at first, how much she looked like Allie. She spoke with the same silk voice, brushed her hair away from her face the same way. Seeing her standing before him after she had passed away twelve years earlier was both torment and ecstasy for Lee. He knew in his mind that Elle wasn't Allie, but his team had produced an immaculate copy of her. The design that Lee had insisted upon using despite protests from Frank. She had haunted him in the beginning, his mind not accepting the vision of her walking the earth. He couldn't understand what his eyes were showing him and refused to accept it. But like a dog in spring curiously sniffs a newly pollenated flower, Lee hovered at arm's length from Elle, watching, inhaling her presence into the empty cavities of his chest. It took only days for him to turn his hesitation into a stroll by her side, his feet in sync with hers.

The lab had scheduled an observation period prior to Walter's involvement to check for issues. She was perfect. During those first weeks after her creation, Lee spent much of his time with her. He got to know her all over again, marveled at her remarkability, relished her company with a desperate boyishness. Moments of hesitation overcame him unexpectedly but fleetingly, and he became consumed with her existence. The memories that he and Allie shared were preserved in Elle, and she spoke of them convincingly. When he was with Elle he felt sometimes as if Allie's death had been a years-long nightmare playing endlessly in his mind, trapped in a coma, unable to wake itself from unspeakable disturbances.

He had trouble sleeping most nights, but for new reasons. Excitement. A wish to remain in a state of consciousness, not wanting to be separated from Elle's consciousness. It felt to him like a new relationship, prepackaged with the comforts of familiarity and trust.

Before the process of creation had been completed, Lee had expected to feel like he was in a dream whenever he saw Elle. But when he cast his eyes on her for the first time, and for many times following, he felt awake, as if not knowing he had been asleep until pulled from his slumber. He had succeeded in recreating Allie, cell by cell, memory by memory. "Plank by plank," as he had described it to Frank. And brought her to life.

And then she was assigned to Walter. To be his companion, to be his aide, his loyal friend. And Lee had to let her go. To watch her only feet away from him, unquestioningly dedicated to someone else. As much as he knew it was the point of the trial to send her off to be a companion to someone in need of one, to see how she fared as part of society, the point of Elle for Lee had never been exactly aligned with that of the lab. He hadn't considered what would happen after her creation. He knew it, but didn't consider it. He wished to have her to himself once again. It was unnatural to him that she wasn't.

Indeed, unnatural for her to be at Walter's side for this reason as well as aesthetic reasons. As a designer, Lee cared very much about the appearance of his designs, noticed when they weren't working in the world and could easily spot where they needed to be changed. He designed with precision. If he noticed something, it wasn't seamlessly integrated in the world. If he didn't notice it, it was perfect. But as he pictured Elle in the world as Allie had been, he pictured her not at Walter's side, but at his own. It had been a difficult transition to see her with another, but not one that he could fix.

Looking out his window, Lee saw the wide, curly hair of his neighbor, Sonja, before he saw the rest of her hurry over to Elle. Her hair took on a strange shape when looked down at from his angle in the window. An unruly sort of rhombus-shaped cap above her neck. He didn't recall it being so large. But he did recall always wishing she would tie it back. As he saw Sonja reach her hand out to Elle, he felt a sudden, intense gratitude for her wash away his petty thoughts, followed by a wave of disgust directed at himself for having such thoughts to wash away.

Sonja knew about Elle, having retired from the lab a month before her completion. With Lee, Frank, and Sonja all involved in the same lab, living on the same block, it was a true wonder that there weren't more rumors about what exactly went on in the lab. And rumors there were. Of course, in a town as small as theirs it wasn't surprising to have neighbors who worked together, and neighbors who gossiped. Particularly among the elderly ladies there seemed to be a hush whenever Lee passed. He supposed that it was human nature to wish to know things, especially if they weren't supposed to be known. But over the years a story seemed to have developed around Lee, and the looks became more cautious and disapproving as he walked past. Perhaps it was the added element of being a widower that gave their whispers intrigue. The lonely widower stuffed in the corner of the road in his big house and his empty rooms. Despite his suspicions about the increasing dramatics of the rumors surrounding him, he had always tried to remain polite. Private, but polite.

Sonja had kept mostly to herself after retiring from the lab, but she heard the whispers too, felt the stigma of the lab, of the unknown, follow her like a shadow whenever she walked. Lee saw it in her gait as she made her way to Elle. He heard what was said about her. The philosopher so involved in her mind that she neglected her physical self. The rich lady with the outdated wallpaper. A catty neighborhood it was.

With her large, blond hair protruding from her head, Sonja wrapped Elle like a mother would a child and guided her protectively to her house. Elle would be safe with her. Lee watched until she disappeared at the bottom of his window frame, and stepped away just as his cell phone rang.

FIVE

....

If the loop of a cul-de-sac has three points—the
most outward before it curves in at either side,
and two points midway between the first point
and the start of the curve—Frank's house sat exactly at
the midway point closest to Lee's house. It was at an
angle such that Frank could clearly see nearly the entire block from his house, and Lee could see Frank's if
he looked left, but needed to strain to see the houses
to his right, including Elle's. His house sat on the part
of the cul-de-sac that had barely just begun to curve.
He had thought of it often as the best place to be located. It was far enough away from the entrance to
feel protected while not at the very farthest tip of the
curve, which felt somehow like it was standing on its
own, separated from the rest of the neighborhood and
vulnerable.

Frank sat at his computer watching scrolls of data move across his screen. His full head of dark hair and small, rectangular glasses were tinted green from the illuminated numbers. His phone lay flat on his desk as he spoke into it.

"Are you home?" he asked Lee casually, with hidden urgency.

"Yeah," Lee replied.

"Then you know what's happening."

"I'm watching. I didn't see what happened."

"Walter just had a massive heart attack." Frank scanned the rapidly incoming data on his computer. He waited for Lee to answer, but no answer came. "He's dead."

Lee stayed silent, processing. "Jesus," he said to himself. He was not surprised. He had seen the body covered with the white sheet being carried on the stretcher. But Frank's confirmation had made it real. Walter was dead. He allowed himself to process the implications of his passing. *A heart attack! After all those months he had wanted to die, he finally found someone to keep him company, to keep him alive. And he goes off and dies.* Lee shook his head, realization creeping into his thoughts. He thought he would have more time.

"Sonja just called here," Frank began. "She's taking Elle for the night, and I'll be monitoring her from here. She should be fine for now, but—you know we never found a way to explain—"

"I know," Lee said cutting him off. He was only just coming to acknowledge it himself and didn't need Frank to remind him.

"It could be bad."

"Let's just see."

"All right. I'll send you a report every hour or so."

Lee hung up and sat back down behind his desk, his legs feeling heavy. He fiddled with the blown lightbulb and it turned back on with a slight twist of his hand. He sat still for a moment, shadows settled across his face. How many times had he sat there in the dark? How many more times would he?

In the otherwise empty bottom drawer of his desk was a single, thin file. It contained his entire body of research on a crucial connection that the lab had yet to implant in Elle. He pulled it out and pored over it as he had done many times before, trying to come up with a formula of which Elle could make sense. A formula to explain death. Not death itself from a first person's perspective, since it wouldn't matter to those people who have already met death. But from the perspective of the living. What, exactly, is death? It seemed a basic question.

But he hadn't yet figured out a way to understand death for himself, and it was proving to be impossible for him to explain it in terms that Elle would be able to reconcile. He had pushed the trial through despite this gap in her connections, hoping that by the time Elle experienced death, he would have found a way to properly equip her to process it.

Walter was not supposed to die just yet. After all he had been through, after his body had fought so hard against his will and kept him alive, for it to give out now after no urging on his part was simply un-necessary.

Another photograph of Elle fell out of the back of the folder. She was looking directly into the camera, smiling as if it had told her a joke itself. Lee picked it up. He stared into her eyes, looking closer, closer, wondering how this would affect her. He feared that he had set her up for failure by not equipping her with the connections she needed to process death.

Exhausted, he fell asleep nearly before he even put his head down to rest. He fell inside her pupils, the dark tornadic void in her eyes that pulled in the world around her. Color. Light. Into her eyes it all fell. Swimming among the connections, the wires, the complex circuitry that made up Elle, he searched for the answer.

Elle

At that moment, inside Sonja's vinyl-floored kitch-
en Elle stood still, staring as if paused. The light in her
eyes went out, leaving behind endlessly empty black
pools.

SIX

....

Days later, Elle emerged from her own house to find that the first snow had fallen. The eyes of the cul-de-sac watched her through hidden lenses. She stepped onto the shoveled streets in a long black coatdress and unusual ankle boots with buttons on the sides, carrying a single red rose. She walked out of the sight of her watchful neighbors who whispered in disapproving but awed voices about how well put together she looked so soon after Walter's death.

She made her way to the riverbank in the woods just beyond the cul-de-sac. Surrounded by complete serenity in nature, she sat motionless, melancholy. Behind her, in the distance, she heard the muffled sounds of a funeral. She held the rose between her hands, clashing with the muted browns and greys underneath the melting snow, feeling each thorn. Footsteps crunched the frozen, moldering leaves.

Lee walked up behind her from the direction of the funeral, ducking under the stray branches of the trees. He wore his usual trench with dark dress pants and dress shoes that weren't meant for walking in the woods. He looked good, Elle noticed, but she didn't look in his direction. Lee sat down next to her, two feet between them, not caring if his coat got wet. They both looked out over the river at nothing in particular through the air, watching an invisible happening of nature.

Everything was cold, still, dead. Much of the river was frozen with patches of motionless ice, but water could be heard trickling underneath, and seen around the edges where it met the grass of the bank. No words were exchanged for some time. They just looked out.

Finally, Elle began to speak. "I don't know what to do now," she said. Her words filled months of those unspoken.

"I know," said Lee.

"I know you know."

Elle was cognizant of her creation, her role in the world, the inner workings of the lab, because of Lee. He confided in her just as he had always done with

Allie. He wouldn't have kept a secret so large from Allie, and felt that there should be no reason to keep it from Elle. Even though he would never have had this particular secret in the first place if Allie had been there, it was the act of keeping something from her that would change their dynamic.

He had told Elle with full confidence about how she would react. The difference with Elle was that as an AI system, she began with no awareness of her self. So the revelation that she was indeed not a being that had a self was not shocking to her, whereas Allie, who believed rightly that she was a human being with a self, would have coped poorly with the same idea.

But just as Allie had an awareness of herself, Lee wished for Elle to have an awareness of herself. Knowing oneself was part of what made up that very self, and he wished for Elle to be as completely made up as possible. By giving her the awareness of her self and her creation, he believed it brought her even closer to Allie. Indeed, made her identical to Allie because she was able to reconcile the idea of her self, and rarely think about it or be affected by it again. She could carry on as she normally would without the burden of a misunderstood self standing in her way.

There was a tense silence between them. Elle continued to stare straight ahead, and Lee did the same.

"It must be hard for you to look at me," Elle mused sadly.

Lee looked down, registering the truth of her words. He noticed how Elle seemed to understand what she was saying on a new level. Seemed to sympathize with Lee's struggle to comprehend Allie's death rather than empathize. After a few moments, Elle stood up and walked down the bank toward the river. She looked into her rippling reflection and addressed Lee, still looking down into the tiny pool between the patches of ice before her.

"I saw you the other day, in the park," she said.

Lee nodded, though Elle couldn't see him. Elle looked out again, no longer at her reflection but at the trees on the other side of the bank, at the late-blooming tadpoles struggling to survive the approaching winter and become froglets. She sat back down, looking deep into the river at the tiny tadpoles milling about beneath the surface.

"It's been a while," Elle said. "I thought you might be avoiding me, beyond what was necessary. It's okay. I can understand why." She paused. "But then, is this really how you wanted it?" She turned around to look at the funeral happening behind her. At the attendees, hunched, crying.

Lee turned to follow her gaze, recalling his own painful memories. He remembered the crowd gathered for Allie's funeral on the very same hill. The same dulcet, monotone voice drifting over the attendees and into the woods on every side of the clearing. He scanned the group of Walter's mourners and spotted a specter of his own face standing beside the casket—Allie's casket—flanked by her friends. The color fell away from the funeral, leaving behind a rusty tint on the land, the people.

He turned back to Elle, perceiving the colors before him once again. A cold wind made its way through the trees causing Elle to shiver. Lee stood and walked over to her at the edge of the riverbank. Looking down at her reflection in the small pool of water, his eyes met hers. They both looked away. They hadn't spoken so openly since the very beginning. Sometimes it was easier to talk to strangers. Though Elle had never been a stranger to Lee, the beginning had felt as new as if she had been.

"I wouldn't know how to live without you." Lee spoke sincerely in a low, soft voice.

"You mean *her*," Elle replied.

Lee smiled at her reflection. "Same thing," he said.

Again, there was silence between them. Elle picked at the ground, contemplative. She listened distantly to the funeral readings in the background, the low hum of the voice, its words indistinguishable, serenading the ground beneath their feet and Walter beneath the ground. But her thoughts were only distantly about Walter, thinking instead of her own existence.

"I wouldn't be able to watch you with someone else if I were in your shoes. But I guess it's not about me losing you, it's about you being lost. Totally and completely," Elle reasoned out loud to Lee.

"Something like that," Lee said. Another breeze blew in. "Are you sure you don't want to go over there? It looks like it's almost over." He gestured toward the funeral.

Elle looked down and shook her head. "What would it do? He's already gone."

Lee held out his palm to Elle as she shivered. "Come on." Elle took his hand, dropping the rose, its petals shrieking brightly against the drab autumn ground. They turned to walk away from the river, still hearing the low, consistent hum of the dulcet voice. Elle looked back in the direction of the funeral, watching the mourning continue.

It was a small crowd, but a crowd indeed. An eclectic crowd of people whom Elle had never before seen. A young, dark-haired woman caught her eye. She stood out, Elle's eyes locking on her, magnetic. *She looks so much like me*, Elle thought. It was uncanny how her hair matched the color of Elle's, how her eyes held the same shape. *Who is she?* Elle looked at her, but didn't find it strange.

As she stared, the woman turned and looked directly back at her. Her face was partially obscured, but her glaring, accusatory eyes pierced through the distance between them, stating clearly from across the field that Elle did not belong. She did not belong at Walter's funeral, she did not belong at Lee's side, she did not belong in mourner's clothes.

Lee didn't notice Elle lagging slightly behind, fixated on the woman. Elle held her gaze and kept walking, unfazed. Her eyes didn't look unkind, her brow didn't furrow in a frown as she stared at Elle. She simply spoke with her stare, a warning. The woman slowly turned back toward the funeral and dabbed at her eyes, as if proceeding to act like she was in mourning due to propriety. Elle took note of this, only then considering that it was the woman who didn't belong at the funeral, not herself.

Still watching the same woman, she said to Lee, "Strange, isn't it? I'll never see him again. But she's walking right beside you." She kept her eyes on the woman as she spoke, then paused and looked at Lee. "Isn't she?"

Lee considered this as Elle walked ahead, considered the implications of suggesting that she and Allie were the same person, but referring to Allie as "she." He moved to catch up to her as the wind blew again, tossing more leaves across the cold, hard ground. They blew still as Lee opened his front door.

....

SEVEN

The sun had set. Once inside, Lee took off his coat and headed straight toward the kitchen to make himself coffee. He waited in the dark for it to brew, cutting the silence. He brought it upstairs to his study, where he put it down without drinking any, walked over to the window, and looked out. Looked down. He wondered what Elle was doing. Wondered if he should call Frank to check on the data, which would give him a clue. But no, he thought against it. She had a right to her privacy.

Does she? Lee thought. *Does she have rights?* He had always assumed that she did. What gave a human rights? Surely not the simple fact that one was human. There were humans indeed with no rights, or with rights revoked.

The wind picked up more as it started to rain. On the outside of his window, he saw a beetle waltzing precariously along the ledge. Lee was transfixed. How strange it was to see a beetle so close to winter. Where was it going? *Perhaps seeking shelter in my study,* Lee thought. It stopped walking and quivered in the wind, shaken by a strong gust. A second later, the wind snapped it completely off the window. Gone. Or did it leap? Fly?

Lee looked out to where it might have disappeared, and saw his elderly neighbor, Mrs. Thatcher, carrying a bag of groceries as she walked to the end of the block to her home. She struggled against the wind, moving slowly. *Just as easily could she be snapped up by the wind as the beetle,* Lee thought, running briskly downstairs. He grabbed an umbrella by the front door, and set out after her.

"Mrs. Thatcher!" he called to her. "Mrs. Thatcher!" The wind carried his voice far away from her ears.

He caught up to her quickly.

"Oh!" She exclaimed, surprised at the sudden intrusion.

"Here, let me help you," Lee said taking her groceries in one hand, holding the umbrella over her with the other.

"Oh you're such a gentleman," she said, grabbing on to his arm for stability. "I don't know where this rain comes from sometimes!"

"It's no problem at all," Lee replied. "This is quite an unusual storm."

"Terrible!" agreed Mrs. Thatcher.

Having run out of neighborly things to say, the time passed silently. Mrs. Thatcher peered at Lee out of the corner of her eye, her smile fading into a snarl. She lifted the corners of her mouth back into a smile as Lee glanced at her, sensing the familiar feeling of her eyes on him.

"It gets dark so early these days," Mrs. Thatcher said. Another gust of wind came through, knocking Mrs. Thatcher into Lee. "Oh my goodness! You know usually I'm very steady on my feet," she said apologetically, embarrassed.

Lee smiled at her encouragingly, but she remained uncomfortable. He walked with her patiently, careful not to rush, until they reached her house at the end of the block. She unlocked the door and turned back around to take her bag of groceries, blocking the way into her home. Lee handed her the bag.

"Thank you so much again," she said stepping behind the front door. Her voice had assumed its usual airs. Lee noticed the light glistening in her diamonded ears. Through the crack in the door he could see Mr. Thatcher sitting with an oxygen mask in a chair.

"I hear Mr. Thatcher's been making great progress," Lee said. "Give him my best." Mrs. Thatcher followed Lee's gaze, and her demeanor darkened.

"He's doing just fine, thank you very much. We *both* are. I don't want any of that voodoo you perform over at your lab coming anywhere near this house. We're both just fine!"

Lee was taken aback by her assault, but recovered after realizing how the rumors must have multiplied after Walter's death. That was the risk of a small town. Everyone in everyone's business. Everyone working in the same buildings, eating in the same cafés. They had always been just whispers to Lee, fueled by the fact that the trial wasn't entirely confidential, just kept quiet. But quiet means that some things get out, and those that do are subjected to neighborly interpretation in the absence of additional information. Usually what Lee heard about his lab was absurd enough for him to not worry. But Mrs. Thatcher seemed quite certain about whatever she had heard this time around, and it sounded to Lee like whatever she had heard was fairly accurate. Aside from calling it voodoo.

He understood her wariness of him, though it saddened him more than he expected. He supposed that was the cost of living a private life, an abandoned life. A scientific life. He wondered how the rest of his neighbors saw him. Did they watch him with Elle? Did they remember Allie? Lee had never been close with his neighbors, aside from Frank. It must have seemed to them like Allie had simply gone away for a few years.

Or did they know? Did they pity him? It seemed unlikely to him that they didn't know that she had died, given how quickly word had spread about Walter. He thought with dismay of what they must think of Elle, having no information other than what they saw.

He looked at Mrs. Thatcher, wondering, wanting to ask her what she knew. Instead, he straightened himself up and turned to leave.

"Of course, Mrs. Thatcher," he said. "Have a good night."

Mrs. Thatcher softened, but watched Lee walk away with a disapproving eye. As he left, she felt that she had been too stern and quick to jump to conclusions. She was both afraid and sorry, and called after him.

"Goodnight."

The wind had died down, but heavy rain still fell. Lee walked back home with his umbrella closed. He looked at the way the rain interacted with his skin, how it fell from the sky in strings of pearls. Lightning flashed silently, then growled softly. A warning. He opened the umbrella and walked brusquely into the dark.

He passed a house on the opposite side of the cul-de-sac, unlit except for one window. He could see clearly into it. An old widow sat alone holding a picture frame, staring straight ahead. From his angle on the street, it looked to Lee like she was staring at the wall. Every so often she glanced down at the frame. She stood up and walked toward the window, putting the picture back on top of its shelf. Through the window she saw Lee, lit by the moon, and waved kindly. She moved back away from the window, hunched, but deliberate. Lee waved after she had already turned, and continued to walk. The light went out in her window, and Lee looked back at it. There were few lights on in the houses of the block. He felt completely alone, muted streetlamps illuminating his solitude.

EIGHT

....

Hours later, Elle stood in her brightly lit kitchen washing dishes. She didn't mind doing so. Unlike in Lee's house, her kitchen was to the right of her front door and had a little window over the sink through which she could look out. She was wearing only a small, pink robe that showed off the smooth curves of her toned thighs. The rain fell heavily but hushed on the window. She liked the idea of storms, of everyone huddled together equally in their homes. She appreciated her little window for letting her see the rain safely, despite it facing the brick side of another house. There was something strange, she thought, about running water inside when it rained.

As she turned off the faucet and dried her hands, one of her stud earrings dropped lightly into the drain. She froze. It was only cheap costume jewelry, but she cherished those earrings for being so versatile with her wardrobe. She tried silently to retrieve it from the drain in her sink, her expression one of empty determination. The rain pattered outside. Its even sound calmed her, as if no time were passing.

"Ouch, shoot. Walter! Walter can you come here?" She pulled her finger from the drain to examine where it had been pinched. Unscathed. She tried again, reaching back into the drain. After some more struggle, she felt the earring. She pulled it out with great care not to drop it right back in, satisfied that she had rescued the earring herself.

"Never mind!" she called again to Walter. She admired the earring and cleaned it off with alcohol, feeling silly when she realized that she held it over the sink as she did so. She put it safely back in, proud. Suddenly realizing that Walter hadn't responded, she walked over to the stairs at the back of the unlit house. The light from the kitchen crept toward them, but she could only see the bottommost steps in front of her before they sank into complete black. "Walter?"

She heard the sounds only of electricity and rain. The combination frightened her. She took a single step up the stairs, looked at her hand on the banister, and recoiled. Retreating from the darkness above, she let out a small, horrified squeal and crumbled into the corner, unconscious.

63

....

Frank looked up at his screens compulsively, even when he didn't hear the alarm sound. He was on edge, certain that he would start seeing jumbled data come through. The strings of As, Ts, Cs, and Gs scrolled seamlessly. He was confused. Elle was processing Walter's death like any human would. Slowly, but without neural trauma. Elle should have started to break down already. Incapable of reconciling the loss of Walter. Left searching for connections with which she hadn't been equipped. She should have been stuck, unable to move forward, lodged between an unstable synapse and the need to escape, to leave the loss preserved in the neuron structures behind her. She was sure to start showing signs of reaching this impasse, Frank just didn't know when.

Asleep in the bed next to him was his young girl-friend, Marigold. He wished to sleep as soundly as she, to keep his eyes closed and invite slumber. But when he closed his eyes to sleep, they popped back open to check his screens. He monitored the details of Elle's existence at every moment, the data informing him of her location, her actions, her mental connections.

At times he was conflicted. He often wondered how Marigold would feel if she could read what the data showed. But, Frank often reasoned, Elle was a creation, and he quickly rejected any reservations, any suspicions of immorality. It was for her own good that he kept such a close watch over her. And, it would only be until the trial was over. Then she would be on her own, away from the watchful eyes of his screens.

Finally, the screen blinked red. *There it is*, Frank thought as the warning data that he had been expecting passed over the screen. His heart seized and fluttered as he read, his eyes searching for key information about irreversible damage to her system. *Am I nervous for the success of the trial, or for Elle?* He wondered vaguely as he searched. He spotted a stutter in Elle's connections, and then a line where no data were recorded.

"Where are you..." he said to himself. He clicked through the wiring of Elle's head, trying to spot which connection had failed and where she had fallen off. He checked the time. Almost a minute had passed. He searched between her synapses, rightly guessing that she had fallen unconscious and was resting in the black pits of her head, running along no wires, passing over no connectors, as if thrown from a diving board into a cognizant void.

He spotted the stalled indicator that showed Elle's cognitive progress lying still, derailed. It was still lit. No damage had been done. He dialed Lee and waited for the indicator to restart itself once Elle regained consciousness.

TEN

....

Lee was lying in bed sleeping heavily when Frank called.

"Jesus," he said when Frank explained. "Can she regain consciousness on her own?"

"She can, and it looks like she will," said Frank. "The indicator is still very bright. But I think you should go over there now in case she's scrambled when she wakes up."

Lee hung up without replying, and was still pulling on his coat when he ran out the front door. Not a minute later he was standing in front of Elle's house, knocking urgently. It was unlit except for a light in her kitchen. What if she was already awake?

"Elle?" he called, pushing on the door impatiently as his numb fingers fumbled to find the spare key on his key ring.

Inside, lying at the bottom of the stairs, Elle was awakened by the knocking. She heard Lee's voice and instantly recognized it, immediately establishing her surroundings. She collected herself and glided over to open the front door for Lee, who barged in as soon as the door opened. Without saying a word, he stood close in front of her and examined her. As he looked her over, Elle remained silent. She watched him, his eyes scanning her body before setting his gaze on her face. Though he looked into her eyes, he didn't see her. He saw a function, part of a system. His expression would have frightened her if she hadn't already figured out what had happened to her.

He determined that she looked fine, broke away, and wandered into the back of the house, giving it a quick walk-through to see if anything was out of place. He kept one eye on Elle, who remained standing where he had left her. Behind the stairs, nothing unusual. The bathroom. The living room. All was well. He made his way back over to the door where Elle was still waiting, and looked again into her left eye, her right eye. Indeed, she was all right. Feeling foolish, he stepped back. He had let her see him lose his composure. Had he frightened her? He wished for her sake that he hadn't been so quick to worry. She smiled at him as his breathing calmed, and he broke his intense gaze. This time, when he looked into her eyes, he saw through the pieces, and saw her.

"What happened?" he asked gingerly, as if she might still break if pushed.

Elle shrugged slightly, unconcerned, the comforting smile still on her face. Then through her smile, her eyes welled up.

"I forgot he was dead."

She threw the words out of her lips like poison, loudly, hating herself for something so unforgivable being true. She turned away so Lee couldn't see her face. Her eyes had welled up so fully that she couldn't see, but she refused to let the tears spill over.

Lee took a moment to understand. *It's not that she forgot*, he thought. *It's that she remembered.* It was something that would make anyone feel guilty. But it also seemed to be the case that remembering had overwhelmed her system. It was when she remembered that Frank had gotten the alert. When she remembered that she had fallen unconscious. It wasn't the forgetting. There was no guilt about forgetting.

He walked over to comfort her, not knowing how to explain what had happened, or even if it would be worth explaining. It seemed to be too scientific an explanation for the circumstances, when she was so clearly distraught on a different level. He thought that it would be inappropriate to try to explain it, and let her instead hang on to him limply. Her embrace felt foreign to him. He touched her gingerly, a stranger. The honey smell of her hair reminded him of Allie. Familiar. Only then, when her face had lost its expression, did her tears fall onto him.

"It's my fault," Lee said, feeling heavy with guilt. "I didn't prepare you for this sort of thing."

Elle let go of Lee and composed herself as she walked toward the bathroom underneath the stairs. She didn't look at them as she passed. In front of the mirror, she pressed herself into the counter to stay out of Lee's sight as she retrieved tissues for her eyes, trying to normalize her appearance. How anyone could ever be prepared for this sort of thing, for the loss of someone, of something, she couldn't understand. She imagined it to be just one of those things that must be accepted, an explanation impossible.

Lee stood at the opposite end of the house, drained. It was not only guilt that weighed on him, but the urgency of fixing what he had done. Whether Elle's negative physical reaction was a result of her forgetting or remembering, there was no reason to think that it wouldn't happen again. Each time risked irreversible damage.

On the end table in the living room Lee spotted a photograph of Elle and Walter. A curious concept it was, to have a photograph of a person who no longer exists. He had no pictures of Allie in his own home. But he had Elle. He wondered what effect Walter's appearance in that small frame was having on her now that he was no longer there. Would a still photograph contribute to her confusion? How a moment in time when he existed could be captured, but not his existence itself?

Elle emerged with tissues and saw Lee staring at the photograph. She stood next to him.

"It's just so strange," she mused. "He no longer thinks of me. Doesn't miss me. Has no memory of anything that's ever happened to him."

There was a tense silence. Elle looked at Lee, wanting to say something else. He cocked his head, questioning her silently. She toyed with the tie of the robe around her waist, torn between the comfort of Lee by her side and the confusion of Walter no longer.

Lee's eyes followed Elle's long fingers down the tie of her robe. They amazed him, her fingers, how silently they moved through space. How perfect they were, so slender. They would be silky to the touch, he knew without doubt. He remembered those hands. Remembered them in spite of the fact that he had never touched the hands before him. But the identical hands that he knew so well he remembered. And there they were in front of him, silk against silk on the tie of her robe. He darkened shamefully and looked away. There was a long silence.

A photograph would capture exactly how they looked in that moment, standing silently across from each other. But Lee wasn't aware of how he looked. He wasn't seeing himself from the outside. An image could never capture the feel of a time, he realized. Though the physical arrangement of their bodies in space in that instant could be captured in a frame, it meant little in comparison. How could the internal, the essence, be captured in a frame?

The thought of the internal not captured by the physical disturbed him. He had structured Elle with the exact physical setup as Allie. Was it indeed possible that he had been able to capture the internal as well?

"It's been a long time since you've been here," Elle said. Their time together had been short before Elle was sent to live with Walter, but her memories of Lee were extensive.

She had known it was coming. She had understood her place that day as Lee handed her over to Walter at the official start of the trial. She was happy to have not only memories from her time with Lee, but from Allie's time with Lee as well.

She had sensed, at first, his hesitation after her creation. His hesitation to believe that she was standing before him, that she was communicating. But they fell back in step quickly. Though they both knew the day would come when she would no longer be at the lab whenever Lee arrived, it seemed like that day existed sometime in the distant future. She never imagined that a change of environment would result in a change of connection. But then he released her to Walter. It didn't take long for him to pull back, to cloud in Walter's presence, and assume the same hesitation that he had felt when Elle walked in front of him for the first time.

It had indeed been a long time since Lee had been to Walter's, preferring to watch over Elle from afar rather than see her in the unfamiliar, unnatural environment of his home instead of Lee's. As part of his life instead of Lee's.

"I don't think Walter liked me much." Lee attempted a joke to avoid what he knew Elle was saying. Though she had phrased it as a statement, it was clear in her voice that she was asking a question. *Will you be able to look at me now that he's gone?*

"He knew what you were doing for him," she said, referring to the loneliness that Walter had felt. She paused, letting the subject die out. "I'm fine though, really. I think I just need to go to bed. Thank you for coming to check on me."

She was still toying with the tie of her robe.

"It's my job," Lee said deliberately substituting his words for "you're welcome." He wasn't sure if he was reminding himself or her.

Elle smiled and stopped fidgeting with the tie. She hadn't noticed the effect she was having on Lee until he let his words slip through the air with an icy coating. She knew the loneliness Walter must have felt. But she had Lee. She had wanted only to pick up their friendship where it had been abandoned. She thought sometimes in moments of fear that their connection had been severed, ruined by the introduction of an unfamiliar party. She still wasn't sure if she ever truly believed that their connection had been lost. Wasn't sure if it could be, given the way that she had been designed. But, seeing him there in front of her, she was sure that it had never been lost, not even faded. It had, perhaps, grown. He was resisting her, she could see. Her body had indeed many years ago been his wife's.

Elle

Lee walked to the front door, hearing Elle's unspoken thoughts as she trailed behind him. He motioned a farewell to her, his voice catching his words before they could become audible, and walked out.

Elle exhaled as he left and locked the door behind him. She listened through the thick wood, feeling that he was still standing just on the other side.

....

ELEVEN

The streetlamp lit up Lee's face as he stood with his back to Elle's house. He wondered what Allie would say to him now. It humored him the slightest bit to think that he could just go back inside and ask Elle if he really wanted to know what Allie would say. Elle would say what Allie would say.

Suddenly Lee realized how close Allie really was. She was in Elle. She was Elle. As true as he could make that be, at least. The realization hit him unexpectedly, as it sometimes did, that he had actually achieved his goal. A goal that had once seemed impossible to achieve, or even to wrap his mind around. He would be hit occasionally with a pang of recognition as he looked at Elle, and the years of struggle after he lost Allie would fall away like a disintegrating dream at daybreak.

In the middle of his thoughts he felt a presence. Not the usual feeling he got as he walked down the street of hidden eyes from inside the houses, but a heavy, physical presence behind him. His mind emptied when he realized that Elle was listening from the other side of the door, and he quietly slinked down the steps.

The sun came up.

TWELVE

....

Only a few hours later that morning, after the sun had a chance to warm the nighttime chill out of the air, Lee walked through the Advanced Artificial Intelligence unit of Cordova Laboratories. He had slept very little after parting from Elle, and was restless. He would have preferred to be working in his own home, in his own study as he usually did, but he hadn't been able to focus there.

Cordova Laboratories sat at the top of a high-rise building in the center of town. It was only ten minutes away from his house by foot, but its clear glass walls and white floors made it seem miles away.

Lee looked through the walls into the different rooms as he walked down the hall. A hologram of the scientist who was standing in front of it. The scientist conversed with the hologram as if it were a body of flesh, and it conversed with him. An image projected into the air, distorted by a hand passing through it, but unable to distort itself to pass through a hand. In the next room, a body scan was taking place. There were no computers in the room. The long strips of data recorded themselves in the air above the researcher's head.

If only, Lee thought, *there would come a time when man possessed few material goods, and instead possessed a single mental storage unit that could be retrieved anywhere, at any time, as long as there was air onto which the object of desire could be projected. Would our sense of touch become less important, as there would be fewer solid objects to grasp? How then, would we describe the state of existence of a pink elephant, which exists only in the mind and is considered then to not exist, if a thing like a book or a map were to exist in such a place in the mind instead of in reality?*

He kept walking and passed a young scientist who greeted him deferentially. His trepidation about being in the lab fell away. He did enjoy being surrounded by discovery, interacting with his fellow scientists, being the head of it all. He had nearly forgotten what it was like to be in control. The lab had been running so smoothly on its own that he had become accustomed to focusing his attention completely on Elle. Not much had changed in the lab, but as he looked in through the glass he could see the progress that had been made, and felt himself to be an outsider.

"Have you seen Frank?" he asked the young scientist, who shook his head. Lee kept looking into the offices lining the long hallway, and was pleased to feel the atmosphere of creation. He remembered once being very much a part of that atmosphere. Running the lab had been one of his greatest joys. It had felt like home to him. He enjoyed waking every day to make the short trip to Cordova, enjoyed working late and through lunch if necessary. And after a full day he would go back home to Allie and recap the whole thing, becoming excited all over again as she became excited about a new research topic or published paper. He had shared the lab with Allie, consulted her on important decisions and valued her opinion. But the joy of the lab had diminished after she died. Though he still loved the work, it had changed. He had changed.

He finally spotted Frank talking to a small group of younger scientists. *Probably recent graduates,* Lee thought, immediately curious about them. *Possibly soon to become part of my team.* Seeing them there, young, bright, eager, he realized just how smoothly the lab was running indeed. Just how little he was needed. It filled him with both pride and worry that the lab didn't need him as he needed it. He shook the thought from his head.

It was easy to forget that Elle was his job. That she was his current project, and that she was a part of the lab. It was an accomplishment that he had built the lab and his team to uphold the highest of standards, and that they were capable of maintaining those standards on their own. It allowed him to be a scientist instead of a manager. *Indeed*, he thought. *It is a fine lab.*

He motioned for Frank to step outside and waited in the hallway while he excused himself from the session.

"Did you call anyone else last night?" Lee whispered.

"About Elle?" Frank asked.

Lee nodded and motioned for him to speak quietly, though he already was.

"No, only you."

He became aware of the room full of young scientists watching them speak through the glass walls. They looked at Lee curiously, having heard of him, but never having seen him. He was different than they expected.

They spoke rapidly, and Lee couldn't make out the words.

"Do you see who that is?"

"Can you believe it? He's the whole reason I went into bioethics."

"He's taller than I expected."

"I saw him once when I was younger. I was visiting the city with my parents, and we saw him at a restaurant. I worshipped him."

"I heard there was a waitlist to transfer to his team from anywhere else in the lab."

"I don't believe that. He handpicks his team."

"I wonder why he doesn't live in the city."

"I've always wondered that too."

"He's too famous. A total recluse who wants nothing to do with his fame."

"That's not true. He didn't seem to mind it in the beginning."

Lee looked back at them, their searching eyes. He recognized the look on their faces. Their lips moving, their heads tilted together, but their eyes fixed on him. He straightened up.

"My office," he commanded Frank.

Frank nodded and went back into the room to dismiss the group while Lee walked away. Their lips stopped moving immediately when he opened the door.

"Could you introduce us?" asked one of the girls in the group. She couldn't have been any older than Marigold, her eyes glistening as she spoke.

"Soon enough, but not today," Frank sighed. They looked crestfallen as they slumped out of the room. He wondered if Lee even knew anymore what effect he had on people. If he knew how impressed people still were with him and his work. How much complete strangers looked up to him.

Lee's office was one of few not made of glass. Unlike his home study, it had large windows on one wall that overlooked the center of town. But it displayed the same piles of papers on the desk, which stood in the same position in the room. His computer sat in the same place on the left side of his desk, so that when he looked at the screen, he could see out the window at the same time. The door to his office was across from the windows rather than adjacent to his desk, but somehow within the walls of the lab it felt right.

He felt safer in the lab than in his own home. His mind was better contained in the lab. He didn't feel the hidden eyes on him. He didn't think each time he sat behind his desk that his door would crack open unexpectedly, slowly, revealing—what?

He had fond memories of the lab and had always found it warm and inviting despite its sterile appearance. There was no constant cold over his shoulder in the lab. It had felt different after Allie died. Everything did. But not like his home.

His home had become hollow, closing itself off and sinking without a fight into the cold emptiness of death, as if its soul had disappeared with Allie's. He felt sometimes like he was sleeping in a museum, closed for the night, the vast empty past surrounding him and birthing a life of its own in the after-hours darkness.

He opened a bottle of Scotch that sat prominently on a tray and poured two glasses, full, no ice.

Frank arrived and stood in the door. "What's going on?" he asked cautiously, stepping inside.

"Shut the door," Lee said.

He handed Frank a glass. Frank weighed it in his hands, partially amused. "These don't feel celebratory to me."

Lee took a drink, nearly finishing half. Frank looked more seriously at Lee, and set down his glass.

"I need your help with something," Lee started.

"All right."

Lee looked at Frank, surprised at his immediate, unquestioning willingness to help.

"You don't even know what it is."

"I review the data every night," Frank said. "And I've known you for approximately forever. Not hard to guess."

Frank never said it out loud, but he knew well that Lee struggled with Elle. He struggled without her, and he struggled with her. So desperately he had wanted to have Allie back, to bring her back, something that should be impossible. But it wasn't. Not at Cordova Laboratories. It was possible indeed, and they had done it. Recreated Allie's mind in Elle. Perfected a physical replication.

She was and wasn't Allie to Lee. Frank could tell by looking at how he interacted with her. He could tell when Lee let himself slip into a complete belief that he was in the presence of Allie, and he could tell when Lee caught himself slipping. It wasn't difficult for Frank to see that his old friend wanted to believe that he had his wife back, but was afraid to. Coupled with his need to remain objective for the sake of the trial, Lee was tortured.

Frank sipped from his glass and waited for Lee to go on. He suddenly felt his chest tightening and recognized the weight pulling his lungs into his stomach. It was the same feeling he often had when Lee spoke of Elle. A nagging weight that he had been carrying ever since he agreed to her design. It was becoming more frequent. No matter how long it had been since Elle was created, he couldn't quiet that tugging feeling.

"When I saw Elle last night she was fine," Lee said.

"That may be true," Frank replied. "But this probably isn't the last time we'll see this. Elle timed out. She hit something like a cognitive wall. Right before she stopped functioning, there was heightened activity, much more advanced than she's displayed in the past, and then she crashed. She burned out."

"Do we know what caused the heightened activity?"

"Actually, we do," said Frank.

Taking a seat behind Lee's desk, he pulled up on the computer the data he had analyzed the night before.

"There was some sort of temporary block, and she forgot—right here—" he pointed, "that her companion died," he said.

Lee took note of Frank's use of the lab's term to refer to Walter.

"But that's not the problem," Frank continued. "The problem started when the memory came back. When she realized that her companion—"

"Walter," Lee interrupted. It bothered him inexplicably that Frank referred to Walter in such terms, as if he were just a test subject. He had been a part of Elle, not just a part of the lab or an unnamed volunteer.

"When she realized that Walter died," Frank corrected himself, catching the crisp tone of Lee's voice, "she was flooded. She started trying to make too many connections, and she burned out."

"She started trying to make connections on her own?"

Frank nodded, seeing that Lee understood the significance. An AI system making its own connections was unheard of. Connections were always pre-formed and implanted. It was assumed to be impossible for it to happen, in fact, after much armchair thinking and experimentation had failed to prove otherwise.

It was accepted that AI systems did not have the same capacity as humans to make their own connections. They could only move along the connections that they were given, follow conditional logic to process things that they had never before encountered. Could they register sarcasm or irony in the words that were said to them? If what was said to them was, "That's funny," but what was meant was, "That's not funny at all"?

There was something in Elle that allowed her to see beyond the connections that she had been given. Indeed, to reason beyond the planted connections and form her own line of reasoning. It wasn't anything that they had hoped to capture, but it appeared that they had by chance. Given that she was not born but built, her reasoning could mean that the mental capability that had long been thought to be reserved for conscious humans was no more than the result of a particular physical structure.

There was silence as Lee absorbed.

"What kind of connections?" Lee asked. *Could Elle have the capacity to reason?* The thought made his pulse quicken. She wasn't just acting like Allie. She was making choices like Allie. And only as a result of those choices was she behaving like Allie.

"It looks like she actually started trying to understand exactly what we didn't equip her to understand. Walter's absence, his death. What death is."

Lee nodded and finished his Scotch, his hope about her situation improving. He looked out the window, catching his transparent reflection looking inside. *Could it just be that understanding death is a necessary connection that we failed to implant, or could Elle really be trying to reason?*

"She seemed to have a good grasp of what happened when I was over there. I think it helps that she knows the backstory of Allie. Maybe it was just a one-time temporary breakdown, and now that she's made the connection—"

Frank interrupted Lee. "She doesn't understand Allie's backstory. She's not wired to understand anything."

Can she be wired to understand anything? Or did our technology just quantify the abstract? She understands, whether she is wired to or not. She understands. Lee held close the idea that Elle understood Allie, that their time together couldn't be reduced to a formula. No! It was not true.

"But she does understand—"

Lee looked at Frank and stopped himself, hearing the tinge of desperation staining his own voice. He recalled the requirement to remain objective and swallowed down the argument threatening to unleash itself in the closed room. It was an argument based not on logic, but on observation. An argument with roots planted in subjective soil was indeed an argument that could not stand upright for long.

Frank watched him, the abruptly ended conversation hanging widely between them in the air. When he finally spoke, he treaded carefully and spoke softly. His friend's struggle was becoming more apparent as the days turned.

"She's not wired to understand."

"Yeah," Lee replied absently.

Frank looked sideways at Lee, concern spread across his face. Lee knew that it was there without needing to look at Frank's face. He hated that it was there. Hated that Frank didn't see what he saw happening in Elle. But then, he did think that Frank saw it and was choosing to explain it by acknowledging what should be the case over what was apparently the case. He had never known Frank to be a narrow thinker. A logical thinker, but never a narrow thinker. He was disappointed to perceive that Frank seemed to think that there was only one logic, despite the evidence against the conclusion that particular logic begot. Wasn't it the case that logic was a man-made way of processing the world around? Wasn't it based on subjectivity? Perhaps it was the case that absolute truths were not truths at all, but only pieces of the truth as far as humans could perceive.

These thoughts, he knew, had no place in the lab. Dangerous thoughts indeed that could very well be the downfall of Cordova if mishandled. No, he would need to remain aligned with the logic that he knew, that was accepted, and analyze Elle in its terms. After all, the point of Elle was not to find consciousness in AI systems, but to provide lifelike, functional companions for the elderly. But if there was potential to discover more, there was no point in wasting the opportunity.

Lee turned over each side of the argument in his mind as he stared silently out the window. His presence having long been forgotten, Frank quietly stood to leave Lee alone, shutting the door behind him.

....

THIRTEEN

As the day turned to evening, the interior of the office became apparent in the window. Lee saw it reflected backward. *What a strange thing, glass. Clear and reflective all at once. The stuff of mirrors.* His face looked light in the window, as if he weren't really there. The books behind him were there. His desk was there. How, if not for mirrors, would Lee know that he was there himself? If he were blind he would still be there, never having seen himself to prove it. He felt there. But what was it for him to be?

He looked at his hand in the window. He didn't feel that hand. He felt his own, not with his other hand, but felt its existence, even with his eyes closed. Lee moved around his office, pensive, a shadow. His arms tingled from his sharp mental focus on them.

The tick of the clock a constant, lurking companion. He felt uncomfortable, hyperaware of his physical body. He concentrated on moving his fingers, trying to bring the command from his brain to the front of his mind. The science he understood. The feeling he did not. He was unnerved.

Did Elle feel her hands the way Lee did? Lee would never know. Only Elle would know. If she felt them at all. Was her mind such that the command Lee tried to pinpoint in his brain was at the tip of her consciousness? Or did she also have the unknown gap between the connections in her brain and her physical movement?

Night descended, and the building emptied. Lee was alone with the clock, ticking more prominently in the silence of the now empty floor. He looked at it, saw it leering back at him. Again he felt unnerved being alone with his body. He realized that in all the times he had looked at the ticking clock that evening, he hadn't noticed the time. He glanced at it again. *Oh that's right*, he thought. He had noticed. Was the information gathered from his first unperceived glance at the time stored in the same gap in his mind as the brain's directive to his fingers to move? Tick, tick, the clock answered, unsatisfactorily. He opened the door to leave, the hair on his arms standing up as he hurried away from his own skin. It closed behind him, shutting out the timekeeper on the wall.

He felt disturbed as he exited the building and walked through the airy center of town into the narrow labyrinth of cobblestone streets. Lit but silent. The data Frank collected on Elle would never show what it was like to be Elle. If she wholly embodied Allie, she must feel. Or think that she feels. Or deduce that she has things called feelings, emotional states of being, reactions, even if she doesn't feel those feelings. Because they are not perceived doesn't mean they don't exist. But would that be true for Elle? Could that be true for a being whose existence is manufactured?

But manufactured to perfection, identical in every way to a being whose existence was full and real and human. *If*, Lee thought, *I can't deny emotional states and reasoning existing in myself, can I deny them in Elle?* He frowned, looking down. With each step he perceived a new stone under his feet, though he felt like he walked in place. He tried to trick his mind into perceiving his forward motion. *Which is true: the existence of logical reasoning only by way of appropriate connections, or logical reasoning by way of the ability to reason?*

He walked with his hands in his pockets, not yet willing to acknowledge them again. The tingling in his arms had only just subsided. He was deep in his own mind when he knocked into another man passing by. The connection of their bodies rattled him.

"Excuse me."

"Excuse me."

Lee looked back at the man scurrying away. What had he been thinking? Where was he going? What would it be like to be that man? Lee tried to put himself in his place, to walk in the opposite direction underneath his flatcap, to have just collided with another walking man. Lee could imagine, but it was just that. It was imagining. It was Lee, still feeling like Lee, walking in the opposite direction. It was still Lee inside the physical shell of the other man. He couldn't get out of his head.

Or had the man run into him on purpose? His heart started to race as he pictured the man laughing as he walked away. Laughing at him. At the man who could be run into, run over, by any other man who passed. The man who would think about the encounter long after it had resolved. Who would feel his chest tighten days after the occurrence at the mere sight of a flatcap.

It infuriated Lee that he couldn't control his pounding heart, his flushing neck, despite telling himself that it was worth not a second more of thought. *Has the man already forgotten?* He didn't imagine the man in the flatcap to be flushing as he was. His hands shaking in his pockets, as Lee's were. An absorbing hatred for himself overcame him. But as he wished himself to disappear into the dark spots between the cobblestones, he walked forth, hoping that whomever else he would pass on his way home wouldn't see through his coat to the unseaming man beneath. He willed the muscles in his face to lift instead of melt, each deliberate step he took feeling foreign and unco-ordinated as he struggled to smooth his gait into obscurity.

....

FOURTEEN

Back at his house, Lee opened the door to his study and stood in the doorframe. He loosened his tie, the light from the hall behind him illuminating his shape. He felt the tie with his fingers, the smooth texture, the sewn shapes. The silk had taken over the feel of his fingers, and he felt his fingers no more. Like mirrors, they were void until the external appeared before them, on them. How did a single finger feel without something to touch? Lee could not tell.

He turned and calmly walked across the landing of the stairs to his bedroom. He slid the right door of his closet to the left, lining up their edges. The open closet revealed a collection of women's clothes, all jammed tightly together. To the left, evenly spaced, were Lee's. He ignored the women's clothes and hung his alongside them. The hangers faced the same way. He took off his already undone tie, shoes, and shirt, and kept on his undershirt, still tucked into his trousers, wrinkle-free. He closed the closet halfway and stepped back, the women's clothes peeking out from the open door. Lee shuffled around the bedroom, looking for something to put in place. There was nothing. He paused. Slowly he approached the closet again, looking at the clothes to his right. He admired them, touched them as if forbidden. Their myriad, feminine fabrics, unworn for years but still pristine. The collars of the dresses all neatly folded, permanently creased. The smell of dust and perfume.

There was a knock at the front door, pulling Lee out of the past. He threw on a sweater and walked down the stairs hesitantly. It was late. Seeing the door, he heard another knock.

"Who is it?"

A high, crisp voice came through from the other side. "It's me."

Lee recognized Elle's voice and opened the door, the same panic he felt the night Walter died threatening again. "Are you all right?"

Elle looked disheveled. She walked inside and took off her trench. She hung it familiarly on the standing coat rack behind the door, and then seemed to realize her place. She did not walk farther into the house.

"Ohhh. I'm fine." Her voice revealed frustration rather than sadness or concern. Lee relaxed slightly.

Elle looked for safety in Lee. He waited for her to speak. When she didn't, he gave in. "Come in?"

Elle took a step forward and stood still again. Her eyes darted from place to place, looking everywhere except at Lee. When she had apparently run out of places to stare and turned to look at him, he was startled to see a burning in her eyes. With great confidence that didn't match her fearful face, she spoke. "I know I timed out."

Lee was only partially surprised. He held her stare for a moment, then walked into his kitchen. Without a word or a backward glance, he put on a pot of coffee and watched it brew. He silently processed Elle's awareness, an awareness that he still wasn't sure was possible. Was it just that he was perceiving her deductions as awareness? He knew that was likely the case, but he didn't try to ignore the nagging hope he felt that she was in fact aware.

The strong, nutty scent of the coffee hit his nose and brought back the feel of morning. Did the scent reach across the room to Elle? Did she inhale it as he did, experiencing the indescribable sensation of invisible, perfumed air hitting her nostrils and creating a sense very nearly like taste that could only be called exactly what it was? Smell. How to describe the sense to someone with no such sense seemed impossible. As death had been impossible to describe. But Elle had the sense of smell. Though Lee could never know objectively what her experience with that sense was like, he would never know objectively what anyone's experience was like, aside from his own.

What curious things they were, senses. The dark brown pool of aromatic liquid emanated heat. The thick sound of the pour. The rich taste. Such a fully formed and distinctive body, all from a little bit of liquid. How else could he describe the color to a blind person, who had always been blind and had never experienced what brown was? It was brown, and brown was it. There was no other way. Its very definition gave it form. He supposed he could give the degrees of light reflecting to describe the color in numbers, but what would it mean? There was only so much understanding one could gain from science without experience. Yes, subjectivity was necessary, in certain cases, to enhance the understanding of science. Indeed. But then, wasn't the experience of science a subjective experience? Wasn't the very act of considering it an act which bestows subjectivity upon it, banning it from the realm of the objective?

The coffee swirled and steamed. Lee remained silent.

When she got no response, Elle repeated herself. But when she spoke next she was unsure, as if each time she said it out loud it became less true, or, at least, less irrefutably true.

"I know I timed out. I forgot he died." She heard her last words for the first time.

Lee looked at her, analyzing her as he waited for the coffee to brew. Her shoulders were lean, close, pushed forward into a shrug. Her eyes looked wide and darker than usual, their blue only a tint within the black.

Elle waited for him to say something. He didn't. He only watched her. Her eyes were cast down, looking away as if ashamed, as if she knew that she had done something wrong. Did she feel ashamed, or did she only look ashamed, holding her body the way one would after saying what she said? The coffee indicated its readiness with a cutting ring, and Lee poured two cups.

"I don't have any more soy," he said to Elle. He remembered how she liked her coffee. Half a cup, the rest milk, but only soy. He handed her the cup anyway. He knew it would be fine. If no soy, black would do, but still only half a cup.

"That's fine," Elle said. Of course it was fine.

Elle looked around the kitchen. Lifeless. The dark, unused living room. The stairs. They reminded her of the previous night. Her face pulled together at the memory. Lee waited.

"What's wrong with me?" Elle asked finally.

The question hurt Lee. Guilt filled him again, seizing his chest. Before him stood a model of perfection, and it was his impatience to begin the trial that had brought her to a breaking point. He should have waited until he had implanted the last connection. But he didn't. And it was hurting her.

It was no fault of hers that she had timed out. Nothing at all was wrong with her. But he saw how the absence of a single connection had caused such damage already, and would continue to weigh on her until there was something for her to hold on to. There was a long pause before Lee answered.

"We didn't write you a way to process death. You burned yourself out trying to understand because you just don't have the resources. Don't worry, I'm going to fix it."

Elle was impervious to his consolation. "How can you fix it if you don't understand how to deal with it either? Isn't that why I exist?"

"I don't know what you mean."

"Well, look at me," Elle looked disgusted as she gestured toward herself. "I'm only here because you didn't know how to let her go." She said this not cruelly, but as fact. "But how do you look at me and think of me as her, when, even if you copy exactly each cell, and each part of each cell, there is—*something*—some part of her that you cannot recreate? I don't want you to 'fix it.' I want to know what that something is that vanished when Walter died."

Lee hung on to her words. *How do you look at me and think of me as her.* He tried to assess their truth.

"You're thinking of it wrong," he said. "You're *essentially* the same. That's what's important. The *essence.* The *process.* The *choice* to move from A to B."

"What do you mean we're essentially the same? What is the essence? It can't just be the process, or the choice."

"But that's exactly what it is," Lee argued.

"But if a copy of Walter were standing in front of me, and he made all the same choices as Walter, and made those choices by going through a mental process, he still wouldn't be Walter. He'd be a copy of

Walter making the same choices. Is the essence of a human being choice?" She seemed to ask herself rather than Lee. "But I can make choices, and some human beings can't make choices. Are they not human?"

"It's not just choice—"

"Then what is it? What is it to be alive that Walter has lost?"

"It's hard to explain—"

Lee went silent. Elle looked dubiously into her coffee cup, staring at her reflection in the dark liquid. She seemed to know that there was no answer. She walked over to the couch, covered in flowered material that reflected Allie's taste. The carefully matched drapes over the windows, closed indefinitely.

She sat lightly on the couch. Across from her was a coffee table, aligned precisely with the center of the fireplace just behind it. To her left were two chairs, the degree of their inward-facing angle measured to a tenth. On the floor, a plush rug. There was not a single wrinkle in the couch or a pillow out of place. The room hadn't been used in months, years. As if she were sitting in a papier-mâché set. She couldn't explain it, but it made her feel like just another prop in the room. Though her heart did beat and her lungs filled with air, it didn't seem like enough. Like there could have been a beating heart without her to house it, sitting on the couch. Just another mechanical happening, like the reclining of a chair.

Lee sat in the chair next to the couch. His presence breathed in the room in such a manner of which Elle felt her own presence wasn't capable. It fooled him, the room, breathing brightness into the colors in the fabrics as he looked at them, returning to their prop-like state each time he glanced away.

To Lee, the fabric was cold and stiff, and made him feel uncomfortable. The drab colors, the cold walls. The only life in the room to him was Elle. She shifted closer to Lee and leaned in to talk, suddenly distant and melancholy.

"I don't know. It seems too simple, that we could explain life in those terms. Process and choice. You can't explain death, right? So how would you know how to explain life? Don't you need to understand what it is that no longer exists in death to understand what exists in life?" She took a sip of her coffee to fill the silence. "How did she die? Your wife?"

Lee shifted in his chair. It had been complicated, choosing which memories to implant in Elle at the end of Allie's life. He knew that there was a gap in Elle's timeline between Allie's death and her creation, but she had never brought it up before. Lee replied with little detail. "Giving birth."

"You have a child?"

In her eyes, Lee could see Elle drawing blanks, cognitively entering the gap at the edge of Allie's death.

"For a moment, I did." He recalled the moment when she had been pulled from her mother's body, when he witnessed the transfer of life from Allie to his little girl. Through his grief came a life, and he wept for both. And then the cord was cut. And it was as if the life that Allie had given her receded, drew back into her body like the transfer was incomplete, and both lives dissolved into the air.

Alma. He named her after she died.

Elle took Lee's hand in hers and smiled compassionately. One eye fluttered, then widened back to normal. Lee caught it, but thought it nothing more than a twitch. She silently urged him to continue, but was no longer listening. The revelation had stirred something in her. *Has he told me this before?*

"Allie was the essential part of *me* that I can't recreate. But I tried. When I designed you, I tried." He looked at Elle and felt the stagnant chill in the air from a room long unused. "Cold?" he asked her.

Elle nodded and swirled her coffee, noticing the prickling sensation on her skin only after Lee drew her attention to it. Waves of electricity ran down her arms indicating cold. The more she focused on each part of her arm, the less the sensation existed on that part. She couldn't quite capture what it was, wouldn't be able to explain it to someone who had never experienced it, but she knew what it felt like to be cold.

Lee walked to the fireplace, aware of Elle watching his back. It made him feel very large and out of place to be in the room, foreign to him after having spent so many years living alongside it rather than inside it. He ran his hand along the gate, lifting the dust into invisible specs that would settle down nearby. The gate looked newly dark, the black iron revealing the layer of old grey that covered the rest of the room. He lifted the chopped wood from the neat pile alongside the fireplace. It released a dry, musty smell as he shifted the reluctant wood. The room crawled with the displeasure of a disturbed cocoon, life bursting forth and receding into the cracks of the walls.

He lit the fire. It shined weakly, the flames uncertain of their reach. As they grew bolder, they brought life into the room, misplaced. The popping of the wood, the scent of fresh ash and burning dust. The warmth that crept over the cold brick, overturning years of stasis. The reflection glimmered in Elle's dark eyes as the warmth reached her face, the flames inspiring a new notion of fervor that she pondered as she stared.

"Right before I timed out last night, I was about to walk up the stairs. It was dark. I saw my hand in front of me on the banister. And I lost my perspective, like I was the hand suspended in space, with no context to tell me if I'm left or right." She stared through the flames, unblinking, her eyes seeing the flickering red flares as smaller and smaller. Less ardent, as she considered herself alongside Walter. "I can't imagine what it would be like to lose him if I actually loved him."

Lee poked at the fire, not wanting to face the appearance of the room behind him that was revitalized by the flame. He felt watched, illuminated, open. The room felt disorganized and large. He wanted to return it to its original state, close it off, and shut himself safely in his study. But he didn't. He walked instead to the chair across from Elle and sat down, pressing his spine into it and sinking low so that its back covered his head. He held his arms inside the armrests. His legs felt exposed, his feet planted on the ground, motionless, blending into the lingering staleness of the unwalked carpet.

Elle was relaxing back into the couch, ignoring Lee's stilted movements for his sake. She tried to quell his discomfort by feigning ease of her own, but her mind raced.

"Why didn't you program me to love him?" Elle mused out loud, wondering more than asking. "Did he know I didn't love him?" She tried to recall times when Walter might have let on that he knew, but she couldn't. She remembered him being very even in his disposition, untroubled, grateful for her company and asking for nothing more. "Imagine your wife going through the motions as if she loves you, but feeling nothing. Would you rather know she doesn't really love you, and is acting like she does, or would you rather die believing that she does?"

Lee didn't respond, knowing that her question was not entirely meant for him. There was a long silence between them as they separately considered the question. Lee's thoughts strayed and landed on guilt. It was a guilt that he had felt often with Allie since the beginning of their relationship. A guilt that he could never comprehend, its source so contradictory and fleeting. It had often made him feel unstable and insecure, vacillating between "what if" and bursts of certainty to correct for the what-ifs. He had felt most unhappy during the periods of "what if," and then desperately afraid to lose Allie and regretful of the time lost on hesitations. His guilt only grew after he lost her. A loss that couldn't be corrected after seeing clearly.

"Sometimes I felt like I didn't love her," Lee said to Elle, recalling the many times of "what if." "But it was the sort of unconditional love where that was insignificant. Sometimes I wished she would leave me. When someone loves you that much, I guess you feel like you don't love them enough. Why couldn't I love her more? But I did. I loved her so much, sometimes I felt mad. Maybe we're only capable of so much love before it turns into something else. Violence, hatred, psychosis. Maybe there's a point along the line where it turns. But we'd be able to recognize a definitive point, no?"

Lee pictured the spectrum of love and hate. He imagined that somewhere in the middle was where one turned into the other, but couldn't pinpoint it, or decide on the same point more than once. "Maybe they all lie in the sphere just outside love, and we just can't tell when we've crossed over. Walter didn't need love. Walter needed company. That's what you gave him."

"Mmmm." Elle closed her eyes, listening to Lee talk. She pictured the same spectrum as Lee did as he spoke, imagining an entirely different point at which love turned to hate. She wondered how many different points would be selected if five more people were asked to do so, and if there were a correct answer. Even if two points selected were next to each other, weren't there an infinite number of points between those two, and an infinite number between those other points? There were, she knew. How precise and inconceivable, impossible, the point would have to be where love turned to hate.

Lee looked over at Elle, examining her features. Her eyes were closed softly and moved little, as if they had simply fallen rather than been pressed together. Her lips were parted only slightly, looking more full. Her head rested on the couch behind her, her neck extended upward, revealing long, sinewy lines that drew Lee's eyes down with them toward her chest. Her shoulders relaxed at once, and Lee recognized the moment when she had fallen into slumber. He leaned quietly over her, holding his feet cemented to the floor. He took the mug of coffee from her limp fingers and set it aside. As he reached for it, he felt the smooth, creamy skin of her hands brush his. He followed their lines up her arms, over her shoulders, and down her slight frame.

The contours of her body were exactly those of Allie's. He recalled the movements created by the curve of her hips, the twist of her back, the turn of her neck. He saw Elle move the same way. He saw them move as one, the curves of Allie meeting the curves of Elle, the bend of their knees together. He looked down at Elle's shape on the couch, seeing Allie's figure meet his eyes. He wished to trace the outline of her body, her pure form.

Abruptly, guiltily, he moved back to break his train of thought. He sank back into his chair and fixated his thoughts on the fire. A draft from the fireplace rustled softly through the thick drapes, their movement old and heavy.

FIFTEEN

••

Days passed unmissed. Lee sat at a sidewalk café with Frank, smoldering. It was sunny but cold, and his movements were restrained by his heavy coat. They watched the people passing by, taking small sips of their coffee. It was Saturday, and there was much movement on the streets despite the imminent winter. Lee imagined that the town was bustling with people anticipating the last decent day before the snow and wind arrived.

The winters had been long the last few years, and the early snow that had fallen that autumn left behind cold rainclouds. The rare sunny day drew people from their homes as if it were the first day of spring. Lee and Frank were no different. The cold metal chairs of the outdoor café were a welcome departure from their own kitchens and home-brewed coffee.

Since the night that Elle had shown up on his doorstep, Lee hadn't entered his living room. He ignored it on his way down the stairs to the kitchen and to the front door, but it sat there, open and used, tormenting him. He felt apprehension about having released the room from its sleep, as if having closed off parts of his house had been necessary for him to coexist with the memory of Allie's death. Lighting the fire had changed something, and it disturbed him. The types of changes fires made were irreversible. Chemical changes. They caught quickly and were difficult to stop.

Lee feared a chemical change had occurred that night in his house. He knew that it was irrational, but felt it nonetheless. He had become wary of the room, the smoke having released something into the air that permeated his entire house. He felt unsure of himself, forgetful. He imagined one night that he couldn't remember whether it was Allie or Elle with whom he had shared an experience long ago. Or was it a dream? He couldn't remember. With the room, he had opened a space in his mind that was empty and unsettling. What it was to be filled with he did not know.

He sat beside Frank, his coffee quickly becoming cold. He saw the heat evaporating into the air through the thick steam, and realized that it wasn't a warm day at all, that it was simply warmer than the rest and seemed positively hot in comparison. They had been discussing Elle, though they hadn't intended to. It wasn't a surprising direction of conversation. Indeed, a life could be truly consuming.

"It's not too late to restart the trial," Frank suggested. We can erase her memories with Walter and restart her with someone else."

"No." Lee dismissed Frank's suggestion shortly, recognizing that erasing Elle's memories would erase all the mental progress that Lee had witnessed the other night. Her apparent ability to reason, to understand. It was something that Lee couldn't recreate. Something that Elle had developed on her own. That alone was significant to the trial and had to be captured. But more than that, Lee admitted only to himself, he had already accepted Elle. The idea of rebooting her reminded him of the grim time between Allie's death and Elle's creation. He wasn't prepared to volunteer for that.

As he pulled his thoughts away from the dark quicksand of those memories, a striking, long-legged woman with white-blond hair passed by. Her leggings accentuated how thin she was, and her high-heeled boots made her look even more so. Her wide, blue parka enveloped her, making her look larger than life and very petite at the same time. She smiled modestly at Lee, her long steps carrying her quickly past him. He caught her eye but remained stoic, forgetting her as soon as she was out of his sight.

Frank spotted her and lustfully watched her walk away, his mouth hung open slightly in shock. Lee stared at him, amused, waiting for him to speak. His fleeting infatuation reminded Lee of when they were at university. Frank was younger than everyone else in their class, and uniquely intelligent. He was quick, charming, and despite his unorthodox looks, he attracted many girls, and was attracted to many of them. Intelligent girls, proper girls, pretty girls. Not unlike Marigold, who was much younger and still only in graduate school, but who was much wiser than anyone Frank had known before.

Marigold was also much more serious than Frank was accustomed to. She valued her knowledge over her appearance and, while naturally quite stunning, preferred to dress in a more classic, plain way. She was petite and didn't often stand out. Rarely did she venture out in high-heeled boots and leggings. Lee knew that Frank loved Marigold, but he also loved seeing tall, beautiful women in extravagant boots and luxurious blue coats. Another rarity in their town, to see such unabashed flamboyance. *She must be passing through*, Lee thought.

When he could no longer see the woman, Frank snapped out of his trance and addressed Lee without skipping a beat. "It's just a reboot. She'll be exactly the same except she'll have a new set of memories for the last year that she spent with Walter."

"You can't just extract the memories of Walter?"

"It's a chain of events. Memories naturally build on each other. Even the memories without Walter will have no context if we keep them. She won't be able to process them. She'd be left with an unbridgeable gap."

There was silence as Lee considered. He looked out into the street, at the strategically planted trees feigning natural growth. At the passersby, old and worn, young and vibrant, and those struggling in between. He looked at their faces, so many that he didn't recognize, and wondered how many of them lived on his cul-de-sac, on the other side, across the short line of planted trees. The unbridgeable gap between neighbors of the east and west. How easy it should be to recognize his own neighbors, but how far apart they remained across the man-made divider. He wondered if anyone recognized him, and if he seemed rude for not saying hello.

Of course they recognize me, Lee thought. *I'm that strange and lonely man whose wife died who runs that lab that brought her back.*

Lee imagined it to be what people thought of him. He didn't know many people outside of his team. It was difficult to tell, but he suspected that they were wary of him. He thought of Mrs. Thatcher, her strange behavior toward him. Not understanding what went on in the lab, not understanding his own disappearance into his home for months after Allie's death, and his constant lurking around the new *thing* that he brought home one day. He thought people might be afraid of Elle, disturbed by her, curious about her. But he didn't know. He never made the trip across the unbridgeable gap between himself and his neighbors, and felt it widen as the days passed after Walter's death.

He felt their suspicions, their eyes watching him as he watched Elle. They didn't understand. How could they? But Lee wondered if they would be ready when the time came to go public with the project. Would they accept what the companions were meant to do? Would grown children buy one for their widowed mothers, lonely fathers, for themselves in the future? Or were the companions too advanced, too humanlike, too "creepy," as Walter had called Elle when he first saw her. Or was that only because Walter had recognized her as Allie walking the earth again?

Another stunning woman with bright red hair passed by, jarring Lee once again from his thoughts. She caught Frank's eye, to his great pleasure, giving him giddy confidence. He stood up slightly in his chair and sat back down, looking like a bounce of joy that a toddler might produce when presented with his favorite cloth lamb.

The loose curls throughout her oversized mane bounced with each movement she made. She walked with her whole body, the twist of her shoulders seeming to dictate the motion of her hips. She slinked past, her hair following closely behind, showing different shades of red as the sun directed all its shine toward her. Frank looked around for the café's sign and address.

"Where *are* we?" He said in disbelief. Lee allowed a small smile to approach his usually set lips. He was surprised himself by the passing of two unusually beautiful women on the same street. Unusual indeed. *They must have come in from the city. Or perhaps they are on their way there.*

Frank continued. He had to remind himself what his argument was for rebooting Elle, his mind reaching to hold on to the image of the redhead rather than trade it in for science.

"If we don't do this she'll keep timing out. She'll never grow—with you or anyone else," Frank added, letting Lee know that he understood that his hesitation wasn't purely scientific.

"Rebooting her doesn't solve the problem," Lee deflected. "We're supposed to be creating companions for the *elderly*. We can't afford to reboot the AI systems every time someone dies. We need to program them to cope with death even if we don't know how to make them understand it."

Lee was right, Frank realized. A reboot wasn't the right answer for AIs coping poorly with death. It was the easy answer, but would be an expensive one in the future.

"I don't know what to tell you," Frank said. "We don't know how to do what we need to do."

"I'm working on it," Lee said.

"I know you are. You have been since the beginning."

"But I'm close. I just didn't expect it to happen so fast."

"You never do," Frank said, sympathetic to how death tends to lurk around unexpected corners and show its face at unexpected times, whether those around it are ready or not. He took the last sip of his icy coffee and leaned back in his chair. He sat with Lee in silence, a sound that was increasingly passed between them as the trial wore on, and wondered if Lee's skewed motivations for finding a way to program the systems to cope would have any impact on his conclusion.

As he set down his cup, Frank noticed yet another beautiful woman pass by. Her skin was very dark and was flawless, her hair so short that it was nearly shaved. Her makeup appeared to have been very skillfully applied, with light colors in the right places that made her look like spring. She did not glance at Lee or Frank, her face set in a determined stare. Frank watched her in surprise, a third wonderfully proportioned woman in their little town.

"Unbelievable..." he said to himself.

Lee again watched Frank watch the woman. He looked back as if to see what he had missed. "Nothing special," he said blandly, disinterestedly, knowing that it would rile Frank, but thinking the opposite. He kept drinking in silence and smiled into his cup when he caught Frank's expression of disbelief.

Out of the corner of his eye, he saw another woman pass by, not like those who had caught Frank's attention. Her head was down and she walked briskly, her entire presence muted. Lee didn't get a clear look at her face before she passed, but he recognized her. He recognized her dark hair and porcelain skin, her slight frame. Her gait. She had walked close enough to Frank and Lee that she would have seen them if she had known them, but she stared at the sidewalk in front of her feet as she walked. It was a walk that he had seen many times before. Though it was nothing special, indistinguishable from other walks to those who weren't so familiar with it, it was a walk that he could recognize from across the cul-de-sac. How it made the body move in space. Lee watched the back of her head, her hair lifting in the breeze as she walked away. Frank didn't notice her.

"Was that Elle?" Lee asked Frank.

"Huh?"

"Who just passed."

"Elle just passed?" Frank asked, confused.

"Right in front of us, right here," Lee said incredulously, indicating how close she had come to the table.

"Someone just passed right in front of us? I must have missed it. I was watching—" Frank trailed off, motioning toward the dark-skinned woman who had passed. "Unbelievable," he repeated.

Lee looked back but the woman was gone. He had been sure it was Elle, but it couldn't have been. If he had been sure he wouldn't be questioning it, he told himself. But he had been so sure.

He shook his head, dropping the subject, and finished his coffee. He couldn't shake the strange feeling that suddenly crept onto the back of his neck. *Or maybe I'm just cold*, he thought, flipping up the collar of his coat.

SIXTEEN

....

Elle burst into her house with flushed cheeks from having been outside all day. Though it had been an unusually warm day for the time of year, the stagnant chill in the air seeped through her clothes when the sun went down and touched her bones, lightly at first so that she didn't feel it, then all at once, as soon as it was inside. She locked the door behind her. Though her house was warm, she was anxious to light the fireplace, sit close to it with a blanket and a book, and let it melt away the day.

She turned to drop her keys in the tiny green Murano glass bowl on the hall table as she shoved off her boots. In the large, decorative mirror above the table, she caught a glimpse of herself. She paused, one fur-lined boot still on. She looked to her side in the mirror, still holding the keys, and leaned in, staring intently into her reflection. Her reddened cheeks. *A lie,* she thought.

Having never seen her skin bleed, she had difficulty believing that her insides were as perfectly matched to the human form as her outsides. But the cold she did feel. Did that feeling come from the inner workings of her body, or from her mind, from the masses of connections that she knew represented a brain? She felt the skin on her face, soft, cool. It would begin to chap soon, her skin, once the winter kicked in. Though the air was rarely dry, the wind would become strong, as if the early winter moon brought with it violent airs that thrived in the dark.

She uncurled one of the thin key rings and held it up. The cold vanished from her mind. She looked at the tip of the ring, the point, and traced the open circle with her finger. The thin wire denting the skin underneath her fingertips. The polished evenness of the curve. The density, the hardness. The smallness and toughness of its silvered material.

When she had felt with her hands all there was to feel, she held the open key ring to her face. The metal felt warm. She ran the curve of the circle over her cheeks, feeling its smoothness, feeling how it pushed in the skin on her face when she ran the wire over her jaw, her eyebrow. She stopped, held the point of the ring just underneath her left eye. She looked at the distinguishing freckle right beneath her bottom lid. She loved that freckle, so unique to her. But no, it was Allie's freckle. A freckle that came from deep in Allie's skin but was merely altered surface of Elle's own. *Is it?* Elle wondered. *Could it be possible that every cell of Allie really does exist exactly the same way, down to the atom, in me?*

She wondered which cell gave her life, knowing that no one cell contained life, that all of them together made up her life, and that without one or many of them she would still have life. It perplexed her to think of her physical makeup, and the fact that she was indeed alive. That not a single cell that made her up was aware of her, but that she was aware of them. Not a single one would care if it were separated from the others, or if all the other cells separated as well and there were no longer an Elle to be a part of. No single cell knew who Elle was, knew anything about life. And yet, it was those very cells, the closest things to her that cared nothing about her, that gave her life. The combination of all those cells that gave her her specific life, her own life, a life different from other lives. If those cells made up someone else, if she traded cells, one at a time, with another body, would her consciousness follow and walk in the shoes of the other? Perhaps it was what she was doing at that very moment. Perhaps she had already traded cells with another. Perhaps those cells made up her consciousness, and she had become Elle from someone else. But she knew that no cell carried her consciousness, that she could shed cells and duplicate cells and would lose no part of her self.

She pressed. And released. A small white line filled in quickly with pink where she lifted the ring from her face. She pressed again, dragging the tip of the wire down across her cheek, cutting the skin. But only an inch did she drag. Her eye sagged as she trailed the wire beneath it. The distorted face that looked back at her scared her. *That's me*, she thought.

She retracted the key ring from her face and looked at the shallow cut. A red line formed but no blood spilled. She looked curiously, horrified and euphoric, touching the mirror where her cut was reflected. *What have I just done?* Her hands moved on their own. She admired their work, feared their work, and had felt them do their work only distantly.

The light in her eyes went out, leaving empty black pits staring back at her from the reflection. The one boot on her foot, the red line in the mirror, and the keys still hanging from her hand.

....

SEVENTEEN

Frank sat up in his bed next to Marigold only half paying attention to what she was saying. On his desk across the room, one of Frank's monitors was recording the usual strings of data. They scrolled through consistently. The screens had been set up so that Frank could see them from anywhere in the room.

"Hey," Frank nudged Marigold.

"Hm?"

"Did you know who Lee was before you met me?"

"Of course I did. Why?"

Frank looked at her, stunned.

"Really?" he said, humored. "Just like that? Of course you did?"

Marigold returned his tone, confused.

"Well, yeah. You can't really help but know who he is, right?"

"But you were so young when he became famous."

"Well, he was a brilliant, successful, not terrible looking, American scientist. That will stick in people's heads for a while."

"Not terrible looking!" Frank exclaimed in shock.

Marigold laughed as Frank's shock turned into a scowl.

"I used to have a thing for him you know," she teased, "before I actually met him."

"You tell me this now?"

"Oh please, I was young."

"Hmph. Young, huh? What about now? Do you still think he's not terrible looking?"

"I do," Marigold replied, her eyes shining. "I mean, underneath all the wear and tear, but yeah."

"I can't believe this," Frank said, turning his nose up. "I'm going to tell Lee."

Marigold laughed. "Go ahead. He'll probably hold it over your head more than anything." She paused, imagining but not remembering a smile on Lee's face. "Why did you want to know?"

"You know that new group that we hired at the lab?"

"No, but okay," Marigold replied.

"Well we hired a new group of scientists—I think there are six or something like that—we just hired them so they're in training right now. So I was teaching a seminar and Lee came by the lab and they all saw him, and they asked if I could introduce them."

"Well that makes sense—he's their employer."

"But it was more than that. I just forgot, I guess, what it used to be like."

Silence passed between them, then all at once, tears started streaming down Marigold's face.

"Mari! What happened?"

"I don't know!" She let out a small laugh through her tears, and then they came harder. "It's just so stupid!"

"What's so stupid?" Her tears caught Frank completely off guard.

"That his wife died! There's just no reason for it! I mean, *why?*" she wailed.

He didn't understand what triggered Marigold's spell of sorrow, but he had seen it happen before. At times, she would be light, laughing, radiant, as she had been moments before. Sometimes, only seconds later, those moments would be followed by periods of intensity and solemnity that he couldn't comprehend, times when her youthful smile was suddenly washed away by a dark and aged wave. Anything could trigger them. A simple statement, a silence that lasted a beat too long. Frank approached the lighter times with trepidation, anticipating the wave that might or might not follow.

Sometimes it would catch him off guard if he was fully entrenched in a lighter moment. He wouldn't expect her mood to swing and would get angry with her when it did over seemingly the simplest thing. But it would, and his reaction would put her into a shell that lasted sometimes for days. It was on those days that he felt like he was living with a ghost, a body left behind, completely disconnected from the rest of the physical world that he understood. He didn't know where she would go during those times. She wouldn't look him in the eye, and when she did, she didn't seem to be there. There would be nothing in her eyes to look back into.

The occurrences were rare, but he remembered them. She was aware of them, and feared their return. She could feel when she was slipping back into that world, but could do little about it. By the time she became aware, she was already slipping, and it was nearly impossible to stop once she had begun. Like the invisible event horizon before a black hole, once crossed, the only way out was through. On these days, Frank lived with the fear that she wouldn't return.

At first he had tried to break it, to fix it and bring her back into the natural world that he knew and that she had known only days, hours, minutes before, but over time he learned that he simply needed to wait until it passed. It would always pass. And when he had her back he would realize, over and over, that she harbored a darkness that he would never understand, retreated sometimes into a world of her own that showed her things that he would never see. And he would realize how much wisdom and weight was behind her most playful moments, and that her light was lighter than he would ever achieve because of how dark her world could be.

He thought of it as he felt her next to him, clouded by the shadows of that world that followed her, waiting for her to slow her step and sink back into them. It baffled him how it could descend upon her at once like a storm could suddenly eclipse the sun. How it could happen to someone like her, this irrational thing, to his bright, sweet, sensible Marigold.

"I know," was all he could say as he held her. Though he didn't.

As suddenly as her tears appeared, they stopped.

"It's just sad to see," she said. "He was such a good person. There was just no reason."

"He still is," Frank replied.

"Yeah, but people don't see that side of him anymore. It's like he's someone else. She was so young. They could have had their whole lives to spend together. They had no time at all. He just carries on without her, and she has no idea."

Frank stayed silent, fearing that he might trigger another episode if he spoke.

"I hate what people say about him," she continued, drying her face. "I don't know why it affects me so much, but it does."

"Because you're a good person," Frank said, choosing the most innocuous string of words he could imagine.

"They're just terrible people. They talk about him like he's a ghost. Like he's not a person anymore. Why are they still talking about him? And it has gotten so much worse ever since—" she paused. "They just don't understand."

"People talk," Frank said. "They'll talk about him until something new and better to talk about comes along."

"Don't you think it affects him?"

"He never says anything about it," Frank replied.

"But don't you think it does? With everything else that he has going on?"

"Maybe he hears it, but I think he's too focused on Elle to notice."

"Or maybe he's focusing on Elle so that he doesn't need to listen," Marigold suggested. "Maybe he would focus less on her if there were no voices he needed to drown out. What about those new designs you were working on?"

"Elle has been good for him. It's a reason for him to get up in the morning. He came into the lab the other day!" Frank reminded her. "Do you know how long it's been since he's been in the lab? He actually chose to leave his house, walk all the way across town, and walk into the lab. Where there are other people."

Marigold looked through him.

"She's good for him? Did you wind up introducing him to those new people in your office?"

"No, not this time. It wasn't a good time—" he stopped himself before disproving his own statement.

Marigold caught it and sat back, her eyes glistening.

The data scrolled unnoticed in the corner of the room. One of the letters in the long strands appeared red, backward. G. The surrounding letters in the strands remained black. All apparently placed together in a random pattern, some letters repeating multiple times in a row, the unlimited repetition creating unlimited possibilities for the arrangement of the letters. The structure of Elle. Her very DNA. Frank read the patterns of the letters like he read English. A language he had created out of the need for constant monitoring. A way to read more efficiently, to spot patterns, to see problems more evidently in symbols rather than in descriptions or words, as in the backward G. It moved slowly across the three screens. Before Marigold could say anything more, the monitor sounded.

Frank immediately looked up and saw the red blinking light. He darted from his bed to read the data. "Ohhh..." he said to himself.

"What's the matter?"

Frank kept reading, pulling up a chart that indicated that Elle had timed out again. The muscles in his face released as his panic diminished. He briefly questioned his next move, then picked up his phone.

Elle had only a small, low-level injury. A bruise, a scratch, a bump. This didn't concern him. What did concern him, however, was that she had done it to herself, which he gleaned from the data as well. It told him that there was a decline in her cognitive functioning. It was happening more quickly than he had anticipated.

As soon as Lee answered the phone Frank spoke, not wanting to delay the unpleasant conversation that he knew was ahead. "Lee this isn't good. We need to start the reboot. She's starting to break down."

Lee sighed. He remained seated behind his desk, his hand hovering over a notebook. From the elongated right sides of the illustrations on the page he could tell when he was halfway between wakefulness and slumber. He had attempted once more that night to find a way to explain death, and found himself drawing what was in his mind instead of writing. Words seemed the wrong approach.

The drawings were of nothing that Lee had actually ever seen. Vast voids, the ultimate simplicity surrounded by chaos, unblinking, two-dimensional eyes, the shapes of letters strung together to form meaningless words. Solitude, in greatness and in smallness. They were all unfinished. He supposed that the drawings might be as close as he would ever come to explaining death. Unfinished.

It irked him that he couldn't remember what he had been thinking before the phone interrupted. As if he assumed incorrectly that he was a still body that had streams of thoughts when the reality was that his thoughts resided in a world of their own. A complete world into which they welcomed him, but when he left, he left the thoughts behind, in their world. He was an outsider in his own mind.

"We knew this would happen," Lee said. "What's she doing?"

"It's not bad, but it's started. It's only going to get worse. We have to start the reboot before it does. We have to stay ahead of it."

"We can't start the reboot," Lee said adamantly.

"We have to. If we don't—"

Frustrated, Lee threw on his coat. "I'm coming over."

"No, no you don't need to come over here," Frank said, beginning to panic again. When Lee didn't answer, Frank tried again. "I'll come to you—Lee?"

There was no answer. Lee was already on his way.

"What's going on?" Marigold asked as Frank hung up the phone.

"It's Elle," Frank said, hearing the obvious words slip from his mouth before he could stop them. Marigold understood.

"Go," she said, picking up a book.

Frank hesitated for a moment, looking for traces of despair on Marigold's face before running down the stairs. There were papers everywhere. Bursting from the small writing desk in the living room, splayed across the couch, piled on folding chairs. He tossed them together and shoved them into drawers, under pillows, anywhere there was space to hide them from

Lee. He hadn't noticed how out of hand the paperwork had gotten.

His guilt rose as he touched each stack of papers. Photographs and notes on Elle. Designs of a new AI system that he had been creating for when Elle was no longer.

He hadn't been thinking of the circumstances that would cause him to need the new design. He'd just had an intuition that it would be useful down the line. The other companions they would need to create if the trial was a success would not be modeled after anyone. They would be their own creatures, have their own unique structures. Like Elle should have had.

When Walter died, Frank thought it would be an opportunity to introduce the new design. He had planned to shut Elle down for good and replace her with the new system. A system that wouldn't be detrimental to Lee, as Frank had suspected Elle was becoming. But he didn't count on Walter's death coming so soon, and he saw how Lee interacted with Elle. He had wanted to show Lee at one time, but held off. He didn't feel right.

He'd had reservations when Lee first brought the design to him, and he regretted giving in. But now, he feared, he couldn't go back. It was done. And yet, he had continued to design Elle's replacement, unsure which way was right. But he knew, even though he had agreed to reboot Elle, he knew that if Lee saw the new designs he would feel deceived. And Frank needed his trust not only for the lab's project, but also because he wasn't sure how Lee would be affected by losing someone else.

When the idea of rebooting Elle came up, Frank had been unsure. His confusion from the beginning, about Elle's design, about how objective Lee was, about how Elle was affecting Lee's perception of Allie, had led him throughout the trial to different conclusions about the best way to handle it when Elle inevitably began to break down. The simplest solution would be to restart the trial with Elle and keep the new designs locked away. For now.

When everything was away, Frank looked around, making sure that nothing looked out of place. *Of course things look out of place,* Frank thought. *I've never been neat in my life.* He walked around uncomfortably, waiting for Lee to arrive.

There was a heavy knock on the door. Frank walked slowly, hesitating before opening it. Lee brushed past Frank, seeming more agitated than he had sounded on the phone.

"You can't reboot Elle," Lee demanded. "She'll forget everything."

Frank had expected this. Lee's hesitation had never been about the trial. It wasn't about needing to program the companions to cope with death, though it was a valid concern for the lab. It was about Lee's attachment to Elle.

Frank scolded himself for letting it get to that point. He had ignored it for some time, but he had known that Lee was no longer objective, if he had ever been at all. He approached the subject carefully, as a friend and scientist. He closed the door quietly while Lee fluttered around.

"Well that's the point," Frank said, calculating his words. "She'll forget so she can move on."

Lee seethed and walked farther into the house, pacing.

"Just listen for a second," Frank began. He could see Lee getting upset. "I know why you don't want to reboot Elle." Frank spoke with compassion. If he showed that he understood Lee, maybe he could persuade him to do what was best. *If,* Frank thought bitterly, *I even know what's best anymore.* Frank pressed on. "But, if we do reboot her, we can expand her capacity for self-made connections, like understanding death. If we don't, she'll push out all of her basic functions and replace them with more complex but incomplete or illogical connections, and eventually she won't be able to function normally."

Lee shook his head. "You're thinking of her as this thing that we can fix. Can we go back and recreate children who are born with defects? We can't just go back in and change them."

Frank spoke quietly. "Look. I get it. If you lose her, you lose Allie all over again. But we're not changing anything. Nothing is going to change. She will be exactly the same, but even more capable of understanding things that Allie would be able to understand."

"But she'll forget! She already knows what it's like to lose someone, not because we made her, but because she experienced it. She knows about Allie, and she gets it. You can't teach sympathy. She's evolving. If you reboot her, she won't remember that she lost Walter. How do you know that she can't handle it? What if she just needs more time to figure it out?"

Frank thought about this. He, again, couldn't tell if Lee was motivated by the idea that an AI system could evolve and have sympathy, or if he was motivated by his own needs. Motivation should have no effect on the outcome, Frank reasoned. If Elle was indeed evolving on her own, even though she'd had a few mishaps, it would be monumental for the lab. *But what about Lee?*

In that moment, Frank realized that he himself hadn't been entirely objective, and he had dealt with Elle keeping Lee in mind. Perhaps a reboot wasn't best for Elle, but was best for Lee. The realization concerned Frank, and he started reassessing his conclusions about Elle.

Lee sensed through Frank's silence that he was persuading him, and didn't push. He relaxed slightly and looked away. He glanced around the room, abruptly noticing how neat it looked. *Marigold must have gotten on his case*, Lee thought. Then he noticed a photograph poking out from a desk drawer next to Frank. He recognized Elle.

"What is this?" he asked, walking over to the desk.

Frank looked over and tried to control his anxiety. *Lee would never open that. He would never look through something that wasn't his.* He sighed with relief as Lee slid the photograph out without opening the drawer.

Standing next to Elle, his arm wrapped around her waist, was Frank.

Lee held the photograph gingerly, feeling his blood bulging inside his veins. He stared at the image, trying to calm himself. He looked at Frank, expecting an explanation.

"This Elle?" He asked shortly.

Frank was confused. "What?"

Lee repeated himself, low, asking less than accusing. "Is this Elle."

Frank looked between the photograph and Lee, astonished. *He couldn't—it's a mistake.* Frank grew concerned again. All of his questions about the best thing for Lee bubbled up again. "Um. Actually, that's uh—"

Lee looked back at the photograph. "Allie?" Lee was confused. Then he got angry. "What were you doing with Allie?"

"Nothing! You were there, Lee, you took the picture."

Lee looked at the photograph again. It was true. He gathered himself and placed the photograph on the desk gently. There was a long pause as he considered the situation. Frank relaxed slightly, waiting for Lee to cave. *Will he grasp the significance of what he just said? Will he see that his own mind is considering Elle over Allie? If nothing else we need the reboot to create the distance. It's become too real.*

Finally, Lee relented. "All right. I get it. But, can you give me a few days so I can at least—try?"

"What are you trying?"

"I just don't think it's right. If all she needs is more time—"

"Two days is probably the maximum if we don't want to risk too much damage." Frank sighed, knowing that in two days Elle wouldn't be able to reconcile Walter's death. It was just passing time. But in those two days, perhaps Lee would come to understand why a reboot was necessary.

"Two days. Fine." Lee shuffled toward the door, defeated. He turned back to Frank. "Sorry about the— before." He gestured to the drawer where he had found the photograph.

Frank waved it off. He shut the door behind Lee, his head lowered. Marigold stood at the top of the stairs.

"Why didn't you tell him about the new design?"

"We're not ready for another one. We haven't finished this trial yet."

"That's not what I mean. I mean you could restart the trial with the new design."

Frank scowled. He was confused enough without Marigold's opinion. He had persuaded himself as much as he had persuaded Lee that they were making the right decision, and he wasn't prepared to do it all over again with Marigold. "And what would we do with Elle?" It was a challenge as much as an actual question.

"She isn't healthy for him." Marigold crossed her arms over her chest.

Frank softened. She was right, but it had become too complicated. As unhealthy as she was to have around, it would be just as bad to take her away from Lee. "Getting rid of her wouldn't help."

"I guess, if he can't tell the difference between Elle and Allie, there's not much we can do. But I think he'll only ever really believe that there is no difference if he forgets that Allie died. I wonder if he'd really like Elle if he didn't tell himself that she's just like Allie. I mean, you say you can tell the difference."

"Yeah. But he's different now too. Maybe it makes sense for him."

"Maybe. It's still not normal." She paused. "You should have shown him the new design."

"He won't let her go."

They were both silent. Marigold watched Frank from the top of the stairs. She saw clearly. The longer the trial went on, the worse off Lee would be. She studied Frank's exhausted, fallen face and knew that he knew it too. They were both stuck with what they had created, and it was spiraling out of their control. She unfolded her arms, softening. "Come back to bed."

"I'll be up in a few."

She looked at him impatiently. Dwelling on it wouldn't solve the problem. He knew what he had to do, but he couldn't. Staying up all night wouldn't give him the courage to do it. Marigold huffed back into the bedroom, frustrated with his passivity. Then she spun back around to face Frank, her expression softer.

"You do see it, right?"

"See what?"

"What it's doing to him." He saw it, he just couldn't face it. "He's slipping. Like I slip. I can see it."

"It's happened before," argued Frank. "It took him months—was it years?—to push through after he lost Allie. But he did."

"But this time you see it happening. It's been happening."

Frank paused, not wanting to admit it out loud.

"Yeah." Frank took a breath. "Why didn't you say something sooner?"

"What do you mean?"

"I know you saw him slipping before any of us."

"I can recognize it in him because I know it so well myself. But sadness is different. Grief. They're terrible, but they're not despair. People confuse them, say they feel depressed when they really feel sad—sometimes very sad. But there are few who go to the depths that depression asks you to go. Until you've been there, you can't fathom what it's like. A world so dark that black seems light, a world so empty that your mind turns inside out. It's an unnatural world that collapses the physical world into a futile speck, dense with the mass of falsehood. It masks itself as simple conversation, a flower bed, a window screen. And while the others look past it and carry their sadness and their grief, it sits in the open, everywhere, waiting to lure the few who can know it into its depths, into a world too big for the human mind, too terrible and too hopeless to be comprehended. And when you come out of it, it terrifies you every day, threatens to pull you back in. And the worst part is you don't even know it's happening until you've passed the point of no return.

"This world has its eyes on Lee," she continued. "And he moves about like a living man—a sad man, but a living man—not feeling his soul slowly turning cold as his mind is released from the living world. He will fall into the world without even a struggle, paralyzed by his unawareness, and soon you will see his body walk out his front door with nothing inside. It will move dutifully through space, but it will be empty, and then it will be he alone who needs to pull himself through, because there will be nothing left for you to grasp."

"But how can we be sure that taking away Elle won't fast-track him into that world?"

"We can't. But if we don't do it, he will without question go there."

"So if I shut down Elle and he goes there anyway, it's just like it would have been with Elle, but it's my fault." Frank shook his head. *How can the cause of his happiness equally be the cause of his despair?*

He pulled out the blueprint of the new design, torn over the right thing to do.

EIGHTEEN

....

After Lee left Frank's, he didn't feel like going home. He walked toward town, welcoming the emptiness. It looked different at night. He had walked through the cobblestone streets at night before, but never had he seen the shops closed and chained, the restaurant chairs stacked, the lights dim. Despite the apparent desertedness, he felt unnerved as he walked deeper into town. The streets grew wider and the two-story buildings were no longer built out from the walls of the buildings next to them. As the town opened to more spacious flatland, he felt that he was being followed.

His walking slowed as he listened for footsteps behind him, near him. He continued forward, past an empty, gated lot, holding his head stiff while his eyes darted around. Breathing suddenly became difficult.

The more aware of it he was, the louder it became. A streetlamp, improbably tall, loomed overhead, revealing his figure to whatever eyes were lurking in the night.

The buildings stretched taller, bending over him like a crouching child holds a magnifying glass to peer at an ant. They were all watching. *There's that scientist,* Lee heard the people in the buildings saying. *That poor, poor scientist. Remember how charming he used to be?*

Lee tried to stare into a window, but they were all dark. Empty. He looked down again. Hundreds of people reemerged in the windows, looking down on him. *Now look at him. Look what he's done to her.*

Lee kept his head down, trying to ignore them. He saw an alley ahead and walked toward it, out of sight. Looked down at his feet as they brushed past the gravel, moving much faster than he was actually progressing. The buildings hissed at him. Teeth gnashed together, chattered, taunting him from above. He moved his feet faster, holding still his upper body as if to disappear. He looked ahead at the alley. Still several meters away. He glanced up at the buildings again, and then straight ahead at his narrow target. It hadn't gotten any closer. He slowed his walking and stopped, staring at the alley.

He heard the buildings. *Ha! Look at him. That poor, poor scientist.*

He moved toward the alley. And stopped. Moved forward again, picking up speed until he was in a jog. He released his hands from his pockets as he jogged faster, breaking into a run.

Where are you going, scientist? You can't run away now.

He ran toward the alley, trying to ignore the voices that echoed around him. He ran, he ran. The alley came no closer. He slowed to a stop, and looked around. The empty lot, the fence, the same buildings looming overhead.

That's right, scientist. The only way out is to go back.

Go back? Lee looked behind him, his shadow standing tall, waiting for him. He took a step toward his shadow. His shadow stepped away from him. A few more steps. He looked around. The fence, the empty lot. More steps, quicker steps. Steps, steps. The empty lot became a building. He looked behind him. The buildings stood tall, their windows black. His shadow disappeared into the dark streets as he walked back into town.

As the streets narrowed, Lee relaxed into their protective enclosure. He walked for hours until the sun just started to light the street. It began to rain lightly through the emerging day. He ambled along, exhausted and disheveled, deciding to take himself back home before the shopkeepers started to arrive. He passed through the rest of the town and cut through to the river before emerging on the outskirts of his cul-de-sac.

When he arrived at his house, he didn't immediately notice Elle waiting on his front step, wearing a slim, bright red trench coat that made her hair look darker and her skin whiter. She was slumped over, sleeping. When he caught sight of her, his disturbing night dissolved into concern. He forgot about his exhaustion from the hours before, her appearance against the red coat striking him. Her limp body against his stairs looked unnatural. It was a sinister sight.

She woke up as he hurried over to her, breaking the unsettling impression that he'd had upon first noticing her. Life filled her skin and her movements became animated. He spotted the cut on her face and knelt down to her, lifting her chin to look at the cut.

"What is this?" he asked himself. There was hardly a scab. Elle tilted her head down as she brushed herself off. Her hands against her coat looked translucent to Lee.

"I'm sorry. I know I shouldn't be out here. I just didn't know where you went and I still haven't gotten used to being alone at night."

She looked at Lee when he didn't answer. Drops of rain rested on top of his head. His eyes looked heavy. His shoulders hunched as if weighed down from the inside. Elle silenced herself as she took in his worn appearance.

Lee unlocked his front door as Elle stood up next to him. She looked at him questioningly, wondering if he wanted to be alone.

He held the door open to let Elle enter ahead of him, then scanned the neighborhood for peeping eyes, and followed her inside. He closed the door quickly behind him.

Across the way, a curtain closed. Lee didn't notice.

Inside, Elle stood before Lee as he shut the door. He moved toward her and turned on the light, angling her so that he could again examine the cut on her face. She stood in front of him, waiting, as if a child at a doctor, careful not to interrupt.

This must be what Frank saw last night. Lee looked more closely at the cut, then at the rest of her face. He saw the breath rise and fall in her long neck, and felt a rare perspective shift as he was overcome by pride at the idea of her breathing. He looked back into her black eyes and gave her a small pat on the shoulder as he stepped back. Neither of them broke the silence.

Lee left Elle standing as he walked up the stairs and disappeared into his bedroom to retrieve dry nightclothes for Elle. His hands lingered over the delicate fabrics, untouched for years. The lace, which seemed like it might crack and disintegrate if moved, still felt soft to his touch. The intricate beading on the red sleeveless dress that Allie had felt she could only wear once, and never did. The silk shirts and outlandish, pastel green fur coat. The hangers all thrust to the side. Her shoes, organized by era on the shelves behind her clothes. Lee picked one up—a navy blue silk slip-on with a curved heel and oversized, jeweled buckle across the pointed front. Allie had made them herself. They wound up being a full size too small for her to wear, which would have disappointed anyone, but she laughed at her mistake. She was just thrilled that she had made her own shoes.

Lee remembered the day he came home and she ran to greet him holding them up. He had asked her to try them on, which she did, knowing that they were too small. Her thin feet spilled over the tops of the shoes, and as she walked around, her steps jarring and stunted, she kept laughing. It had made Lee laugh with her. He remembered her wide, white smile, a smile that he had never seen Elle produce. A laugh that he had never heard Elle release.

He moved the hangers aside, picking plain cotton clothes from Allie's collection, spare sheets, and a pillow from his own bed, and laid them out. He looked at the clothes, for a moment seeing Allie's shape fill them out before carrying them downstairs to Elle.

When Lee returned Elle still hadn't moved. Standing cold and uncomfortable in the doorway, she was relieved when she saw the dry clothes. She started removing her wet outer garments right where she stood, not wanting to trail rainwater through the house. Lee averted his gaze, but Elle took no notice. Out of the corner of his eye, he caught slivers of Elle's lissome movements as she stepped out of her clothes. A piece of her hip, her thigh, her arm.

"Thank you!" she said to Lee, grateful for the warmth of the soft, dry fabric against her chilled skin.

Elle saw that Lee wasn't looking at her. It made no sense to her. She felt no shame, as Allie wouldn't have, and instead found it unnatural for Lee to be uncomfortable.

She finished dressing quickly to spare Lee, who had unfolded the couch and was busily fitting it with sheets. He kept his eyes down and determined, even after Elle had gotten dressed, feeling embarrassed not only that Elle had disrobed before him, but that she had noticed his refusal to look at her. He fumed at himself into the sheets.

When there were no more wrinkles to hand-iron, Lee turned to look at Elle. In her nightclothes, it was as if Allie were standing in front of him again. She glowed as Allie had once glowed. Though she looked no different, no pieces of her face looked different— each crease that Lee noticed looked identical to the ones Allie had—she looked somehow different. Perhaps it was the shade of clothing that she wore, or perhaps it was the familiar look, a look that he had seen so often at night, a look that he had become comfortable with and fond of. The silk string of the bottoms always coming loose. How the cotton of the shirt seemed to match the feel of her skin underneath. He paused, conflicted, knowing that if he advanced toward Elle she would find it natural and wouldn't resist. He shook his thoughts, reminding himself that she was Elle and not Allie, and that it would be wrong to do so. Would it? If she was able to make her own decisions, wouldn't it be her decision? Or would it be manipulative, to design Elle to make decisions that Allie would have made? Did she really have a choice then, in what decisions she made?

He finally peeled himself away. He turned out the light and walked upstairs, tortured. Elle settled into the sheets, feeling the distance that was just created between them. She no longer felt tired, but fell into a deep, comfortable sleep only minutes after she lay down.

Hours later, in the mid-morning darkness of a house with all the blinds drawn, there was movement. Elle slinked around in the shadows, disoriented. Had she slept through the day? Was it night again? The heavy curtains kept out whatever light might have given her a clue. Holding a mug of freshly brewed coffee, she slowly tiptoed up the stairs, knocked, then cracked open the bedroom door.

Lee was nowhere to be found. The large bed, its puffy white comforter and ruffled pillows, was still meticulously made. The drapes had been opened, leaving only a thin, white curtain closed across the windows. The sunlight beamed in. She turned to the opposite side of the hall and saw light seeping underneath the study door. From where she stood, the steps leading downstairs appeared to fade into a black abyss. It frightened her that she stood in the light and looked down into the dark. She felt vulnerable. She walked toward the study door and listened through it. She heard nothing.

"Lee?" The whispered "L" made a sound so small that only the breathy "ee" hung in the air. A sound that could easily blend into the walls. It sounded like it had come from behind her rather than from her own lips. She clutched the mug with both hands close to her chest. "Lee?" The loudness of her second effort startled her. She glanced over her shoulder toward the void where the stairs should have been. She suddenly felt as if a single step in any direction would plunge her eternally downward.

There was no response from inside. Elle cracked open the door and peeked in. Lee was sleeping on his desk, half-full cups of cold coffee lining the window-sill, his desk, the shelves. Elle wondered if he ever ran out of coffee mugs, or if he just kept buying them when they were all dirty. A man with four plates, four bowls, and four tall drinking glasses who had at least three times as many mugs. She found it charming.

Elle put the coffee down on the edge of his desk and saw paperwork underneath his hand. He had done that before, fallen asleep right on top of his work. She wondered what he was working on that had exhausted him. Looking more closely, she saw blueprints of herself. The full outline of her design, the degrees of her angles, the color, in numbers, of her skin, eyes, hair. She was fascinated. How much of this work was about her? She looked around. On the bookshelves she came across thick reports and review logs from the data team. She carefully pulled the most recent from the shelf and opened it. She flipped through, skimming the pages, not understanding what she was holding but intrigued nonetheless. She became wide-eyed as she flipped to one particular page, a loose sheet shoved between two pages folded sloppily on itself, revealing only part of an image. She stared at it, adjusting the book so that she could balance it in one hand and open the rest of the folded paper.

Suddenly, gently, Lee put one hand on her arm from behind and one hand under the book that was dangling from Elle's fingertips. She jumped, not having realized how much noise she was making rustling the papers.

"Careful. There are loose pages here."

"Oh I didn't mean to snoop! I just brought you some coffee and then I saw—me—on your desk there."

"It's all right."

"Sorry—"

Lee shook his head nonchalantly to dismiss the subject, and replaced the book on the shelf for her. He walked over to retrieve the fresh coffee from his desk. Elle stood still, thinking about what she had just seen. She was hesitant to address Lee.

"You didn't—no never mind."

"What?"

"I just thought I saw something. It's okay."

Lee took the book back off the shelf and handed it to Elle.

"Go ahead."

Elle sheepishly flipped through to find the page. She grabbed for the paper with the image she had seen. A detailed, hand-drawn, pencil sketch of a girl about twelve years old who closely resembled Elle unfolded.

Lee took the notebook from Elle and looked at the sketch. His face hardened and his eyes dimmed, but Elle couldn't place his expression. She watched Lee, concerned that she had found something that she wasn't supposed to.

"I didn't mean—" Elle began to apologize again. Lee was far away, reminiscing about the sketch. "Is that me?"

Lee shook his head.

"You drew it?"

Lee nodded. "Almost a year ago."

Elle hesitated again for a moment. "Who is it?"

"It's my daughter." Lee paused. "Alma." He said her name definitively, as if saying her name made her just a little bit more real. Elle looked at Lee, shocked. "It's what I imagine she would look like if she made it to twelve." His hardened expression fell piece by piece, sliding one quadrant of skin down his face at a time, leaving behind cracked streaks of internal age.

"I'm sorry." Elle stood uncomfortably while Lee looked at the sketch. "Did your wife get to see her before she died?" Lee shook his head again. Elle appeared to be processing, calculating information, trying very hard to reconcile this information. Lee assumed that it was because Elle didn't really know what she meant when she spoke about death.

She changed the subject. What he had said reminded her of something that she once knew, but she wasn't sure what it was. She couldn't shake the feeling that she had done something wrong. "I brought you coffee," she said, gesturing toward the mug already in Lee's hands.

"Thank you." He noticed that Elle was wearing the same clothes that she had worn the day before, now wrinkled from drying in a pile. "I want to show you something. Come." Lee took Elle out of his study, across the platform into his bedroom. Elle glanced around, the first time setting foot in his even-lined bedroom.

It looked staged. There was a wide dresser between the two windows across from the closet, and a tall dresser on the wall across from the bed. A bathroom door, closed, was in between, next to the tall dresser. End tables were on either side of the bed, though only the one on the left had belongings neatly piled on top of it. A cushioned, armless, wooden chair sat apparently unused in the corner. Trinkets were sparsely placed on top of both dressers. A jewelry box perched on top of the taller of the two, a lace cloth laid out underneath. A bed skirt. A thick, wall-to-wall rug that was the exact white color of the bedding. Elle looked closer at the gossamer, white curtains hanging over the windows, noticing how sheer and delicate they looked against the harsh early sun. Allie's presence was everywhere, as if Lee didn't belong in the bedroom at all. Elle's attention turned back to Lee, who was facing the closet.

"Go ahead. Pick something. It's all your size." Elle caught Lee's attempt at a joke and smiled widely, relieved that the deep, frowning wrinkles in his forehead had smoothed out since putting away the sketch. She slipped toward the closet, having caught a glimpse of the luscious colors and textures that poked out, but stopped as she approached, feeling a wall come between her and the clothes. She recalled Lee's reaction to her wearing Allie's nightclothes. She still felt that there was a slight distinction in his mind between her and Allie, and wondered if it was a necessary distinction to maintain by dressing markedly different and appearing in a way that Allie never had before.

"Is this too..." Elle trailed off.

"It's fine. They're just clothes."

She looked once again at the fabrics peeking out from the closet, unworn and cast aside, and was convinced. She rummaged through Allie's clothes, concentrating on the details of each piece. Although she knew that she and Allie were the same size, the clothes seemed exceptionally tiny. Having never perceived herself as particularly small, Elle held up a lightweight wrap dress against her body to compare. Her reflection stared back at her. A different reflection from the one she had seen the other night, that dragged the key ring down her face. Perhaps it was the light in the room, or the bright, patterned, jersey fabric contrasting sharply with her dark hair. But when she looked in the mirror, she had trouble recognizing her own face.

Lee watched her, amused, expectantly, mistaking her pause for awe. Elle put the dress back and held up another, trying several different ones before finally making her decision. Each time she stood before the closet, the strange feeling she'd had diminished with the sight of the eclectic fabrics. More clothing than usual seemed to fit into the corner of the closet. *Prob-*

ably because the clothes are so small, she thought. The choices seemed to appear endlessly, as if the neglected shirts and skirts shoved aside had suddenly clamored forward, showcasing themselves to an interested eye for the first time in twelve years.

She emerged from the closet with clothes draped over her arms and looked at Lee as if for permission. Lee held up the shirt.

"Why did you choose this?" he asked.

"I don't know. I love the color. And the little feathers. But I can choose another one if this is—"

"No no, it's okay." Lee looked at Elle curiously. "What shoes did you pick?"

Elle showed him.

"Interesting."

"What? Do they not match?" Elle asked.

"They don't match at all. Allie wore them together all the time." He ran his hands over the small feathers of the shirt. After all that time, they were still soft. *Which connection was it that made her pick this shirt and those shoes, the same way Allie did? Or was she just recalling a past memory? If she hadn't had that memory of Allie's, like Allie didn't have any memory of the combination when she first put them together, would she have made the same decision?* Lee questioned where the application of a memory ended and choice began. *Is Elle just following along the connections that we built for her, or is she actually making decisions?* "Go ahead, get dressed. I'll wait outside." He started walking toward the stairs and closed the bedroom door.

Moments later, Lee stood outside looking out at the sky. Blue despite the cold air. His eyes had lost their amused shine. There was a breeze. A leaf floated down from a tree. Another one followed. He looked at another tree, almost bare from the deadening autumn season. He focused on each leaf falling, one at a time. With a stronger breeze more leaves fell. Cause and effect. There was no decision to be made on the part of the leaves. But then again, there was never going to be any way to tell whether or not the leaves made decisions. He would never know what it was like to be a leaf. Perhaps their logic was different. *We really are so sure of ourselves aren't we. Thinking that the logic we can understand is the single and correct logic that exists. How can we know what we don't know? People question their faith in faith, but not their faith in science.* Another leaf dropped and twirled around in the air, the only indication that there existed at that moment an unseen force called wind.

Elle opened the front door behind him, cutting his thoughts. He took her in. She once again had that look, the familiar look of Allie that he thought she'd had already before wearing her clothes. *Could the exterior on top of her exterior really change that much the way she appears to me? What is happening in my brain when I look at her dressed in Allie's clothes? In Allie's skin? Does each layer of exterior unearth Allie that much more?*

He looked at her for a moment with a slight fear in his eyes. It passed quickly as Elle smiled, and he dissolved once again into the complacent unease to which he had become accustomed. He had never felt that way with Allie, but didn't notice any difference in the way he felt. It had become normal. A new normal. A normal that was determined after he himself changed. The whole of his surroundings, his position in the world, had shifted. But like a speck of dirt roiling around the deceptive eye of a tornado, there was no way to tell up from down or the distance traveled beyond the swirling walls of the surrounding invisible storm.

"Ready?" he asked.

Elle nodded and they set out, walking slowly next to each other in comfortable silence.

"Where are we going?"

"I'll show you." Lee caught sight of the patterned shoes walking next to his without looking down. In his obscured periphery, the pattern appeared grotesque, unattached to legs, and took on the semblance of a dysmorphic face.

"Is it far?" Elle asked, intrigued.

"Just a few blocks."

Silence again. Lee ignored the face walking next to him on the ground. He knew that it was his brain playing tricks on him, trying to make sense of it. *Perhaps that's how Elle sees the world—things she can't make sense of.* Lee imagined a terrifying world full of inanimate objects, contorted in a way that tried to reflect logic. He focused straight ahead on the cluster of trees that fanned out into a wide strip of densely wooded area separating the quiet cul-de-sac from the lights of the town. The approaching cover relaxed him, the tall trees redirecting the sun to either side of the strip.

Elle kept up, knowing but not minding that she was overdressed for where it looked like they were headed. She felt ownership of the clothes. A certain freedom in them. A self that she recognized.

"I never come down this way. It's so isolated," she said.

"It's quiet. I don't know that isolated is the word."

"Maybe I'm just comparing it to the rest of the town."

"Maybe." Lee went silent again, watching Elle as she absorbed everything new around her.

"Oh look at this!"

They came upon a set of stairs in a small haven of things that were still somewhat green, thickly shaded and holding layers of moisture.

Lee led her up the rock stairs where they came to a bridge overlooking a busy street multiple stories below. They emerged on the opposite side of the wooded strip.

Elle looked out in wonderment. "I didn't even know this existed!"

"Not many people do."

"How do you know about it?"

"I don't remember how I found it. I just always remember it being here. Every once in a while I come up here just to be alone."

"You *live* alone."

"It's not the same. In my house, my mind is cluttered." There was silence between them as they looked out, only a foot apart.

"Did you ever bring anyone up here before?"

Lee nodded. He leaned out over the bridge, remembering.

"How many people?" Elle already knew the answer.

"Just one." Lee didn't have to look far to picture her dark hair, her light skin, her outlandish style of dress.

But he looked in his mind rather than at Elle to recall. He wanted to remember the pure form.

"So you wanted to be alone with someone?" She knew only recently what that was like. It was why she had turned up on Lee's doorstep the night before.

Elle looked out again when Lee didn't answer. "It looks like a painting. It can't be real. I didn't even know this existed!"

Lee looked at her sideways, noticing that she repeated herself. But she was marveling at the view before her. He thought it must just be her expressing a type of speechlessness that included words, and it made him happy to see her appreciate what he had shown her.

She looked young and vibrant staring into the mist. Her usually subdued beauty was striking against nature—the sunlight, the wind, the trees behind her. She took it all in, the solitary companionship from the peaceful point above the whirring town, as Lee stayed aside out of sight. She inhaled the cold air as she felt the hot sun on her face, and became curious about what other secrets the woods held. She turned and looked past Lee.

"What's over that way?"

"I'll show you."

Lee helped her step over the branches and around the mud. They had retreated back into the middle of the woods and were making their way alongside the town, walking deeper into the strip.

As thin as the strip was, it was inordinately long. Someone who attempted to cut through from the cul-de-sac to town could make a wrong left turn and be walking for days, whereas he could cut through from side to side in minutes. It could be very disorienting halfway through to town, where the cul-de-sac could no longer be seen and the streets of town could not yet be. It only took a minute to get past that point of no reference, but it took less than that to lose the way and start walking parallel to the outside.

Lee led Elle easily, keeping the rock stairs somewhat in sight. He knew his way through the woods, but never strayed too far from a permanent fixture that he knew well, just in case. Disorientation could descend at any moment in the woods, with this tree looking just like that tree—or was it that tree?—and it could cause the mind to unravel, making one's own mental bewilderment even more menacing than the surrounding woods.

Elle abruptly stopped. Holding a branch up out of her eyes, she stood up straight, stiff, as if a second branch were pressed into her back. Her eyes squinted together in an alarmed frown. Her toes curled in her shoes, butting up against an unseen wall that marked the edge of the earth, the edge of stability. She imagined the floor eroding and disintegrating beneath her feet. The dirt caving in like a waterfall when it hits the glass boundary and directs itself downward instead of horizontal, changing the shape, depth, and tilt of the spherical earth. She stood on a small island, holding her branch for balance.

"Where are we going?"

"I'm taking you to the other side—what's the matter?"

"I don't know. I just suddenly got a bad feeling."

"A bad *feeling*?" Lee shifted closer to Elle and reached up to grab her hand, wrapped tightly around the branch. She let him. "It's okay, I know where we're going," he said.

"No, I want to go back. I don't like this. I don't know what this is. I didn't even know this existed."

Again? thought Lee.

"Come here." Elle obediently stood still in front of Lee as he examined her eyes, just as she had done not long before. Her dark irises throbbed. The protective lens over her eyes appeared to quiver when she looked this way or that to separate from what it was protecting in a cowardly retreat.

A bad feeling. What is going on inside that head of yours? Lee wondered. She looked uneasy but not alarmingly so, and the shake in her eyes had stopped. "Okay, you're okay. Let's go."

Lee guided her back to the stairs, holding her gingerly. She became more sure-footed as the woods thinned and the edge of the cul-de-sac became visible again, and dropped her arm heavily from Lee's grasp. Careful to not be insulting, but anxious to regain control of her composure.

The chaos of the small town entered their ears as they left the little oasis. From the other side of the woods, the sound wafted overhead and settled down clearly where they stood. Feeling disappointed at his marred attempt to share his quiet retreat with Elle, Lee started wandering toward the town square.

Elle resisted the moment he took a step away from her. "Why don't I head home. I don't want to overstay my welcome."

"Not at all."

"No I should shower, the plants need water."

"I'll walk you."

"Oh it's only a few blocks away. Really, you probably have other things to take care of. I don't want to impose."

"Okay, well, if you need anything..."

Elle dipped her head in a sort of self-conscious "thank you" and walked away, the brightly colored shoes misfit below her inward-facing shoulders. She turned and gave him a little reassuring wave, with the same staccato movements that Allie used to make.

In that moment, Lee recalled parting from Allie on those very cobblestones just before she had become pregnant. The memory crept up on him unexpectedly, unleashed from a cobwebbed corner of his mind. *How did I not remember this until now? How did I not remember one of the last moments of Allie before it became Allie and Alma?* He remembered it clearly. Her little wave, her loose, straight hair—she must have just gotten it cut, as the ends were more blunt and chopped than usual. He tried to visualize the features of her face, what she had been wearing. Though in his mind she was wearing clothes, and looked like herself, Lee couldn't picture either when he focused on them individually. *Allie and Alma. Alma.* He would have called her "Allie" for short.

He waved back at Elle, erasing the image from his mind. When he closed his eyes again, he pictured Allie. Her brightly colored shoes, her feathered shirt under her heavy coat, waving at him on the cobblestone street.

She was gone when he looked up.

....

NINETEEN

Later that day Lee arrived back home. The only
light that was on came from the inside of the
refrigerator as he unpacked a bag of fresh fruit
and vegetables. His house felt empty again. Elle had
folded up the sheets and left them on top of the
couch, still displayed as a bed protruding into the living room. The coffee table had been pushed to the
side and was jammed haphazardly against two chairs.

Lee observed the room from the kitchen, registering how quickly Elle had come and gone. The sight of
the folded sheets left him with a longing for something over and done too quickly to capture, the scent
of the remains still raw. They looked strange. The
whole room looked strange, with the coffee table out
of place and the newness of the sheets presenting
themselves in a room where nothing new had existed

for years. He left the sheets folded on the couch. *Five, six, seven.* He counted the stairs as he walked up, feeling their irrefutable solidity vibrate through his soles to his knees.

Standing in front of his closet he saw the empty hanger from the shirt Elle was wearing. He saw it swinging, though it was not, as if it still felt the effects of having its shirt plucked off hours before. He closed his eyes and inhaled. The motion around and within Allie's side of the closet earlier that day had released her scent from under blankets of stiff dust. It had always lingered faintly, but was newly filled with fresh profundity. Lee wondered if a little bit of Allie's scent disappeared into the air with each movement of her clothes, as if her clothes were like a moldering chest that kept safe the last remains of her, catering to the weakest of all senses and disintegrating imperceptibly with each brush or flick of the hand until the last of her was gone, released from the chest.

He willed the swinging hanger in his mind to stop. To stop releasing the scent and waving it away like a renewable perfume. He wished to never forget her scent, and wondered why he had never noticed any scent of Elle's. Perhaps the scent of Allie really was just the fragrance of a specific perfume. In a moment, the feeling had passed, the flavor of the air had changed, and the clothes had locked away the aroma once more, protecting and preserving what was palpably left behind of Allie.

Lee took off his own clothes carefully, deliberately feeling each piece of fabric between his fingers, inhaling slowly so as to not disturb his own scent settling deep into the threads. He hung them with as little motion as possible. There would be no one there when he died to stand over his clothes and inhale the last bits of his fleshed self. He thought of Alma, of leaving Alma, with nothing but a faint trace of his scent. A sense so weak that what it sensed always needed to latch on to something else in order to be perceived. Scent in a void was no scent at all. Alma, who never had the chance to develop her own scent. What would she have been like? What if Allie had gotten pregnant only a week later? Would Alma still have turned out to be Alma? The incredible odds that Alma was the one who was produced, carried to term and born, only to succumb in the last moments before her first moments. Had she recognized the scent of her mother for those few moments? *Though we all were, once, newborn babies, we will never know what it's like. Is it a failure of memory, or is memory something that we develop, a kind of fake, a false account of things that we have been trained to experience and understand in certain terms?*

For her birthday, her first day on earth, Lee had bought Alma a science kit. She wouldn't be able to use it for many years, but he bought it anyway. He would answer her questions. "Why" would be explained properly, along with "how." He would show her, they would work together on homemade science experiments. The day she was born he knew she was like him. Her mind. What she would grow into. He felt less alone. That she understood in a way that Allie never had because she wasn't like him. He felt like there was another one like him, who would not only question the world, but seek answers. And those answers oftentimes were difficult to grasp, and made it difficult to walk the earth comfortably like so many do who do not question. She was like him, he knew. And he was sorry and ecstatic at the same time. Sorry that she had been given his mind, which sometimes threw him into a manic frenzy when he was faced with the enormity of some concepts, but ecstatic because she wouldn't have to face it alone. He would be there. He had been there. As long as he was around, she would have someone who understood.

And as long as she was around, he would have someone who understood.

When Alma died too, he felt a sublime aloneness, a oneness, a single hand clapping eternally on an earth full of vigorous applause.

He circled his bedroom. Sat on the bed. There was nothing to put back in its place, no adjustments to be made. A prison of purposelessness. Nothing to be done, no one to undo it. The stillness around him was striking. A leaf fell outside the window, peering in at the moving man in the still house. A dollhouse with plastic doors and glued down windows trapping the live man inside. The great eye of the leaf bore down on him through the window. He sat still on the bed, waiting for the leaf to pass before he breathed.

He walked out onto the platform at the top of the stairs and put his back to the wall, feeling safe with no windows in sight. At the bottom of the stairs he once again faced the folded sheets. They mocked him with their square stillness, pretending that they had not just known a life and didn't still hold it in their fibers and folds. Standing in front of the last step, under the highest ceiling in the house, in the center of the open floor, the room widened around Lee. His back needed a wall behind it. Floating slowly behind him, coming down from the bedroom, Lee felt himself hovering. He felt separated and stretched to fill the wide space of the house. To spread enough life through the paper walls to cut through the cold, square stiffness of his prison.

Behind the sheets the fireplace called. He debated. He wanted to shrink into the walls unnoticed and become part of the deadened house. A lit fireplace would be a second life, and would confirm his existence, unwanted in the quiet house. Without bending his ankles, he walked past the folded sheets and waited for a moment after he reached the fireplace to let his hovering second half catch up. He stood to the side of the fireplace rather than in front of it, with his back to the wall. He kept his breathing low to minimize the disturbance and draw little attention to his presence. Because of his position against the wall, adjacent to the fireplace instead of before it, his movements were stilted as he ignited the flame. It circled the shadow of his face and projected him onto the curtains, illuminating his floating second half in a dark outline of absence in the shape of his body. Seeing the shadow on the curtains made him conscious of the light necessary to see the dark. He felt aware of himself standing in the light of the flame as he looked out into the dark room, wondering what was staring back, awakened by the pattern of his beating heart where it did not belong.

A knock on the door broke his thoughts, but he didn't move. His eyes fixated on the door, and he prepared himself for the threat lurking outside to make itself known by way of voice. His heart beat faster, giving him away. He felt his will shove back into the wall from within his bones, but his body remained motionless. He was still lit by the fire. He needed to move. Just two steps to the right and he would be out of sight. But his body was rigid. His mind moving slowly. Another short knock, then the door opened slightly. *Unlocked!* He panicked.

"Lee?" Frank called quietly.

The room fell apart around Lee. His second half snapped back into his body, popping his ribs and expelling the hidden breath held in his lungs. The dark corners of the room, less acute, looked grey in the late-afternoon light.

"Come in."

Frank opened the door fully and stepped inside, seeing Lee standing awkwardly next to the fireplace, painted into the wallpaper.

"I was just passing by and I saw your light pop on. Elle went to her place?"

Lee nodded.

"How is she doing?"

"You don't know?" *That's the reason you're over here. Because you do know.* He wanted to ask what the data showed, but thought it might be easier if he didn't.

Frank nodded, knowing that Lee understood. It was time. Lee motioned for Frank to make himself comfortable. He shut the door behind him and locked it, marking that Lee had left it unlocked. *A new sense of security, or an uncharacteristic slip?*

Lee walked into the kitchen and filled two glasses with Scotch. Frank observed him from behind, noticing his tense shoulders. *He's going to do it. He's going to agree to the reboot.* He felt cautiously hopeful, knowing how stubborn Lee could be.

"I don't want to waste any more time if she's only going to get worse," Lee said.

"So you want to—"

"Yeah. But I don't think it's right to just erase part of her life. She's no longer just what we made her. She's aware. She's *feeling.* And she'll be aware of whatever decision we make."

"Well, I don't think she feels—"

"She feels. This isn't about being selfish. It's about doing what's right."

Frank's confidence was beginning to falter. *What's right? For whom? Right and wrong don't apply to AI systems.*

"So what do you want us to do?" Frank asked.

"Is it possible to pinpoint each memory she formed from the moment she met Walter, and extract them one at a time?"

"Oh, wow. I mean, that's a year's worth of memories."

"Can it be done?"

"It *can*, sure. But what good is that? We talked about this already, the chain of events."

"I saw it today—what you meant when you said she would forget the basics. But just a cold reboot—it just isn't right. She has a sense of her self, has a personhood specific to that self. She recognized herself. If we take out one memory at a time, but we *replace* it with a new one, she can adjust to the new memory without really losing anything. The context will still be there. She'll have the same amount of knowledge that she has now, the same type and number of connections that she has now. That's what we're targeting. I can build the memories that will be used to replace the ones we extract. If we have some old memories to help formulate the new memories, then once the new memories are created, we can erase the old memories, and the only thing she will be forgetting is Walter, not everything else that she doesn't need to forget." *Like me*, thought Lee.

Frank considered this. "Like her identity," he said, understanding. "Okay, what about her environment? She's been living in Walter's house."

"He has no family. He donated everything to the lab when he signed the release—I guess as a thank you—or maybe as a way to preserve it all—"

"Or to preserve the memory of him..." Frank was starting to wonder if erasing the memory of Walter was indeed the right thing to do. *But, it's not a real memory, is it, if it's not inside a real person?*

Lee ignored Frank. "She'll stay in his house. As the memories of Walter are removed, they'll be replaced with modified memories that include his house so that the environment is a constant. Otherwise, I think it will be too disorienting."

Frank sighed, considering the options. There no longer seemed to be an easy way to fix the problem. "This is an interesting approach. But I think the team should know about this. There will be questions..." *That you're not willing to answer...*

"I agree. We're doing it this way because—" Lee paused to think of a persuasive reason to give to the team that wouldn't call the decision into question. "We're studying the effect on Elle as a whole, of removing and replacing connections in a one-to-one ratio. There should be no noticeable change—to her or to us."

"And why are we studying this effect?" *"Why" will be the first question they ask*, Frank thought.

Lee shrugged. "Repairs."

"All right, well. I'll get this set up. I need tonight to sort through the data, and then we can get started before any real damage is done. I'll send you notes on what we're targeting first. This will require some delicate choreography. If either of us misses a step, the whole chain of memories could be disrupted."

Including those with you. Lee heard it though it wasn't said. He finished his Scotch, feeling the fire he saw through the bottom of his glass disappear into his throat.

TWENTY

....

Weeks later, the autumn season had settled in deep. Winter hung thickly in the air. Snow had fallen weakly and turned into rain as the temperature rose, and solidified into dirt-filled chunks of white ice as a cold front burst through. Elle and Lee walked together up a hill, partially green from the ever-moist skies and partially mud from the confused snow. They laughed at each other, out of breath, and collapsed at the top of the hill. Lee felt a strange mixture of sweat and cold roiling inside his coat as the moisture from the ground seeped through the material.

Elle's eyes were closed. She lay on the hilltop ground next to Lee between patches of leftover snow where the fall rain hadn't washed them away, looking peaceful. She didn't care that she was probably lying in mud. She liked the fact that she had felt cold upon stepping outside that morning, and after walking up the hill, was grateful for some of that cold to be trapped inside the earth to cool her off. She opened her eyes and turned to Lee. His arm was extended out toward her own outstretched arm, but not touching.

"I saw a bee the other day," Elle said.

"A bee?"

"I know. It was just walking around, so lost." She looked back toward the sky and closed her eyes again, remembering.

"It wasn't flying," Lee assumed given the season. "It was probably dying."

"Do you think it went out one day in the summer and forgot where it was, and just started wandering around trying to remember where it came from?"

Lee turned to look at Elle but didn't respond, just listening.

"It looked so sad. I've never seen a happy bee. When they fly around they look angry, and when they walk around they look sad. It's their wings."

Lee noticed how much less expressive Elle's face looked when she spoke with her eyes closed. He closed his own eyes and pictured her face instead.

"I never tried to interpret the emotions of an insect before," Lee joked.

"No?" Elle responded seriously. "Hmm."

Lee shifted his hand slightly so that it was just touching Elle's. They lay in silence. Neither one moved away. Lee opened his eyes slowly, sensing that he would feel Elle's hand touching his more fully if his eyes were open and seeing. Sad and blue, they glistened as he looked up into the daytime sky.

Lee was reluctant to mar the moment by reliving a past memory. The present seemed so much more real and true than what was in his mind, but it was essential. He had taken her to the hilltop for a purpose.

"Do you remember coming up here before?"

"Mmm...was I here before?"

Lee nodded. It still pained him slightly that she didn't remember despite him deliberately having removed the memory. *If she hadn't asked about Walter that day, she would remember.* Lee blamed Walter bitterly for his presence in that particular memory and consequent removal from Elle's storage.

"It was the first time we met, just the two of us, outside the lab." Lee knew that it was a difficult task to remember the first time meeting anyone in specific circumstances, but it wasn't just like all the rest. He hadn't known at the time that it would be one of those experiences that would be stored forever in the front of his mind, ballooning into one of his fondest memories. It was the first time that Lee had spent time with Elle as Elle, and saw her as real.

"Was it?"

"I took you up here to show you how the town looked from above, how organized the streets were even though they feel confusing when you're small and walking through them."

"Do they feel confusing to you too?" A hopeful frown flitted across Elle's face. "You would think I'd be familiar with them by now."

"Do you remember what it looks like from up here?"

"I can picture it."

That doesn't mean anything. You could imagine anything that doesn't exist. Remembering something that does is different.

Lee didn't know how to proceed. He wanted to describe what happened after he showed Elle the view from above, but he didn't want to ruin it by saying it out loud. It was a memory too precious to him.

He dug into his own memory and replayed it silently. How he had pointed out his house to Elle and how she couldn't pinpoint which one he meant. How he had positioned her in front of him and leaned over her to follow her eyeline as he pointed to his house again. How it was only after he had let go of her shoulder that he felt his hand on her, felt the heaviness of her bones underneath his palm, the fullness of the space that she took up. At that moment, when his brain sensors finally processed the touch, she became real. The hand that rested on her shoulder had never forgotten the sensation. The sensation that confirmed what his eyes had thought was a trick, a mirage, a specter, was concrete.

"It's going to get dark soon."

Elle didn't open her eyes, almost asleep in comfort. "Yeah."

Lee paused, also feeling lethargy coax him into slumber. "We should go."

"Yeah."

Lee peeled himself off the ground, sitting up. He looked over at Elle, examining her. Her chest rising and falling. The puffs of warm air from her nose. He stared at her neck, a piece of flesh exposed by her loose scarf, and up to her eyes, which were wide open and looking at him, startling him. They stared at each other, and Elle sat up, her face close to his. He did nothing, breathing deeply. He had to recreate the memory.

"You can see my house from up here," Lee said.

"Really?"

He helped Elle stand up and pointed in the direction of his house.

"It's right there," he said, anticipating her not seeing it.

"Oh..."

Lee was surprised. "You see it?"

Elle hesitated, her eyes searching the town below, then shook her head without looking at Lee. He smiled, relieved that he would be able to recreate the moment, delighted that she would pretend to see something that she didn't for his sake.

Just as before, he positioned her in front of himself, and leaned over her shoulder to share the view from her height. When he saw what she saw, he rested one hand on her shoulder for stability, and pointed with the other.

"There," he said softly. He saw Elle no longer searching, but looking directly at the house.

"That's not at all how I would have pictured it looking. It looks so different."

Lee pulled his hand off Elle's shoulder and stood up straight next to her. He searched her face for a sign that his rare touch had impacted her like he was sure it had impacted her the first time around. At that moment he realized that he couldn't remember what had happened next, but he supposed it didn't really matter. They would both remember the surrounding moments differently, if at all. But their shared memory, the experience that was important for her to remember as a way to remember her bond with Lee, had been preserved. He was satisfied. Below her eyes glistening from the cold air, her nose started to bleed slowly.

"Oh!"

"Here," Lee said, pulling a pack of tissues from his coat pocket.

He felt aware of his concern for her, and realized that it was exactly that concern that she wouldn't feel for him ever again if the memories they shared were simply erased. He appreciated Frank profoundly in that moment for agreeing to extract and rebuild one memory at a time. To think of Elle walking the earth with no memory of him was worse than her not walking the earth at all. He equated it to how Allie might have treated him if she'd had Alzheimer's. Not remembering the love she'd had for him, not caring if she caused him pain, not missing him though he would desperately miss her. And it would be all in her mind, a past once held in her mind, lost. How it could affect her whole personhood frightened him. He couldn't deliberately inflict that on Elle. How frightening it must be to lose oneself slowly like that. And he couldn't inflict that on himself, to be coldly forgotten.

Elle dabbed at her nose as the bleeding stopped. "This has never happened before. Thank you."

"It's this weather. You're probably dry."

A drop of water fell on Elle's face, confusing her, as her mind had just been processing liquid on her face as blood, but the raindrop landed above her nose instead of below it.

"Oh, what is happening?" Elle pushed her head back into her neck, trying to see the liquid on her face to determine what was going on.

Lee looked up.

"I felt another one," said Elle, realizing that the new liquid was not coming from her own face, but from the sky.

The single drops of rain quickly turned into a downpour. Lee and Elle ran back down the open field of the hill, trying unsuccessfully to shield themselves. Lee, running slightly ahead of Elle, heard her giggling at their bad luck. The sound of her laughter wrapped him like a coat and made him smile. For a moment as they ran, Lee forgot about why they were in the rain, about the question of whose laughter it was behind him. He felt like he belonged right there, running downhill in the torrents, with that familiar voice he so loved close behind.

As quickly as he had forgotten, it came back. In a single moment, recalling much faster than it could have possibly happened, he saw himself telling Elle about the process.

"We're going to replace one memory at a time."

"Will it hurt?"

Will it hurt. The question resonated in his mind. At the time he thought that she had meant physically. And he assumed that she had meant to ask will it hurt *her.*

Sliding down the last few steps at the bottom of the muddy hill, they ran across the gravelly road into a crowded café. Lee held Elle's hand so that she wouldn't slip on the marble floor. Elle looked around self-consciously at the dry patrons, aware of how she and Lee looked bursting into the café, sopping wet and dripping all over.

No one cared. Lee walked up to the counter, dropping Elle's hand. It had felt natural to him to hold her hand. Unexpectedly so.

"Do you want something?" he asked Elle as he gazed up at the chalk-written menu.

"Just some tea. Are you getting something? Look at those croissants."

She looked closely through the glass at a platter of freshly baked breads and pastries, reminding Lee of a child. *How Alma might have gazed at those pastries.* Lee pushed the thought out of his mind. After so many years, he had mostly learned how to keep his grief in check, stored away in a safe place in his mind. But every so often it crept up on him, usually when he was happy, just to be sure it wasn't forgotten.

"Do you want a croissant?" He knew that she did.

"Do you want a croissant?" she asked him in return.

"If you want a croissant I'll get you a croissant."

"I don't want it by myself."

Lee stepped up to the counter. "A cup of tea, a black coffee, and a croissant."

Elle beamed. While Lee paid, she turned to look around the café. A man was staring at her, frowning. She held his gaze for a moment, then continued to scan the people. She looked back at the man. He was squinting and swaying slightly. He looked away.

The barista handed Lee a number. "Put this on the table so your server will know where to bring your drinks when they're ready."

Lee turned around to find a table with Elle. The café was cozy, but fit a surprising number of people. Small tables with too many chairs huddled around them combined with heavy winter coats made maneuvering difficult. Trying not to get everyone wet, Lee and Elle weaved past the staring man's small, round table. He looked up when Elle passed, and called out, "Lee!"

Lee doubled back, recognizing the voice.

"Eamonn!" Lee walked up to the table to greet the man, a pot-bellied, jovial, red-faced man with sparkling, drunk, Irish blue eyes and a meaty face.

"How the heck are yeh?" His smile was wide and crooked from alcohol. "You know Benny 'n' Didi."

He motioned barely in the vicinity of two men who were sitting around his table. At Didi, a tall, thin Frenchman, and the hulking Benny, just as tall as Didi and nearly as wide as he was tall.

Lee nodded toward them courteously, even though he had met them only briefly once before. "Of course. Benny. Didier." They mumbled in return.

Eamonn turned his attention back toward Elle. He was mystified. The drinks were hitting him hard. "And this—I didn't mean to stare—"

"This is Elle."

Elle smiled politely but didn't say anything. Eamonn drunkenly stared at her. He seemed to be processing her slowly.

"Elle!" he said to Lee. "Well you certainly have a type don't yeh?" He turned to Elle, taking in how much she looked like Allie. "Lovely to meet yeh! Join us! We just ordered another round of cider. My God, yer soaked!" He turned to Lee and playfully scolded him. "Wassamatta with you, you don't give the lady an umbrella? Come! Sit!"

Lee looked at Elle apologetically, trying to gauge her reaction. Allie had known Eamonn for years. Even though Elle had those memories, she had never met him herself. To Eamonn, she assumed that she was supposed to appear as though meeting him for the first time. Elle looked complacent.

Benny pulled over two more chairs and Lee placed the number on the table. The barista swooped in instantaneously and set Elle's tea in front of her just as she sat down across from Eamonn.

"What've yeh got there?" Eamonn asked.

"Just some tea."

"Tea?" Eamonn bellowed in mock-horror. "Bring her a cider! You want some cider?"

"No, I'm all set with tea."

Eamonn pretended to be suspicious of her, then smiled.

"Good! Tea is good for yeh. So," Eamonn settled back into his chair, curious about Elle. "How did you two meet?"

Lee and Elle glanced at each other. Eamonn looked shocked at their silence.

"What, you don't remember? My God! I could still tell yeh how I met my Rosie."

"Rosie's his dog," Didi said dryly, as if he had explained that very fact to thirty people already that week.

"Oh but she's more than just a dog," Eamonn started with a surprising level of speech clarity. "Do you know, when I met Rosie, she jumped into my arms like she'd been waiting for me her whole life."

"He saw her at the kennel when she was a puppy and took her home," said Didi.

"She keeps me company, little Rosie."

Elle's eyes lit up with excitement. "What type of dog is she?"

"A teacup poodle," said Benny. "Can you imagine this one with a teacup poodle?" Elle caught the irony of the massive man who said it.

"I love dogs," said Elle. "I wish I could get one of my own."

"So why don't you get one of your own?" Didi said as if he had solved all of her problems.

"Oh I couldn't take care of a dog. I wouldn't know how."

"Why don't you come over later and I'll show yeh how. Rosie would love you."

"She's not going to come over later," Didi sighed.

"He's a dirty old man!" joked Benny. Elle smiled, indifferent to the stale line.

Didi nudged Benny, and they both stood up and ambled toward the door.

"Quick smoke," Didi said.

Eamonn chuckled to himself as they left. "I'm only kiddin'. So really, how did you two meet?"

"Eamonn," said Lee. "This is *Elle*."

Eamonn looked at Elle, realization striking, and sobered up fast. Lee patiently watched Eamonn scan Elle.

"*Elle*. So it *is*. My God, I didn't really think—this is amazing. Does she know?"

"You can ask her."

"Do you know?" he asked Elle.

"Yes, I know."

"But if she knows—doesn't that make her—off?"

"How so?" Lee asked.

"I mean, if she knows she's—*herself*—then she knows she's not—who she looks like. She's aware of herself, right? Then, she wouldn't think exactly like— who she looks like—because who she looks like never had that awareness—because she had no reason to have that awareness—because she was the first—*version.*" Eamonn struggled to make sense through his many glasses of cider. Lee understood.

"We've never had secrets. This is no different. Frank knows also."

"Frank! My God, how long has it been?"

"It's been a while."

"I don't mean to stare, but this is really impressive. I mean—I don't even know—it really doesn't change her? Being aware? Would she know if it changed her?" Eamonn addressed Elle, "I'm sorry—I just—do you *feel* like—like her? I mean—would you know if you didn't?"

"Eamonn—" Lee started.

"Lee!" Eamonn exclaimed, thoroughly fascinated. "My God. Companion for the elderly. She's gonna kill me."

Elle smiled.

"More cider?" she offered Eamonn, seeing how flustered he had become.

He smiled back at her, amused, her small words calming his jumbled thoughts. When he saw Benny and Didi walking back he immediately dropped the subject. He was well aware of Lee's struggle to cope with Allie's death, and had been there for Lee when he first thought up the idea of Elle. But between Lee's withdrawal and Eamonn's heavy travel schedule, they had lost touch, only checking in briefly every so often, mostly on the part of Eamonn to make sure that Lee was okay.

"Anyway," Eamonn looked at Elle, his jolly expression returning to his pudgy face. "You gonna eat that? We don't want it to go to waste. Only if yer not going to eat it."

Elle handed Eamonn the rest of her croissant and he wolfed it down, leaving one last bite and holding it out to her.

"Last call…"

"No, thank you," said Elle.

Lee stood as Eamonn finished the last bite. "We should actually get going. My socks are soaked. Really great running into you. Are you in town for long?"

"A bit. Staying at The Chevalier. Only place Rosie would accept."

"Pff. Only place that would accept Rosie," said Didi.

"I'll stop by for a drink," said Lee.

Eamonn stood and embraced Lee, speaking low and seriously into his ear. "Chevalier. 2F. If you need anything."

Lee managed a tight but appreciative smile.

"And you!" Eamonn opened his arms wide as if to display Elle. "Lovely to meet yeh." He gave her a small kiss on the cheek. When he pulled away, a look of repulsion flitted across his face. The flush of his drunken cheeks paled slightly, and the skin on his nose crept upward involuntarily as his flesh met hers.

Lee followed Elle out of the café with his head down to make himself small. His tall figure just looked hunched, like old, crooked bones made up his insides.

Eamonn sat down, watching the door even after Lee was out of sight. Didi and Benny relaxed back into their chairs, quietly sipping their cider.

"Freak," muttered Eamonn in part awe, part jest, and part trepidation.

"What?" shrugged Benny. "She seemed nice."

Eamonn sighed, debating whether or not to elaborate. As disturbing as Lee's life had become, he felt loyalty to him. And to Allie, whom he had admired greatly since the days when she and Lee were still only dating. The man he had just seen, with sunken cheeks and downcast eyes, was far from the man he had known years ago. The illustrious scientist, the artist, the best of friends.

Benny and Didi looked at him curiously, waiting for him to answer.

"His wife died many years ago. Completely crushed him. He lost his mind."

Benny and Didi looked in the direction of the door, trying to picture the man they had just seen, broken. After a moment, Didi shrugged it off.

"Maybe his new girlfriend can take his mind off her. Very pretty."

Eamonn stayed silent, not willing to disclose any more. He felt both pity for Lee and sadness for the memory of Allie, knowing what Benny and Didi did not. They all drank.

TWENTY-ONE

....

That night Elle stood alone in her house, looking once again into her mirror. She moved her finger down along the thin red line on her face where the key ring had cut into her skin. The scab had long ago healed, but the red mark remained. *What happened there?* She assumed it was one of those marks that seemed to appear out of nowhere, like a mysterious bruise on a leg that is the first and only cognitively acknowledged sign of having bumped into something.

She traced the red line over and over, watching it widen as she irritated the surrounding skin. As she dragged the tip of her finger down her face, she felt a familiar spot that had been noticed not by any sense other than awareness, just beneath her eye. A small freckle. The moment of recognition caused a disturbance in her head that shuffled her memories like stacked storage boxes upended after the moldering, bottommost box is pulled. Boxes of dusty past experiences toppled and spilled into her consciousness. From them surged forth a conversation between Lee and Frank discussing her procedure.

"What's next?" asked Lee.

"The park, right before he died. Remember?"

"I remember."

Frank's voice echoed inside Elle's head. "Remember?"

She looked away from the mirror. She remembered that she soon wouldn't.

TWENTY-TWO

••

fternoons at Cordova Laboratories tended to be quiet. The mornings were when most of the scientists aimed to finish their heaviest fieldwork for the day, and many spent the afternoons locked away in their offices writing. It wasn't uncommon to see a wall of closed doors and an empty lab emitting not a single sound between the hours of two and seven, when the sun had gone down and the scientists would once again emerge from their own heads. Or even later, as a new group of scientists would only come into the lab at that time and start working under the solitude and space of the night. There seemed to be more hours to work during the night at the lab, though there were in fact just the same amount of available hours during the day. It was a necessarily solitary lifestyle at times.

There were always small groups of scientists spread out through the lab at different times of day, all looking to be solitary in the presence of someone else.

That afternoon was particularly quiet. It was just after lunchtime and the lab had emptied out. Frank sat behind a desk with three monitors suspended from the wall. Lee stood over his shoulder. There was a wide glass window in front of them through which they could see into the Procedures room. An operating table was bolted to the center of the floor. On the wall near the door was a large, white cabinet that hung over a countertop with a sink, trays of beakers, test tubes, clamps, and a monitor. It resembled a sterile medical chamber. The all-white floors, ceiling, and walls meant that only whatever was lying on the table could give the room depth.

Behind the glass was Elle. Her eyes were closed, her skin blended into the white sheets that covered her body up to her chin. Her hair was pulled back into a tight knot on the top of her head and plastered down with a thin, writable, clear gel covering that extended down over her forehead.

A scientist moved around behind the glass between Elle and his tray of tools wearing white latex gloves, fastening a syringe to a steel apparatus with mechanical arms above Elle. Frank clicked on a highlighted cluster of brain receptors. He blew it up on his first screen and clicked on one of the branches, which also highlighted. He deleted the highlighted branch, leaving a visible gap between two other branches. From a folder on his desktop called "Replacement Memories," he located a single memory and dragged it to the gap, carefully adjusting it to fit perfectly where the gap had been created.

Lee noticed that it wasn't connected to the other receptors, but simply appeared in its place. He said nothing.

"And here is the altered memory..." Frank said to himself as he finalized the replacement. He gave a thumbs-up to the scientist, who pulled a screen over Elle's face. When he looked down through the screen, it showed him the inside wiring of her head. He spotted the new memory that Frank had replaced, and brought the screen low and close to Elle. He locked the device in place and tapped the new memory. Two tiny red dots bloomed on the gel over Elle's forehead, indicating to the scientist where to inject the needle. He pushed aside the screen and pulled down the arm that held the needle above Elle, angling it as best he could in line with the first red dot. He pressed another button. As if magnetic, the needle found the first red dot on the gel and locked itself onto it, adjusting the angle of the needle. On the screen, he selected an option to fill the syringe. A single tube was drained from a row of vacutainer tubes that sat in pairs inside a shelf within the belly of the apparatus. Only two tubes still contained liquid. The syringe filled with the liquid from one tube.

Lee watched an image of the tube drain on Frank's screen.

"Now we just need to fuse them together..." Frank remarked.

With one more tap on the screen, the needle plunged into Elle's forehead, precisely through the center of the red dot. When the syringe was emptied, the mechanism withdrew, discarding the needle into its own sharps container and resetting itself for another injection. The red dot that had been punctured disappeared from the gel. The scientist replaced the syringe with a new, empty syringe, and pushed the apparatus back in place over the second red dot. As before, the mechanical arm locked itself into place above the red dot and adjusted the angle of penetration. The mate to the tube that had just been drained started to fill into the syringe. It administered itself once again through Elle's forehead.

Lee watched it play out on Frank's monitor, seeing that the injections targeted each side of the memory, fusing them where the new branch met the old.

Frank waited for the syringe to empty and the device to reset itself. When the scientist gave Frank the signal to proceed, Frank clicked on a small cloud on either side of the replaced memory and typed in a command, refreshing the page on his desktop. The clouds smoothed. The receptor had fused with the other receptors. He unhighlighted the new branch, minimized the image, and swiveled around to look at Lee, the last replacement of the day complete.

"And there you go."

Lee examined a receptor cluster on the screen that looked darker than the others.

"What is that?"

"Where?"

"Right there," Lee pointed. "The dark spot. Blow that up."

The enlarged dark spot showed a receptor stemming from a point labeled A linking to point C, skipping point B. It lay over the existing connections between points A, B, and C. A piggybacking connection that looked dark when the image was small, but was really two connections, one on top of the other.

"That's strange..." Frank pulled himself closer to the monitor. He zoomed in on the connector and saw that the receptor fell just short of reaching point C. It was an open, dead connection stemming from A.

"What is it?" Lee leaned in to see.

"It looks like Elle tried to make her own connection. But look—the connection is just short. And she skipped point B. That's probably why she fell short. She skipped the gas station and ran out of gas."

"Can you tell how she started? Go over here." Lee motioned to Frank to blow up the connector at point A. Nothing looked strange, it just looked like twin connections came from point A, one thinner than the other.

"It's a weak connection," Frank said. "That might be why it didn't register on the monitor. It kind of sprouted and died."

"But what does that mean?"

Frank highlighted the dead connection and deleted it.

"It means we're looking at proof of why all of this is necessary. She tried to walk along her own connection, but fell into the abyss when she reached the unattached end of it. She either couldn't complete the connection or it was stretched too thin. Either way, it couldn't support what it needed to." Frank pressed the intercom. "Consolidating new memories."

The scientist nodded and Frank pressed a button on his keyboard. His screen went black, then strands of letters and numbers started to appear. A progress bar read thirty minutes to completion. The scientist turned off the light above Elle and moved the contraption aside. He backed away from Elle and took off his gloves.

Lee looked into the sterile room at Elle. Free from the white light, the halo around Elle had diminished, leaving her looking like a limp, life-sized doll. She was completely motionless, her breathing not even visible.

Up close she looked like a wax figure, the remains of the gel melting off her face and head, shrinking into itself and dissolving into the air. But even closer, her eyes appeared to shift back and forth behind her closed lids.

Lee watched her for a moment. The dead connection had unsettled him. *What if there are more? What if there is an entire dead connection graveyard in her mind that we are missing, just sitting there, decaying, shriveling up, poisoning the rest of her mind?*

Frank sat back casually, not paying attention to Lee, satisfied with how smoothly the replacement had gone. The plan seemed to be working. Nothing strange was coming through in the reports, and the physical memory replacement was flawless. It was a small weight off his shoulders.

He unwrapped a thick sandwich and stuck a straw in a large takeout cup. Keeping the volume low, he turned on music while he waited for the memories to consolidate, keeping an eye on the progress. The scientist waited in the room, cleaning up and glancing at Elle every few minutes.

Suddenly, quietly, Lee turned around and walked out of the room, leaving Frank alone. Frank looked back at him curiously, then turned his attention again toward his desktop, unconcerned with Lee's abrupt departure. The data scrolled.

....

TWENTY-THREE

Weeks passed. The clouds of the daytime sky rushed into heavy, overcast nights, and opened back up into clear blue as the days rolled routinely forward. The replacements continued, one by one. Needle by needle.

Lee and Elle walked together through the deserted park. It had been only months since Lee had watched Elle take the same walk with Walter. Her navy blue peacoat and pale pink scarf stood out amidst the dull browns of the dead season. The blue darkened her hair to black and the soft pink around her neck made her look fresh, like a newborn, uncontaminated. There were no lines from unwanted knowledge across her porcelain face, no downward brow above tired eyes. Her step was youthful and unaware, unburdened by her own existence.

Above the greys of the trees Elle spotted a bird. *Is it a small bird, or high in the sky?*

Lee followed her gaze, growing uneasy at the silence shared between them.

"What is it?"

"A robin, I think. Isn't that what they are? The ones with the red?" There was a shift in the way that Elle spoke. Her voice sounded less fragile, less melancholy, more pointed.

Lee noticed only for a moment, and paid no attention. "Yes, but just because it has red doesn't mean it's a robin."

"That's the only way I know how to describe it. If it has red, it's a robin."

"What if it's a robin with poor pigmentation? Is it still a robin?"

Elle laughed. "I wouldn't be able to tell."

They walked together once again in silence. The branches around them, leafless, motionless. The stillness rang in Lee's ears as his mind churned trying to find something to say. Nothing was worthy. He walked close to Elle, feeling a mixture of nervousness in her presence and serenity with her at his side. His nerves, he knew, stemmed from his hyperawareness of what was happening in her mind. He both protectively observed her and let her company fill him, as the pull of observation and the pull of familiarity tore tensely in opposite directions. Their coats brushed past each other at the sleeves. Lee noticed as if it were his own skin, but Elle paid it no mind.

He spotted the swing set through the trees moments before Elle.

"Ohhh!" Elle looked brightly at Lee and then ran toward it, hopping on and pushing herself off. Lee watched her, her hair flipping back and forth with her movement through the air. "Come sit next to me!"

Lee walked over and sat still on the swing, watching her. He blinked and the grey park turned to a bronzed memory of Allie on that very swing, looking at Lee as she rose and fell. Her legs kicked the same way, slightly crooked because of the turn of her head.

Elle amused herself, kicking harder to see how high she could go, surprised by how much effort it took. She laughed out loud as she swung down, and as she rose, she looked up in time to see the robin fly over once more. Her smile faltered as she saw the red of the robin, questioning what she thought was an intrinsic quality of being a robin, but returned once the robin passed. She kept swinging, never once feeling compelled to look at Lee despite feeling his eyes fixated on her.

"Am I ever going to get you to leave now?"

Elle laughed. "Nope. This is it. I'm staying."

Lee looked around the park as Elle continued to swing. Dead branches, frozen ground. Browns, greys, gloom.

He turned back toward Elle, in her blue and pink, looking very much alive on the swing against the colorless, motionless background. And very much out of place in the world around her.

TWENTY-FOUR

....

That night the sky was dark but revealed scattered stars. The park was silent, the moon ascending overhead. Elle and Lee lay next to each other beside the swing set. Lee was perched on his elbow looking at Elle. He studied her, each crease around her eyes carefully placed. She took no notice.

He leaned over, then hesitated, suddenly aware of his free arm and unsure what to do with it. Elle was face up on the ground, both hands behind her head to form a pillow. She was unfazed by Lee leaning over above her. He put his free hand down on the ground between their bodies and rolled inward. He kissed her briefly, then lingered for a moment above her lips as years of unused kisses meant for Allie awakened before he backed away.

Elle smiled at him politely, having simply accepted his gesture, neither returning nor refusing it. She playfully tossed a piece of mulch toward him. His face lit up.

The lamps in the park started to switch off. One by one, making their way closer to the swings, they extinguished. Just before the last light turned out, Elle looked over at Lee. All went dark.

....

TWENTY-FIVE

Eamonn stood alone in the street outside Frank's house. The chill in the nighttime air left the cul-de-sac deserted. Scattered lights from inside the houses shined dully through the shadows. The clouds above churned darkly in the velvet sky. He held a piece of wrinkled paper in his hand with an address written neatly in the corner. He looked at it, then looked at the number on the house. Glancing once more around the empty street, he proceeded up the steps. He listened from outside the door, hearing Frank's mumbling voice and a female's that he didn't recognize.

Ha! Typical, Eamonn thought, not surprised that Frank had female company. Nostalgia suddenly overwhelmed him as he thought back to many years before at university. It was where Lee had met Allie. He re-

membered seeing Lee's face when he finally introduced her to everyone, knowing right then that Allie
was going to be around for a long time. *Not long
enough.*

He knocked and heard the voices quiet. Only then
did he consider how late it was. The voices started
again, Frank talking louder as light footsteps came
closer. The door swung open and Frank appeared in a
robe, a young, blond woman in a matching one sitting
at the kitchen table. She looked at Eamonn through
Frank. Frank, in shock, recognized Eamonn, who
stood silently, nervously folding and unfolding the
paper he held in front of his chest.

"Oh my God—" Frank started.

"Er—" Eamonn started.

Frank lunged forward and pulled Eamonn into a
hug, breaking into a smile. "Ea-man!"

Eamonn felt his nervousness dissolve at Frank's
warm greeting. The years spent apart melted as they
exchanged long-lost greetings. Frank looked un-
changed, his boyish face still framed with the same
square glasses, topped with the same thick hair that
spilled onto his forehead. Not even a new grey strand.

Frank looked at Eamonn in disbelief, expectantly.
"What are you doing here?"

"Uh—"

"Come in!"

Frank stepped aside as Marigold, curious, made her way to the door.

"Mari—this is Eamonn, from school. My girlfriend, Marigold."

Marigold recognized the name and shook his hand.

"I hope he hasn't told you too much," Eamonn joked.

"Oh but he has," she replied, matching his tone.

"Really?" Eamonn was genuinely surprised. Maybe Frank had changed a little bit after all. "I'm glad to see you finally tamed him. I never woulda thought he'd pick just one. You wouldn't believe—"

Eamonn suddenly felt Frank's eyes on him, willing him to stop taking. Eamonn understood. Marigold didn't know half of it. "Uh—popular guy."

"Are you visiting?" asked Frank, changing the subject. Although he suspected that Marigold had some idea of his promiscuous younger years, he didn't need to confirm it. "Have you seen Lee yet? He lives just down the block. Tea?"

Frank talked quickly as he motioned for Eamonn to have a seat at the kitchen table.

Eamonn hesitated. *I guess we're getting right down to it then.* "Actually, I did see Lee. And I saw Elle."

Frank looked piercingly at Eamonn and tried to gauge whether Eamonn understood what exactly Elle was. He asked cautiously, "You saw—Elle?"

"I did. She's...unreal." Eamonn chose his words carefully and pointed to Marigold. "She know?"

Frank nodded.

"Good. It would be rude to barge in here and start speaking in tongues."

Marigold sat down next to Eamonn. Frank stood back, not comfortable enough to sit.

"Look, since we're on the subject, I want to get right to the point," Eamonn started. Then he paused, catching himself. "Beautiful home," he said to Marigold as an aside, not wanting to be rude.

"Thank you."

"I'm only here for a few more days, so we'd have to act quickly," Eamonn started, wasting no more words.

"What are we acting quickly on?" Frank's elation at seeing Eamonn was starting to sink.

"Look, you and I—we—there's no one who knows Lee better. But you spend every day with him. Me? I bump into him after how many years and I barely recognize him. He's not good. *She's* not good."

Frank was silent. Eamonn watched him, concerned that Frank was too close to Lee to see what was happening. Marigold leaned into Eamonn, speaking in a soft but serious tone.

"I think you're right."

Frank stepped over to the table to silence Marigold. "Wait wait wait."

Eamonn sat back and smiled. "She agrees with me. I like her."

"Lee is fine," Frank argued. "Has he changed? Yes, of course he has. His wife died. That would change anyone. But he's *good*."

"No. Not what I saw. What I saw was a man who's only a shell of what he used to be." Eamonn leaned closer, lowering his voice as if someone unseen and unwanted were listening. "Have you ever watched them together? Have you ever seen the way he looks at her? She *terrifies* him. He looks at her, and—*fills* himself with her."

As he spoke, his words became more true to him, filling him with guilt that he had been gone for so long while his friend unraveled.

Frank listened intently, thinking only slightly that Eamonn was being ridiculous. Of course it had been a little strange for some time, and Lee had struggled, but Frank had not once seen any sign of Lee being terrified of Elle. He searched Eamonn's face for a hint of knowing exaggeration. There was no sign of a smile.

"She doesn't terrify him," Frank argued.

"She's a ghost. Her flesh may be soft and her voice may be dulcet, but those alone do not a wife make." He paused for a poetic moment, then spoke seriously once more. "The man needs to grieve! He needs to grieve. Or he will waste away," he warned Frank.

Frank pictured the disturbing images of Elle cutting her own face. He pictured the mirror from Elle's point of view, but saw Lee in the mirror, looking old, thin, worn. The cut showing up on Lee's face as Elle dragged the key ring down her own. The damage Elle inflicted on herself as a result of incomprehensible grief.

"And what if he doesn't understand how to grieve?" Frank asked.

The room was heavy. Eamonn was silent. His stony face held the answer. Frank, Marigold, and Eamonn slouched over the table as the night wore on, as it does, around them.

The next morning, the sky was a cloudless, royal blue. Lee woke early, the sun streaming into his room through the thin, white drapes. He sprung from his bed only seconds after he opened his eyes like a schoolboy on the first day of summer vacation. Only one day before had his routine felt like an elaborate drudgery. His tube of toothpaste heavy. The dread of wetting his face only to need to dry it again. But overnight it had changed. He bounded into the bathroom and slipped back into his regimen. He started washing his face, but stopped after looking at the greys in his hair. He grabbed a towel and brought it to his bedroom, laying it down in the center of the floor where he started doing sit-ups and push-ups. One. Two. His lips met hers. Four. Her long, low lashes. Six. His chest beating on top of hers. He felt like he would never get tired. But he stopped, went back into the bathroom, and washed his face again, brushed his teeth for several beats longer than necessary. He felt alive and fresh. Minty.

He walked over to his closet and pulled out a light blue sweater from the back, an unusual pick compared to the five dark-hued sweaters he rotated through every week that were within perfect reaching distance. He blew dust off some of the clothes on Allie's side that had been stuffed into a corner, and moved his clothes to his side to make more room for hers. He stepped back. The closet was separated exactly in the center.

Reaching into Allie's jewelry box on his tall dresser, he plucked out a new-looking wristwatch. A tiny, tired serenade played as he held the top of the box open. It sounded tinny and distant, as if it knew it was playing for the wrong person. Two gold necklaces, one with an "A" charm dangling from the center, and one with an "L," rested faithfully next to each other in the velvety red cushion inside the box. AL. He read them as a single, unbreakable word, touching them sentimentally. Pulling on his coat, he slid the "L" necklace into his pocket.

....

TWENTY-SEVEN

Lee walked the few steps to Elle's house, the scent of the moist bark on the trees transporting him back to the evening before, under the swings in the park. He couldn't describe the sounds he had heard, the shape of the trees above him, or the taste on his lips after they met hers. But he would recognize the sounds if he heard them again, the shape of the trees above him if he looked up at the right angle, and the taste left on his lips after meeting Elle's for a second time. Just as he hadn't noticed the scent of the trees before he encountered it again, he knew that there were triggers for his other senses that would jump-start his memories, which fluttered by in a blur, unable yet to be captured.

Voices from behind him hushed as they passed. Normally he would have felt exposed standing high on the steps above the passersby, as if on a pedestal of ignominy. Instead he felt bold and turned around to face his neighbors directly.

"Ah," he said. "Mrs. Thatcher. Mrs. Grove. Lovely to see you."

The two women hurried past, looking at their feet. Mrs. Thatcher glanced up and forced a smile, which surprised Lee. She slowed her step and took a breath.

"Good morning," she said with a shaking voice. It was unexpected, as the last time Lee had seen her she had called his work voodoo. Lee was pleased to see that her perspective was changing, even if he didn't understand why.

Mrs. Grove led Mrs. Thatcher away with a look of horror in her eyes.

"Come now," said Mrs. Grove quietly so that Lee wouldn't hear. But with her hearing loss, she spoke louder than she intended.

"Don't!" said Mrs. Thatcher to Mrs. Grove, pulling her arm away. Lee witnessed the exchange and con-templated how cranky Mrs. Thatcher could be at times, and how pleasant she could be at others. She was difficult to crack. The two women continued to whisper to each other as they passed Elle's house, glancing sideways at Lee.

He heard the sound of Elle's light footsteps coming toward him from beyond the door and stood up straight. Only then did he realize how difficult it was to push his shoulders back, to lift his chest, after months, years, of not. He wondered when he started slouching, and if others noticed it.

Elle opened the door and flashed a delighted smile when she saw Lee.

"Well hello," she said to him, standing in the doorway.

"I was just going to go out for a walk, and—" Lee faltered for a moment feeling foreign in his artificially unrounded shoulders.

"It is a beautiful day, isn't it," Elle commented, noticing but not understanding Lee's discomfort.

"It is. I wanted to stop by and ask if I could take you to dinner tonight," Lee managed to say with the grace and confidence that he had once been used to. He felt compelled to continue speaking but stopped himself to give Elle a chance to answer.

"To dinner? At a restaurant?"

It occurred to Lee only then that Elle had never been to a restaurant. She had the memories of a restaurant experience from Allie, but not the experience itself. *Is there a difference?* Lee wondered.

"Just a quiet restaurant. There's one that I used to go to quite often, but," Lee faltered again before continuing. He was struggling. "But I haven't had a reason to go in a while."

Elle understood. She realized then how upbeat he seemed underneath his discomfort. It faded in and out, but it was pushing through like the sun on a cloudy day. He looked at her with such pleading behind squinted, quivering eyes that it was impossible for her to refuse.

"I'd be happy to join you for dinner."

....

TWENTY-EIGHT

That night, Elle sat across from Lee in a dimly lit corner table of a restaurant in the city. It was a large, elegant restaurant with tables on the ground floor as well as a section of tables raised slightly above the rest, which Elle thought was more for aesthetics than for practicality. The hostess had seated them right away and appeared to recognize Lee. Her eyes had lit up when she saw him, but since she didn't say anything, Elle couldn't be sure.

In the city, Lee was still as much a celebrity as he had been during his earlier years at the lab. The small-town gossip had indeed reached the city folk across the thin divide of trees, but unlike the residents of the cul-de-sac, who had witnessed Lee's deterioration, the businessmen and women of the city held Lee in high regard. Younger women, like the slender hostess who looked to be in her late twenties, were intrigued by the mystery of his situation. They heard about his genius, about his dead wife, and labeled him a brooding bachelor. Wealthy, handsome, and in need of a new wife.

Elle hadn't heard any of the talk surrounding Lee, but Lee was aware of his reputation beyond the trees. It was part of the reason he so seldom ventured into the city. He preferred the anonymity of the small town to the excited whispers of the other patrons, though, he considered with dismay, he had indeed become a subject of gossip in his small town as well.

"I hope you didn't mind the cab," Lee said to Elle.

"Not at all. It's not a far walk, but everything feels miles away when you're walking in heels. I'm glad you called a cab."

They picked at their food in comfortable silence. Lee had gotten dressed in a suit and would have been out of place if he hadn't. It somehow made it easier for him to keep his shoulders pushed back. When he looked at Elle sitting across from him in her dress, in the heart of the city he once frequented, he was reminded of how his life had once been. How he had been comfortable being known in certain circles, how he never had to say his name twice. He had become quite well-known worldwide, among academics as well as the general public, since the work he did in his lab was often what people imagined, dreamt, or thought possible only as a result of huge studio sets in California. He preferred to think of himself as being more "internationally popular" than famous, and had enjoyed the benefits of his status during nights out in the city. But he was always happy to return to his small, quiet home on his anonymous street, just to the left of where people would have expected him to reside. He never pictured himself in a penthouse in the city, or turning his name into a larger brand. He had always only wanted to work on his research, and go back home to spend time with his wife.

"Oh my goodness," Elle said looking around the restaurant. "Isn't that Mrs. Thatcher?"

Lee spun around in his seat and spotted her immediately. Indeed, frail old Mrs. Thatcher was seated across the restaurant at a table with five other ladies.

"I never pictured her going farther than the market!" Elle said.

"It is strange. I always think of our neighbors as never leaving the town, but I suppose everyone has a night out every so often."

Just then one of the ladies at Mrs. Thatcher's table glanced in Lee's direction and leaned in to gab to the rest of the table. Mrs. Thatcher slowly turned to look, and when her searching eyes landed on Lee, her face shut down like a switch had been flipped. She squinted at him. Her mouth drew together into a tight line. And then she looked at Elle, sitting across from Lee. As soon as she laid eyes on her, Lee saw her face fall.

"Why is she looking at us like that?" Elle asked Lee.

Lee felt his shoulders slump back toward their usual positioning. He wanted to melt into the floor, disappear from sight, and then suddenly felt intense hatred for Mrs. Thatcher.

"She doesn't like what we do at the lab," Lee responded.

"But she doesn't know what you do," Elle protested.

"Well, she thinks she does."

"She doesn't like me very much, does she."

Lee sighed.

"No, she doesn't. But only because she doesn't understand you. Anyone else who saw—you—after so long would probably have some questions too."

"Why don't you answer some of those questions? I know it's just gossip, but look at how she's talking to that table. Word spreads. Whatever she's saying could hurt your reputation."

"I'd rather not say anything until we go public. Let them talk. If the lab stays quiet, it's just that. Talk."

"She's coming over here," Elle remarked.

Lee wiped his mouth and said nothing as Mrs. Thatcher walked up to their table, slowly but assuredly. She looked at Lee, then glanced at Elle.

"Hello," she nodded at Elle with a forced smile.

"Hello Mrs. Thatcher," Elle replied brightly. The use of her name seemed to startle Mrs. Thatcher, and she leaned away from Elle slightly. She regarded her for a moment, then turned to Lee.

"Hello," she said to Lee, unsure where to begin. Lee said nothing, but dipped his head to her.

"Well I realize that this is an inappropriate time to bring this up but—well I wanted to—*apologize*—for judging something that I didn't understand."

Lee's eyebrows shot up, surprised. She continued.

"Well I still don't quite understand it, but I do, at least, a little more now. What people are saying around town—it just became clear to me that it was all nonsense."

"Well I appreciate you saying that," Lee said to her, waiting for the catch.

"You see, my husband hasn't been doing very well lately, and somewhere along the way I realized that the end is no longer sometime in the future. It could be any day. On good days he's still there, still himself, but most days—well, he told me not to buy green bananas anymore."

Elle stifled a giggle. Sad as it was, it was wonderful that Mr. Thatcher had kept his sense of humor.

Mrs. Thatcher caught Elle's look and glanced at her, cracking a small smile in return.

"Well anyway, I just wanted to say that I understand now, why—this—was all necessary." She glanced again at Elle without gesturing toward her. "And if you're coming up with any more, he might be a good candidate," she said with a meaningful glance.

Lee took a moment to consider what she was saying.

"Mr. Thatcher?" Lee said, confused.

Mrs. Thatcher nodded. "He's really a good person. It wouldn't hurt to keep him around."

Lee was perplexed, but wanted to avoid the topic entirely.

"I understand, Mrs. Thatcher."

She pulled her lips back into a tight line as if trying to prevent herself from saying any more. As she turned and walked away, Elle whispered to Lee.

"A good candidate for what?"

Lee shook his head. "I think she's a little confused about what we do in the lab."

"It sounded that way, didn't it? I think what she sees is a certain—immortality."

Lee looked back at Elle, wondering if she had become a bit saddened by their short conversation with Mrs. Thatcher. It was sad indeed to see a soon-to-be widow planning her life beyond the death of her husband before he was in the ground rather than spending her last moments with him. There was a selfishness he hadn't recognized before in grief.

"Before we go on speculating, I'll talk to her about it. See what she's really thinking," Lee said, wishing that the conversation would end.

His mind started spinning at the thought of immortality, which he knew was simply a concept dreamt up in the minds of men and women grasping at their present. Their past. A future that they would forever know instead of existing alongside it with no consciousness. He glanced at Elle to look for signs that she was calculating, as he was. That she would time out again in the face of reasoning about such a concept.

"How is it?" He pointed to her food, changing the subject.

He didn't listen for her answer, but instead wondered why he had to run into Mrs. Thatcher right then when he just wanted to be with Elle, wanted to build on the time they had spent together in the park, free from talk of the lab, of herself, of anything that would eventually be replaced or altered. He wanted a pure memory.

As he thought of the previous night in the park, Mrs. Thatcher's odd offer melted away in his mind. Across the table, Elle's red lips reminded him of their soft, fleshy texture. As she chewed, a slight smile remained painted across her mouth. He noticed how natural she looked in her dress, in the spacious, candle-lit restaurant. How her arms were bent over her plate holding her knife and fork, how they cut with no hesitation or stumbling. He wouldn't have noticed if it had been anyone else. He felt light. Not once did he think about Allie.

Later that night, after leaving Elle at her house, Lee sat quietly inside his own kitchen drinking tea. After the noise and the crowd of the city, his house felt particularly lonely. It was only ten o'clock, not late enough to be tired, but too late to continue socializing. As he watched the minutes go by, he thought of Mrs. Thatcher's proposition. It made him curious in a way that resulted in restlessness.

He took his coat and walked the few steps down the block to a bench in the center of the cul-de-sac. The open air cleared his mind. It was a welcome change of scenery despite the cold. For the first time since he could remember, he hoped to be seen. He hoped to be seen by Mrs. Thatcher on her way home from the city. It couldn't be long now. It was getting late.

The lights went out in Elle's house, causing Lee to feel abandoned.

As if on cue, Mrs. Thatcher's cab pulled up to the drop-off point at the opening of the cul-de-sac, and her shadowy figure emerged alone. She began her slow march toward her home on the opposite end of the cul-de-sac. Lee thought about how much walking his neighbors were really required to do. It made sense that there were so many elderly folk on his block. They tended to stay in shape well past the point of the usual decline. Like Mrs. Thatcher. She moved slowly, but capably. Not a bad hip or knee, only a small hunch in her back, but she walked indeed with steady footing, and took her time as if she had time to spare.

She passed behind the bench. Lee wanted to call out to her, but realized that he might scare her. He tried anyway, keeping his voice low so that the sound of it wouldn't be jarring in the silence of the sleeping cul-de-sac.

"Mrs. Thatcher," said Lee.

She looked up and spotted Lee under the blown street lamp.

"My goodness, you'll freeze out here. What are you doing?" She made her way over to him.

"Actually I was hoping I would catch you."

"Is that right. Well it's a bit late—"

"Could I make you a cup of tea before you turn in for the night? Or perhaps a quick nightcap?" Lee offered.

"Well, I suppose it would be all right. My husband's aid is scheduled to end her shift soon though, so it'll have to be quick."

Mrs. Thatcher followed Lee up the stairs, then stopped before walking through the door he held open for her.

"You know, I don't know that I've ever been in your house," she said.

"Oh that can't be true," Lee replied casually, though he knew it was true indeed.

"No, I believe this will be the first time." She looked at Lee as if they had an understanding. "I'm very glad to be here now," she said.

It made Lee hesitant to let her into his home. Clearly Mrs. Thatcher took it as a friendship offering. It irked him to think that the thing he had in common with Mrs. Thatcher was loss, whether long ago or imminent. Something so personal. She couldn't understand it as he did.

She stepped inside and waited for Lee to turn the lights on before looking around. She hadn't expected it to be so neat based on how he walked around—the scraggly man who so often looked as if he had been awake all night, who wandered through the streets of the neighborhood at odd hours, never a smile on his face. She had expected his home to reflect this, and was satisfied to see that it didn't. But as she looked closer, the house felt colder to her. It wasn't a disheveled house because it was an unlived-in house. Like an old gallery, where furniture was not to be sat upon and dishes were not to be touched.

"Well," she said putting a smile on her face.

"Tea?" Lee offered again.

"Yes, please. With milk, if you have it."

"Of course."

Lee hung Mrs. Thatcher's coat for her and led her to the kitchen. She sat in silence for a moment as he prepared two cups of tea, like a child waiting to be fed.

"Isn't that a wonderful restaurant?" she asked to break the silence.

"It is."

"I'm so glad I ran into you there. You know, I've felt terrible about the way this neighborhood treats you. About how I've treated you."

It was difficult for her to get the words out, and Lee noticed. They were insincere, saccharine, dripping with self-serving asks and favors.

"The neighborhood treats me just fine," Lee replied, ignoring the last part of her statement.

"Oh but the things they say—it finally became clear to me how having too much time can melt a brain," Mrs. Thatcher replied with a smirk. She was trying hard to make herself out to be a comrade. Lee saw through it.

"I suppose that's what happens when something is misunderstood and not explained. Rumors start."

Lee set the tea down in front of Mrs. Thatcher and sat across from her.

"So," she said to Lee, sipping her tea.

"I'm going to be blunt here, because I don't want you to get the wrong idea," Lee said, suddenly wishing that he hadn't invited her inside.

"What is it?" Her eyes darkened for a moment, then brightened once more as she set a deliberate smile on her face.

"What exactly do you think the lab can do for you?"

"Well, if I am to be honest—I know, we all know, that your wife died. And yet, she walks around, not a day older than the day she died years ago. It's not really her, of course, but you've brought her back somehow. I don't want to be without my husband, and I don't want him to be without me. So either we both go on living, or we both come back."

"That's not what we do at the lab."

"But you could."

"Even if we could, you wouldn't know it. There is no transfer of consciousness—neither you nor your husband would know if whatever versions of you we 'bring back,' as you say, were looking right into each other's eyes."

"But they would know, right?"

"They would. You wouldn't." Lee realized suddenly that Allie had no idea that Elle existed. They were so intertwined, it seemed only natural that Allie would know of Elle. But of course, that wasn't possible. "Mrs. Thatcher, I appreciate your interest, but I can't really discuss this any further at this point. When the time is right I would be happy to revisit the idea and clarify a few things to make sure that we fully understand each other."

Mrs. Thatcher dropped the smile from her face.

"When the time is right? The time is right now. He doesn't have long to live you know."

"I understand. But the lab is not prepared to do what you are asking."

"When will it be prepared?"

Lee heard the desperation seep through the layers in her voice. He recognized it. He felt it as she spoke. It was unthinkable, how people could change in the face of death, in the face of experiencing a death and living beyond it, carrying it along until the relief of their own death frees them from the remnants of others. It seemed cruel to turn away Mrs. Thatcher without reassurance. To allow her to face her husband's death by herself, and to face every day after with his death on her sleeve.

"The time will be right in time," Lee said, choosing his words carefully.

He led Mrs. Thatcher to the door and helped her with her coat, noticing how narrow her shoulders were, how frail her bones looked up close.

"You know," she started. "Even though Walter did finally pass away, he died happy. It was as if his body refused to let go until he had that one last taste of happiness, and you gave it to him."

Lee couldn't help but interpret her words to mean that he had assisted in Walter's death. He wouldn't ask her what he wanted to know. What she thought was Elle's relationship to Walter. What she thought Elle was. Why she was. Questions from him might invite her to ask questions of him that he wasn't prepared to answer about the lab's dealings with preservation versus creation. He realized that because he had created Elle in Allie's image, the purpose of the experiment must have looked quite different from what it actually was. He remembered at once the original purpose and saw how something that was identical to his late wife could confuse onlookers. It wasn't about preservation of an old companionship, it was about creating a new companionship.

And Elle is an exception, he realized with guilt. *Can I go on saying that she's a part of the trial if she's unlike what we would be creating in the future?* He thought of Frank and pushed the thought aside. If Frank didn't object, no lines were crossed. It was what he told himself.

He looked at Mrs. Thatcher as she pulled her coat around her shoulders. She had been so afraid of Elle at first, and he suspected that she still was to some extent, but had come to be so eager to have a companion of her own. Or rather, to turn her likeness into a companion. She seemed to be struggling with her own mortality as well as the idea of being left alone. Perhaps it was the idea of dying alone that troubled her. The loneliest journey of them all, one that everyone must make alone. She didn't want to be separated from her husband even after their death, even after there was no more consciousness, when she wouldn't know whether or not she had been separated. But she would know before that time came, and that was what mattered to her. It was a sort of being buried together. But in her case, she wanted to leave behind the image of her and her husband together.

Lee wanted to help her, understanding her sudden fear and confusion, having seen the dispassionate, in-discriminating face of death lurking just around the corner. Her corner.

Perhaps, he thought, *I could help her.* Not to create a companion in the image of her husband, as she thought she wanted. She needed a companion who could take care of himself, who could take care of her as she aged. A companion designed in the image of her husband wouldn't be able to fulfill those needs. Indeed, Lee suspected that the person whom she once knew and loved, whom she was so keen to hold on to, was already long gone, no longer part of the crum-bling body that sat in its wheelchair day after day, speaking only rarely in a voice that she didn't recog-nize.

Death comes well before we even realize, killing everything about a person except the person himself. Before we even begin grasping to hold on to the person we once loved they are already gone, and it's too late.

The thought made him melancholy. He recalled the many times he had the chance to be with Allie and

worked late at the lab instead. There was no postpon-
ing of time, there was no refilling of hours lost, spent
apart, in fights. They were simply gone. Time eroding
lives every second without break, without slowing for
a breath, without waiting if a husband is late for dinner with his wife.

He wanted to reach for Elle. It seemed silly that he
had spent the hours after dinner apart from her, alone
is his house watching the time tick on.

Then a thought passed through his mind that disturbed him. What would happen to Elle after he died?
How would she go on? It came as a surprise to
acknowledge that the lab hadn't thought about the distant future, about what would happen to the systems
when they did manage to explain death to them, and
what would happen when the original team of scientists was all gone. Would the original systems still be
around, ageless, with memories of their creators?

His mind reeled back to Mrs. Thatcher, who was
looking at him curiously.

"Are you all right?" she asked him, looking at him
the same way she had months before when he terrified her.

"I'm fine, sorry, I was just thinking," Lee replied,
pulling himself together. "Let me walk you home."

"Oh that's all right, I can manage."

Lee was relieved. He wanted suddenly to be alone, to be under his sheets with the bedroom door closed, to feel like the rest of the house could fall away and he would be safe in the bedroom, as long as the door was shut, locked.

"We'll talk again soon," he said to Mrs. Thatcher as she left.

"Oh I hope so," she replied in a serious voice. "I am counting on it."

....

TWENTY-NINE

The next day Lee woke early and sat behind his desk writing feverishly. Something said the night before had implanted itself in his mind, growing like a weed in his conscience while he slept. It had occurred to him that Mrs. Thatcher's request might be exactly what he needed. The thought of releasing Elle's data to the public didn't sit well with him. The idea that she would be analyzed, that the study would be questioned due to the exceptions made during her creation and trial, or worse, that she would be sent off to be someone else's companion.

But if he created a second system, his own design, not based on any living human, he would be able to release that design to the public, study the companion as it would be, and keep Elle to himself. Once she was rebooted, he would have Frank unplug his watchful screens and let her live her life privately. The new companion would be the system to watch. The one that would be released to the public first. There were statistically more female widows than male, so a male companion on the market would do more immediate good. Word would spread while they worked on the first female companion. He would fix Mrs. Thatcher's situation and his own with the new male companion. His hands began to shake with unfamiliar excitement. Urgency, perhaps. He scribbled quickly on a notepad, then threw down his pen and left for the lab.

He jogged up the elegant steps at the front entrance of Cordova. The movements felt foreign in his body. For the first time in years, he noticed what surrounded the lab. The plaza was decorated with dying but still vibrant potted flowers. Against the smooth, grey, stone steps, they looked that much more inviting, their colors appearing deeper and more saturated. Off to the side, a small, circular, marble fountain was spitting white, foamy water.

The building itself was only twenty stories high, but looked massive compared to the rest of the two-story town in the middle of which it sat. Perhaps it only looked massive to Lee, who realized that only an hour before, if asked to describe it, he wouldn't have been able to. He looked beyond the lab to the point just outside town where the buildings became taller, more city-like with their brick faces and small windows stacked for what looked like miles into the sky. He peered at the skyline, feeling his heart beat faster in his neck. His eyes felt wide as if they were taking in more than they were built to take in, to make up for everything that they had missed when their lids were hung heavily before them.

But in the center of town, the modern, twenty-story, all-glass building was an anomaly among the tiny, square cafés with canopies over four-table patios, and the shops with awnings over each window and a shopkeeper living upstairs. If he hadn't felt the presence of the cold stirring up winter, he might have mistaken the season for spring based solely on the appearance of the lab's sparkling, concrete landscape. To his left he noticed a freshly painted but worn signpost surrounded by a wall of concrete. "Centre-Ville," it said. He wondered how long it had been there. Looking around, he saw no one else taking note of the sign, and imagined from their indifference that it had been planted there for months, years.

Once inside, the sleek, tube-like, glass elevator shut its doors and waited for him to choose a floor. He marveled for a moment at what he had built. A lab so advanced that it was nearly invisible with incomprehensibility to pedestrians and passersby. The difference between the lab and the townspeople had fascinated him when he was younger, when he noticed. As if two different worlds, two different times, were living side by side, the lab in its own technological bubble in the center of the commons. Not a glance in its direction. Not a sidestep too close around the reaches of the lab grounds.

As soon as he pressed the button, the elevator swept him up fluidly. If he hadn't been able to see out through the glass, he wouldn't have even known that he was moving. He wondered, if not at his surroundings, what he had been looking at the last time he ventured into the lab.

When he arrived at the top floor, he spilled out of the elevator, briskly making his way toward a private office. He knocked on the open door. One of the scientists on his team, Julie, looked up.

"Meeting in Conference Room A in two minutes."

Before she could respond, Lee was already down the hall in front of another office, and another, rounding up the entire specialized team of five scientists who had been assigned to Elle's trial. He waited for them in the conference room, Julie entering right behind him, and took a seat around the table. Frank filed in with three other scientists. He looked weary and watched Lee speak through lowered eyes.

"I know Frank and I have been keeping you somewhat in the dark, but I think we're ready to move forward."

The announcement startled Frank. He had been distracted, turning over and over in his mind the conversation that he'd had with Eamonn. "Wh—um. What are we moving forward with?" Frank asked, not attempting to hide his cluelessness from the rest of the team.

"I'd like to get started designing other units. There are some changes we need to make—I have some notes here."

Frank, shocked, leaned in to address Lee, thinking that he would fill him in.

"Lee, what are you doing?"

Lee disregarded him and pulled out a file.

"I'd like to start with Mrs. Thatcher, seventy-seven. Her husband is dying, but she's still healthy. Moves well. Solid mind. Unfortunately I don't think there's much time, so even though this will be the first male we design, we'll need to do it quickly. We'll need a fully functional companion for her in...six months."

"That timeline seems fine for me," said Julie. "But what about Elle?"

"What about Elle?" Lee echoed nonchalantly.

Another scientist, a young computer programmer, spoke up. "Can we see the reports now?" He spoke clearly but with a pencil in front of his mouth. Lee noticed, attributing it to age.

The scientist who had overseen Elle's physical memory fusion chimed in before Lee responded. "It would help to examine Elle too, to see what's breaking down physically."

"She's fine, physically," said Lee defensively.

"Okay. Okay. I think this may be a bit premature," Frank said. "We haven't finalized anything yet with Elle."

"I could start outlining a male in the meantime," said Julie. "Otherwise, six months—when do you think the trial will be complete?"

Lee looked at Frank for a response, not knowing the answer himself. Frank hesitated and looked directly at Lee, relenting.

"I think one more month."

The news hit Lee, even though he had known it all along. In a second, his motivation disintegrated, and he felt her slipping away.

One more month. And the reboot will be complete. Then what?

He thought back on the time that he had spent with Elle, and it suddenly seemed far away. As if he were replacing his own memories instead of hers. As if he were fading instead of Elle. Faced with the idea of soon having completely overhauled Elle's memory from the past year, the very amount of time that she had walked the earth, he felt his pulse quicken, but his eyes no longer took in the expanse of his surroundings. The room narrowed.

"A month? Oh I can definitely work with that. No prob," said the programmer. Lee noticed the baggy coat he wore, the glasses on top of his head causing his hair to spike. He thought of him in the photograph that had been taken of the whole team that first day, the photograph he knew so well, and was struck by how recent that day was. How much younger he had thought they all looked upon first rediscovering the photograph, but indeed, they looked the same. *Is it just me who has aged so much?*

"All right then," Lee closed, sounding more assured than he felt. The faces in the room all looked up at him expectantly. Feeling their eyes on him, he deliberately did not meet their gaze. He wanted to disappear. His chest felt tight. The room felt hot. The whiteboard behind him crept sideways, expanding, surrounding him, overtaking the entire wall. It grew brighter, brighter, releasing all the light of the sun into that single room, blinding him. As he looked away from the whiteboard, he met Julie's eyes. Her round, brown, oversized eyes. Deep, swirling, empty pools in her face that looked right through him. Her cheeks hollowed, as if made of sand falling through an hourglass. Her chin clung to her drooping lips. Her eyes, wider. He could see the rings in her eyes spinning faster as they absorbed more of her face. The rest of her features disappeared, swallowed by her eyes. They were all that was left, those big, spinning eyes. They would come for Lee next.

He broke his gaze and the room went silent. The brightness of the whiteboard overwhelmed his sense of sight, and the rest of his senses deadened.

This must be the sound of implosion.

The pressure in the room thickened, squeezing his chest tight, tighter. His toes, his fingers, his head scrambled to make room for the blood fleeing his constricted middle. Then the pressure encased his toes. His fingers. His head. He was sure that he would burst, but the pressure completely enveloped him. Could a person's cells, with no room to release pressure outward, become so small and close together that they could disappear? After all, weren't there an infinite number of points between two cells, and between two sizes? Infinite possibilities to become closer, smaller, before disappearing completely into a puff of past.

Lee imagined his bones, powdered. Would powdered bones mix with blood to form a paste? A man of clay. If he were to implode, he would lose no parts. Not a single atom would go missing. But he would be rearranged. *How strange,* he thought, *that although I would be made up of the same parts, their arrangement would matter. Would I be me if I were arranged differently? Would consciousness be the same as what it is to me now?*

The pressure increased. *How can I possibly bear it!* But there was nowhere to go. His instinct told him to flee the pain, but he was trapped. The instructions from his brain jumbled on their way to his body, and he did not try to move. He knew that the pressure would strengthen if he struggled, like a boa constrictor wrapped around his neck. *Can a person die from pain?* He knew that his feeling of pain was simply the firing of c-fibers. If he rid himself of c-fibers and were trapped in the same imploding room, he would not die from pain. He would die from the rearrangement of his atoms. But then, what if the imploding room stopped right then, held that pressure eternally on him? His atoms would not rearrange. With c-fibers firing rapidly, he would be in excruciating pain. With none, he would not. Would he die in the first case? He imagined so, and he imagined, in that moment, that it would be due to a different type of death. Not a physical death, but a death of will. *Where does that will reside if not in the physical body?*

For reasons unknown to him, at that moment he recalled a day he had spent with Elle months before, back in the beginning of the trial before she was assigned to Walter. Lee had taken her to a pond, observing her movements, how she walked, how she moved within the space around her. He had still at the time been wary of her, somewhat disturbed by her, even, like she was some sinister object that followed him around. For all of his wanting that she would bring back Allie, it was too good. It was uncanny. He'd had moments when he didn't believe that she was real, but believed that he had lost his mind and started seeing the thing that he wanted most in the world standing right in front of him. He hadn't touched her, afraid of her, afraid of her existence. She made no sense in the physical world, and it unsettled him.

He hadn't realized it back then, but the time at the pond was a breakthrough. She had spotted ducks in the pond and moved closer to watch them. Normally ducks float upright. But these ducks kept diving in place, their tail feathers suspended above the water like buoys, and their webbed feet straight up in the air, kicking as if they were swimming. They did this repeatedly, lifting their necks out of the water and turning themselves right side up, then plunging down again, kicking their feet, one by one. It wasn't so much the dive that had captivated Elle, but the swimming feet in the air. She had watched them for nearly an hour, laughing each time she saw the feet as if seeing it happen for the first time. Lee had watched her, and the feet, and felt his hardness melt and flake off right there alongside the pond.

How could I have forgotten? And how could I have re-membered if I had truly forgotten? He remembered it as if it had been a paradise. He would never want to go back, for fear of ruining it. *My memory lies to me,* he knew. *It is the memory I don't want to ruin, the favorably twisted memory.* His mind, his intellect, the thing he had most relied on as a believer in science, a follower of logic, could no longer be trusted.

He wept inwardly at the death of his mind, the arrangement of his body. For Elle, who would miss him when he was no longer around.

She won't miss you. He didn't think it himself. A voice in his mind arranged the words for him. *If she doesn't remember herself, she won't remember you.*

Herself! Lee replied to the voice. Then a thought crept into his mind, a thought that was followed by such guilt and fear that Lee no longer felt the pressure on his body, but concentrated in his head. He had spent weeks making sure that she remembered him, remembered their bond, remembered everything she had discovered about loss without remembering why, but he hadn't thought to make sure that she remembered herself. Her creation, yes, The facts, yes. But what about her *self?*

The self is just a compilation of memories, experiences. Nothing beyond.

Memories that you're altering.

Lee was indignant. *Memories that we're altering so she doesn't self-destruct! Memories that we're replacing with memories that will preserve her!*

Ah, preservation. Isn't that where the mess begins?

Lee hated the voice. He hated that it was inside him, that it spoke so bluntly of Allie and his desire to preserve her.

He wanted to hold on to her for just a little longer.

And he would. All at once he became grateful for the voice that had warned him about Elle losing her self. He knew now what he was up against. He wouldn't let Elle go. He wouldn't let her forget herself.

The whiteboard shrank, sucking the light back from the room and locking it inside itself. His chest expanded, the weight of the pressure on his body snapping, releasing him. The blood poured back through his body in one painful rush. He looked at Julie, her eyes looking back at him from a full-featured face. He looked at the clock. Six seconds had passed. Lee searched in himself to find the correct voice. He tested it by clearing his throat with an audible "ughn" trailing at the end.

He addressed the team. "That's it."

Notes were gathered and bodies shuffled out the door. Frank stayed behind, as Lee suspected he would. Six seconds was enough for Frank to notice that something was awry.

Frank stood, slowly gathering his notebook, stacking and restacking his papers, putting the cap back on his pen. It had been subtle, but Frank had caught the moment when Lee tuned out. He had seen the same empty expression many times before. It came in waves and lasted sometimes for weeks. It had stopped once Elle had been created, leading Frank to believe that this was an Elle-induced episode rather than an Allie-induced one. It concerned Frank, who thought back again to what Eamonn had said, to what he had suspected but ignored for Lee's sake since the first day the concept was conceived. He prompted Lee to see if he wanted to talk, though he knew he wouldn't.

"Lee—"

"Yep?"

Frank paused, contemplating what he should say next. It was clear that Lee did not want to talk. He wasn't about to press him.

"Okay." Frank started to leave.

Lee provoked Frank. He wondered if Frank had suspected it all along, that the reboot could potentially be useless. His resistance, his apparent loyalty. Lee felt a moment of clarity that came with the realization that Frank could no longer be trusted.

"Eamonn's in town," Lee stated, trying to catch Frank. Catch what, exactly, Lee didn't quite know. He just *knew*.

Frank heard the tone in Lee's voice and shrank. How could Lee have known of his conversation with Eamonn? Reason told him that he didn't know, that he just assumed, that he was simply baiting him. A wave of fatigue overcame him. He didn't want to battle.

"I know," Frank replied, resigned.

Lee was not surprised.

"He mention Elle?"

Frank nodded, uncomfortable.

"What'd he say?"

"She turned out nice," Frank said shortly.

Lee turned to face Frank.

"That's it?" He asked.

Frank nodded.

"Hm," Lee said, looking away again.

Frank walked toward the door.

"She did turn out nice, didn't she," Lee said without turning around.

Frank hesitated, but left without answering. Lee was alone. Standing before the whiteboard, he paused briefly, then picked up his coat and left, emptying the room except for the buzz of the lights above him. As he walked through the hallway, he heard Julie's hushed voice.

"Do you think he's all right?"

He passed by the open door of her office and saw Julie with the other three scientists standing in a group. They caught his eye as he passed, and a tense quiet fell over the room. Lee gave them a small nod as he walked by and felt their eyes on him until he stepped into the elevator.

No better than the neighbors! But he could write off the neighbors gossiping because they had no information and nothing better to do than to make up stories about him. But his own team? He felt betrayed and ashamed, wondered if he would lose their trust, if they still saw him as a leader or as a sad fool.

He realized then that Julie's question could have been one of concern, and it would be a valid question given the pressure he was under, even without the related circumstances. Perhaps he was looking too much into it. But he replayed it in his mind, the wide, silent eyes of his team as he passed, and the shame washed over him again. He recoiled from his own skin in the elevator as it carried him down, down.

....

THIRTY

That night Lee walked alone outside in the dark. He hadn't gone straight home, but instead wandered through town, retracing steps that he knew well. The anonymous ease of the familiar comforted him. The same cobblestone streets, smooth in the same spots with wear, the pattern of the awnings on the cafés. It was all very expected.

He thought back as he passed over the same stones to a time shortly after Allie died, before his consciousness felt the impact of her loss, when he tried to carry on as normal.

There was one café that he used to visit frequently, back when he used to hold meetings outside the lab. Any meetings that were scheduled to take place outside his office in the lab he would schedule there. Particularly if he was meeting someone new, he was sure to be on firm footing if they met in his usual café. He knew what drink to order. How the coffee would look on his lips. That he had to stir it diligently for it to cool off enough to not sear his tongue. Everything around him was familiar, routine, so that he could think less about his surroundings. About how loud the music would be. If too loud, it would be difficult to talk. Whether or not the place would have room to seat two. About the silence as he read over the drink menu. He followed this routine so that he could focus on his thoughts and conversation with the person sitting across from him.

Or the person he was waiting to meet. In the months after Allie died, if someone was a minute late to a scheduled meeting, he panicked. *They're not coming,* he would think. And he would go further. *Something happened.* Though he could have been meeting with someone he had never met before—a new hire, a fellow scientist or professor—he would imagine that person having had some sort of accident, being in the hospital, or worse, having died a week before, unbeknownst to him. He would be the person on the calendar who was unaware, just one piece of what was supposed to be a part of that person's future. An unmet connection dangling limply along a clipped timeline.

If he had been asked to sit down inside a new café, it would have all been too much. How large was it? What was the arrangement of the seats? How crowded did it usually get? Questions that not knowing the answer to would have prevented him from setting foot inside, from even approaching the foreign door. No, the recognizable stones over which his feet moved were far more favorable.

He moved slowly compared to the world around him. As he walked along, morning turned to noon, noon turned to dusk. But the spin of the earth had left him lagging behind as it washed others rapidly forth. Mouths moved rapidly to form words, shops were entered and exited before he passed the front door. He seemed to be catching up with the past, experiencing it only when it had gone. As if the past were always a few steps ahead of him.

He approached his cul-de-sac, a dark pocket clinging to the edge of town. The light in Elle's house peeked out through one window. *All the things that could be going on in the rest of the house and she would have no idea. She only knows what's happening in that single room.* He imagined intruders lurking on the top floor, strangers emerging from the many unlit corners of each unused room.

Through the window he peered in from the darkened street, aware of his own intrusion from beneath the shadows. Only her legs and the bottom of her dress, cutting her calves across the middle, could be seen through the half-closed blinds. She walked back and forth in the kitchen. Cooking, Lee presumed.

Then, another pair of legs appeared. Another female, wearing the same type of dress. They walked back and forth, in the same manner as Elle. *Or do those legs belong to Elle?* Lee tried to distinguish between the two pairs of legs, the legs he knew so well, but they looked identical. The second pair of legs followed closely behind the first, mimicking their movements only a beat behind.

They seem to be quite close, thought Lee, marking how the two pairs of legs seemed to move as one. *How do I not know of this person?* A quiet fear brewed in him, that there were parts of Elle that he didn't know, that didn't show up in the data. He knew that she was aware of how he monitored her, but he wondered then if she had been aware enough of his watchful eye to adjust herself around it.

He remembered a lesson that he had learned years before at university. The very fact that one enters a room to observe that room changes the room being observed. It would never be possible to observe the room as it stood in the absence of observation. It would be a mistake to proceed as if the room hadn't been changed. Lee had struggled with this concept throughout the years when objectivity had been crucial. It was an impossible requirement.

Both pairs of legs abruptly walked out of the window frame. Only in their absence did he notice their dance-like movements as they shifted back and forth, crossed over each other, swayed. Four fleshy ribbons moving in patterns across the floor. Lee waited for a moment for them to return. They did not.

His focus turned back on himself. He realized what he must look like standing in the street, staring into Elle's window. Had someone been watching him, as he watched Elle? The darkness illuminated him. He felt caught, afraid to move lest his motions give him away. He averted his eyes first, as if to be able to say that he had been looking down the whole time. Confusion overcame him again as he walked forward toward his own house, shedding the feeling of vulnerability more completely as he moved farther away from Elle's.

From their second-floor balcony, Frank and Marigold watched, calmly sipping tea from floral-patterned china. They pitied Lee.

"He's acting strange today. He was acting strange at the lab too," Frank said to Marigold.

"How so?"

"I don't exactly know. He started talking about creating a companion for Mrs. Thatcher—"

"Mrs. Thatcher!"

"I know. He seemed to be almost manic for a moment, and then he sort of, just, went blank."

"What do you mean manic?"

"His eyes—there was something in his eyes. He was breathing heavily, and he was looking everywhere around the room, and then, just like that, he went blank. Sometimes I think I'm monitoring the wrong party," Frank said, half in jest.

Marigold watched Lee standing motionless outside Elle's house. She hesitated, thinking of the right words to say before she spoke, slowly, quietly.

"Step back for a moment," she started. "Forget about what's on your screens and just look at what's in front of you. Not at the data, or in your books, or at Elle. Just look."

And he did. And with that look, Eamonn's words replayed in his mind, and all at once he realized the gravity of what he'd had a role in creating. It was more than a recreation of Allie. It was an atmosphere around and within Lee.

"We played God and can't handle it," he said.

They watched Lee, their eyes fixed, staring in his direction, but their minds elsewhere.

"He looks awful," Marigold observed.

Frank sighed and put down his cup.

"You know," she started carefully. "I know I'm not privy to everything that's been going on with the trial and all, but maybe that's a good thing. I can see from an outsider's perspective what's happening to Lee. Eamonn saw it, he told you exactly what he saw."

"It's obvious what's happening to Lee."

"But then why can't you do something about it?"

She could see a flash of anger flit across Frank's face as she asked.

"You think I haven't been trying?"

"I know you've been trying," Marigold said, trying to soothe him before it turned into an argument. "But let's look at the facts. You are Lee's closest friend. And to have his best interests in mind right now is, amazingly, not what's best for him."

"It's just become so complicated," Frank admitted.

"But that's why it needs to become uncomplicated. Whether he knows it or not, Lee is relying on you to do that. He is too close to the situation to see it clearly. If it goes wrong, he would turn to you to explain why, right? Which says to me that he is trusting you to keep it from going wrong."

Frank was silent. Marigold waited a moment before continuing, careful not to press too much.

"Lee is, we have to admit, compromised. He is no longer—and never really was—objective. So if we eliminate him from the trial, what does that leave? He is a man, your closest friend, who is emotionally attached to an AI system."

"It's more than that, Mari—"

"It's more than that if you consider factors that shouldn't be considered."

"But you have to consider them."

"You *can't* consider them. This is what you know. There is an AI system that is self-destructing. You can reboot, which gives you a chance to figure out how to deal with it in the future, or you can not reboot, which will destroy the system completely. There is a third option—what Lee suggested. Memory replacement. This option still doesn't solve the problem for the future, and it takes time away from solving that problem. If it will never be solved, you need to figure out a way to prevent the systems from destroying themselves whenever their elderly companion dies."

"We can do that in the future, but not with Elle."

"Right. So the question right now is whether you reboot or proceed with the memory replacement. If Lee were not a factor here, you would reboot, right?"

Frank nodded. "But he thinks that's unethical."

"Does he? Or does he have no other substantive reason for not wanting the cold reboot?"

Frank inhaled deeply and faced Marigold.

"I know, I know all of this," he said, trying to control his voice. "But you can't—I can't just eliminate Lee as a factor. This is the situation that was created. This is the situation that we need to fix. Whether or not Lee *should* be a factor, he is. I can't cut him out and make decisions as if he's not here."

"The best decision you can make is the logical one."

"I know!" His frustration burst forth and continued running out of him like a waterfall. "But it's not logical! It's not logical that Elle exists. It's not logical that the lab created something so much like Allie that she even *thinks* like Allie. We shouldn't be able to do things like this! It's not logical what happened to Allie. Why the more complicated of two futures fell into her lap and killed her when the simplest future is the more probable one. Whether we do the reboot or the memory replacement, it doesn't matter. What matters is Lee. That's the complication. That's what I need to figure out. Lee."

Marigold listened patiently, calmly, as Frank spit his words at her. He didn't look into her eyes as he yelled, showing her that even while he was yelling, he was sorry for it.

"If that's what you need to figure out, look there." She pointed to where Lee was standing, staring into Elle's window. "You see that man there? It's him that you need to figure out, right? Look at him. What is there to figure out?"

Frank followed Marigold's gaze toward Lee. But he didn't see Lee. He saw the remains of a man, destroyed, unstable, standing in the street, carrying on as if there were nothing wrong. But everything was wrong. He could make out Lee's stance from his balcony, his withered posture that made him look like a frail, old man. He pictured his face, how drawn it had become, how hollow his eyes were, how they lit up when they saw Elle and waited, trembling for her next appearance before them. That man wasn't Lee, that man who skulked outside windows in the dark.

He slumped in his chair, accepting finally what appeared in front of him. The man he had helped to destroy when he helped to create Elle.

....

he next morning, the blinds in Lee's study split open with a jerk of his fingers. He peered out from the window watching Elle's house, the blinds slithering back and forth. The streets were quiet, as expected. When spring arrived the people would emerge, shedding their winter skins anxiously for summer garb that it would still be too cold to wear. Their voices would carry up to his study, hushing as they passed his house, as if he were some fragile shadow that was not to be disturbed.

It was a peculiar street, Lee noticed for the first time amidst the absence of sounds that he imagined would usually be heard in a quiet, friendly neighborhood. There were no children. There were no chipmunks scurrying, no dogs harrumphing at their tied leashes in the yard. It seemed to be a plasticine town, a town only there to pass through, only alive at night when the yellow lights of the houses flicked on from inside. A town stuck in a quieter time. There were no cars, but there was, in the end, no need.

Everything was within walking distance, and there was nothing beyond. Though there were many residents who lived and worked in the dense part of town—the city—who did have cars. But the city had always felt like an add-on to Lee, a strange modern addition to a quiet town. The isolation made him feel claustrophobic and wide open at the same time, as if there were indeed something beyond that he just couldn't see.

He looked at the face of the houses slung around the curve of the street, and confirmed once more to himself that his was the safest. It wasn't at the end, which felt too open, but it wasn't at the bend, beyond which lay unexplored, and thus potentially predatory, territory.

After some time, Elle emerged. She walked in the direction of Lee's house, but continued walking along the curve of the cul-de-sac, bypassing him. From the slit in the blinds, he could see her eyes set in front of her, her brusque movements. She looked troubled. A moment later she stopped in front of Frank's house and waited on the steps. No doorbell ring, no knock. She waited.

Frank met her on the steps. There was no friendly greeting, no exchange of hellos, no cordial embrace. They talked for a minute, standing apart on the steps. Lee wondered if Frank had ever actually touched Elle, verified that she was real and wouldn't disintegrate with the skin on his hands moving through her phantom body.

He watched Elle nod as Frank spoke. The intensity of their conversation seemed appropriate only for two individuals who were much more intimately acquainted than they were. He wasn't used to seeing Elle so serious. Even when she was sad, it seemed that she maintained a hint of a smile on her face. An accomplishment, on Lee's part, to have been able to capture such an expression and recreate it in Elle. Frank's hands were animated just enough for Lee to tell that he was explaining something rather than arguing.

Marigold poked her head outside and joined the conversation from behind the door. When Elle saw her, the hint of smile finally returned to her face in the form of a greeting. Shortly after, Elle gave a little wave—that familiar little wave—and kept walking. She walked toward the dirt road outlet that cut the loop of the cul-de-sac in half. A space that had made the neighborhood feel less closed than it would have if it hadn't been there. It led to a path around the outside of the cul-de-sac, behind the houses, directly into the center of town. He had never walked it himself, but always imagined it to be like walking along the edge of the earth, on a little warning ledge just before a drop into nothingness.

Frank watched her walk away, then snuck a glance in the direction of Lee's house. Lee's instinctive reaction was to pull away, but his body stayed motionless as he reminded himself that he was behind the blinds. From that distance, it would just look like a bent blind, a mistake. Frank walked back inside.

Lee continued to dress as he mulled over the exchange he had just witnessed. What could Elle and Frank possibly have to discuss right before another memory replacement? He expected Frank to call as usual when something happened with Elle. But he didn't. Vexed, Lee picked up a briefcase, and left his study.

THIRTY-TWO

Elle marched up to Frank's house. Her intuition told her that Lee wasn't the one to help her. She couldn't figure out why. But something was off, and she was afraid. She wasn't only losing her memories, but seemed to be uncovering snippets of memories that she couldn't piece together. What if something was wrong? She thought with great heaviness about how she didn't have the right to stop the memory replacement, though if she asked Lee he would probably give her the choice. But before proceeding to the lab that morning, she needed to tell Frank. If something was wrong, he would be able to fix it.

As he stood before her waiting for her to speak, she didn't know anymore what she was asking.

"Something is happening, Frank," she said. "It's just not right."

"How so? What's going on?"

"It's like, for the memories that are removed, another one pops up."

"Well, those are the replacement memories that Lee's creating. It'll seem a little jarring until we're done replacing all of them, because they're all interconnected. They build on each other. So for a while, some things won't make sense."

"No, it's not that. It's not a new memory. It's a memory that I already had. That's what it feels like. Like it's just being dusted off."

"Do you know what it's about?"

Elle shook her head.

"It's still unclear. But what does it mean? Don't you know what it is?"

Frank took a breath. He had an idea, but he couldn't be sure until he looked more. If it turned out to be what he suspected, he would have to find a way to bury it deeper. He looked at Elle's eyes, shining, looking back at him, entrusting him with her mind. He couldn't lie to her.

"I can't be sure. But I will look into it. I'll look today during the procedure."

Marigold appeared in the doorway.

"Is everything okay?" She hadn't expected to see Elle. She had never seen her up close before. In a way, Elle had seemed like a myth, a mirage that Marigold saw from afar, that she heard about. But there she was, right in front of her. Her eyes pierced Marigold's, and suddenly Marigold truly felt the concern expressed by her question. *Poor Elle*, she thought, catching hints of fear flitting across her face. She was something. Almost intimidating, in a way. *She's just so real.*

Marigold suddenly remembered visiting her grandfather in his nursing home when she was ten years old. She had been walking out the front door and turned around at the calling of her name. Coming toward her, only feet away, was an old man. His arms were reaching toward her. His hair as white as his face. His jaw hung open, slack. The movement toward her had surprised her, and she had felt a cold fear wash over her and retreat immediately once her mind registered that it was a man. She had felt embarrassed that she had been afraid. Why should old age instill fear? The man was a person.

She thought of it now and realized that persons of such old age were rare. There were those who walked the streets, who could be seen and were recognizable, and there were those who were locked away, unfit for the streets, unable to handle the cold, and thus, unseen. It was an unfamiliar old that she had seen. It was the unfamiliar that had frightened her.

And Elle was unfamiliar to her. Nothing like Elle had ever walked the streets before. It wasn't part of Marigold's visual vocabulary. As she stood on her doorstep, the same fear that she had felt as a ten-year-old bubbled up inside her, coupled with the same sorry feeling she'd had for the old man, trapped in a world unnatural to him because being in his natural world was unnatural to everyone else in that world.

Elle was trapped, in a way. Though no one chose to be born, as Elle hadn't chosen to be created, there was something that seemed unfair to her, unethical, about bringing her into the world. When Marigold asked in that moment if everything was all right, she had intended it initially for Frank, but as she opened her mouth and locked eyes with Elle, her words redirected themselves to the sublime creation standing before her.

"Hi Marigold," Elle said amiably. Marigold felt delighted and targeted at the same time.

"How are you?" Marigold asked Elle.

"I'm fine. I just wanted to check in before today's procedure. I hope I didn't wake you. I know how voices carry."

"Not at all," Marigold said, smiling. It was the most she had ever conversed with Elle. She liked her immediately.

"Well, I'll see you at the lab, Frank." She gave Marigold a smile like a wink, and left.

Marigold watched her leave. "Wow," she said to Frank. "I didn't realize she was like that."

"Like what?"

"I don't know, like that. She's so...*nice*." Marigold heard the juvenile simplicity of her words.

Frank understood. "She's very easy to like. You would have liked Allie," he replied, thinking of how easy it must have been for Lee to fall in love with her. At the thought of Lee, he instantly filled with worry. If the memory that Elle thought she was uncovering was the one he thought it was, she was right to come to him first. But she couldn't have known that. Either way, he was lucky that she did.

As he turned to walk inside, he saw the blinds of Mrs. Thatcher's house snap shut.

"What is it?" Marigold asked when Frank hesitated.

"Mrs. Thatcher."

"What is it with that woman?" Marigold asked, annoyed.

"What, you mean you want her to stop sniffing around and whispering about Elle? What fun would that be?" Frank joked. He followed Marigold inside, wondering just how loud the neighborhood whispers sounded to Lee.

....

THIRTY-THREE

An hour later, Lee and Frank were back in the lab staring intently at the display of computer screens in front of them. Frank was isolating tainted memories. The whole team of scientists was on the opposite side of the glass peering over Elle. They examined her limbs, her skin, her eyes, as the room was being prepped for the start of the day's memory replacements. Lee felt nervous having the team scrutinize Elle like that. What if they saw something? What, he did not know.

As he saw her limp body displayed on the table, once again surrounded by the sterile white walls of the Procedures room, he remembered just a few days before reassuring Elle.

"We're getting close now," he had said. "You'll be back to your old self in no time."

"Good as new." She had replied cheerfully, but Lee detected something more in her voice. A wistfulness, a nostalgia, a return of the melancholy that had been so abundant in her eyes whenever she thought about giving up her memories. A resignation to the idea of soon being new.

Frank's eyes were set on the screen in front of him. Lee watched him closely, waiting, growing more suspicious at his silence about Elle's visit that morning. When Frank showed no sign of volunteering any information, Lee pressed.

"Elle stopped by this morning?"

"What? Oh. For a minute." Frank stared at the screen in front of him, willing himself to project nonchalance so that Lee wouldn't grow suspicious.

"What for?"

Lee noticed that Frank hadn't blinked for some time, concentrating on the screens. His head was pushed forward toward the screen. Lee wondered why he didn't just enlarge the image.

"Um—she just wanted to know what the plan was for today. What we would be replacing."

"We already went over that."

"I guess she forgot."

He deleted another receptor connection. Lee looked from Frank to the computer screen. *He seems unconcerned. Maybe I'm not asking the right questions.*

He remembered the extra pair of legs that he had seen in Elle's kitchen the night before.

"How's Marigold?"

Frank looked up at Lee, caught off guard by the sudden change of topic.

"She's all right. Studying hard."

"So she doesn't get out much."

"I mean, not often, but she manages." Frank couldn't follow Lee's train of thought. "Did she say something to you?"

Lee shook his head. Frank stared at him for a moment, waiting for clarification, or a follow-up question that would explain Lee's interest in Marigold. Lee said nothing. Frank went back to work.

Lee stood over Frank's shoulder for another beat, then began to pace as he supervised every click of Frank's mouse. The fact that he had gotten no information out of Frank shifted his suspicion toward jealousy. If it was true that Elle had gone to Frank's house that morning to ask about the memory replacement for the day, then she had made a choice to bypass Lee's house, to walk farther in the opposite direction of the lab to Frank's house to ask him instead. Or had she suddenly become close with Marigold? He pictured again the legs from the night before. It didn't seem likely. It didn't make sense to Lee.

"Lee?"

"Yeah."

"Can I ask—why the sudden interest in creating a companion for Mrs. Thatcher?"

"It seems like the right thing to do, no? Isn't that the point of this? To create companions for the elderly?"

"Well yes, but aren't we jumping ahead a bit?"

Lee shook his head. "The sooner the better. We're ready. All of this—" he indicated toward Elle. "This is just ironing out the wrinkles."

"There are still some rather large wrinkles to iron out. Such as—how to fix a system when it witnesses a death."

"That doesn't mean we shouldn't start designing now. We will have time. I'm working on it. I think I'm close."

Frank eyed Lee.

"How close?"

"Not close, but I'm working on it."

Frank sighed. "I just don't think it's a good idea. Where is this coming from?"

"We've been working on this for years. It's time to release it to the public."

"We haven't finished the trial yet. We're still working on Elle. We have to complete the trial with Elle, fix whatever issues there are, and then start producing more. We can't just start over," Frank argued.

"You wanted to start over with Elle," Lee said.

"Yes, but we already have Elle. Restarting the trial with Elle would have just been a matter of a reboot. Which we're technically doing anyway, in a way. But you are talking about restarting the design process entirely." He didn't mention that he already had blueprints for a new design. They weren't complete enough to be useful, and it would be impossible to finish them before the team started designing the new companion.

"Don't you think that's something that we need to do no matter what? Elle is not an accurate representation of how this is going to work. It's going to take time to create the DNA. We won't already have it at our disposal."

"We have all that ready," Frank said. "We just need to put all the pieces together once we have the design. And once we have a fully successful trial."

Frank watched Lee become increasingly agitated as he spoke.

"Lee?" he said again. "What's this really about?"

Lee sighed as he paced. "We're going to complete the trial with Elle."

"Right..." Frank prompted, following.

"But then what? When we determine that it is a successful trial, then what?"

"Well, the original thought was to release the first successful system to the public," Frank said.

Lee waited for Frank to understand. Frank simply looked at him blankly.

"We can't do that," Lee stated. The thought of releasing Elle to someone else, of giving her away to be treated however she was going to be treated, to not be able to watch over her, to lose her again, he couldn't fathom.

Frank's face did not change.

"I know," he said.

Lee was surprised and confused at once. He looked at Frank, searching for an indication that he wasn't really following what Lee was saying.

"You know?"

"Of course I know," Frank replied.

"What did you think was going to happen after the trial?"

"Well, I hadn't really gotten that far, but I figured we would decide on something when the time came."

Lee felt relief that he wasn't aware he needed. "If you know, then why do you think it's a bad idea to design the male companion?"

"Really just for the reasons I said. Nothing more. We need to use what we have to iron out the kinks before we begin creating another."

Lee was skeptical. "That's it?"

"That's it. We do have a protocol to follow," Frank reminded Lee.

"You're right. We'll have the team work up what they can in the meantime so it's ready when we are, but we won't compile the next system until the trial is finished."

"Lee, I'm behind you on this you know. I want this to work. I wouldn't point you in the wrong direction. You need to know that."

"I do know that," Lee replied truthfully. He was nevertheless glad to hear it from Frank.

"We have to just stay the course for now. We can't get impatient. Nothing is going to happen to Elle if we do this carefully."

"You're right. You're right."

There was a long silence. Frank contemplated asking his next question.

"Why did you ask me about Marigold before?"

"What? Oh. No, nothing. I thought—I saw some-one with Elle last night. A woman. But I didn't see her face. I thought maybe it was Marigold."

"Why would you think it was Marigold?" Frank asked, confused.

"I don't know. It was just the first thing that popped into my head. And you didn't tell me any-thing, so I thought..." Lee trailed off.

"That's strange, actually," Frank said. "That didn't show up on the data."

"That someone was with Elle?"

"Yup."

"Huh. Is it capturing everything?"

"It has been. Maybe it was just a shadow?" Frank asked warily, looking at Lee with a small, concerned wrinkle between his brows.

"I don't think so. But if nothing showed up, I guess that's what we should go with."

It seemed strange to Lee that he was so willing to believe the machine data over his own eyes, his own memory. He began to pace, picturing the pair of legs trailing Elle's.

Behind him, Frank heard Lee sighing and breath-ing more heavily with each step. *Maybe he needs a break from all of this.* Frank turned to Lee.

"You don't have to stay for the rest of this. This is all straightforward replacements. Nothing fancy happening."

"I'll stay."

"You sure? There's going to be nothing really for you to do. The whole day is just—this. Physical updates won't be ready for you to sign off on until tomorrow. Go ahead. Take a break."

Lee considered this. *Is he just trying to get rid of me?* Reason quelled his rising paranoia, noting the sincerity in Frank's voice. He sighed once again, acknowledging his fatigue. He glanced at Elle and saw how peaceful she looked on the table with her eyes closed, shutting out the commotion around her.

"All right. Let me know how it's going, though. How much longer do you think you have?"

"Couple of hours. I think I'll be done by three. They're actually almost done with the exam, but then it'll take some time to write up. Elle will be out of here by three though."

"All right. If you need me—"

"Absolutely."

"My cell."

"Right."

"All right."

After an awkward pause, Lee reluctantly left. Frank watched him go, then returned his focus to his screens, noticing how loud the clicking of the mouse sounded against the silence of the empty room.

He quickly scanned Elle's connections for the memory that she had described, and spotted it. There, partially visible underneath layers of replacement memories, was the memory that he had implanted and hidden in her circuitry long ago. He quickly arranged it so that it was buried deeper, careful not to shift any of the other connections. It wasn't the time to reveal it. Lee had enough to worry about.

....

THIRTY-FOUR

Lee walked quickly down the steps of the plaza, stopping at a food cart on the sidewalk. He wondered if the foot traffic in front of the lab was really enough to sustain a food cart. The cold soaked into his fingers quickly after the warmth of the lab. He bought a coffee, once again feeling out of place amidst the unfamiliar. The cup burned his hands. But he knew it felt hotter than it actually was because his hands were so cold, so he kept his fingers spaced out around both sides of the cup and held tightly. He inhaled the steam, heating his face more than his insides.

He spotted an empty bench and sat down, ignoring the cold on his legs. The lab was still in sight. He noticed how invisible it seemed as the pedestrians strolled past it without a glance, curving their walking paths around the plaza as if repelled by a magnetic force. He drank his coffee, watching. He focused on their legs, like he had focused on the legs in the window of Elle's house. Their legs walked randomly. Only because he knew that they walked in patterns of two did there seem to be some sort of order to the movements. Only because he knew what walking was did he understand the pattern. He noticed how strange it looked to see only the movements of the legs without considering the rest of the body. There seemed to be so much effort that went into the motion for what seemed to be little progress. The heels lifting off the ground at a precise time as determined by the toes of the opposite foot. The weight shift, side to side, in an effort to move forward. A strange movement indeed. A movement that seemed ancient and unfit for the advanced humans who scurried through town.

He thought again about the pairs of legs he had seen the previous night, and noted how differently they moved from the legs that moved before him now. *Or perhaps*, he thought, *I am remembering wrong*. The legs that he had watched moved in sync, the second pair trailing only a moment behind the first like a lazy shadow. As he thought back, he wondered how he hadn't noticed how unnatural their movements were when they were right in front of him.

Had there really been two pairs of legs at all?

An elderly lady being walked by a younger woman approached his bench. Lee immediately gave up his seat, then eyeballed the elderly lady. Lee thought that it was quite cold to be walking her outside, but she was wrapped completely. Only her eyes and the very tip of her nose were uncovered. The younger woman smiled up at him. She was pretty. Lee smiled back. Her movements made him think that she was a caretaker rather than a family member. There seemed to be a polite distance maintained between the two when they interacted. The younger woman propped up the elderly woman before settling down herself.

Lee searched for a mote of recognition in the elderly woman's eyes. Usually the older population recognized him as the scientist who created the companion for Walter. Her eyes were empty. He focused on her face, the many lines around her eyes, the cracks in her skin, the outline of her skeleton becoming apparent through the sinking of her face. She was quite old indeed. And yet, here she was, walking around town.

She probably wouldn't have remembered anyway if she had at one time known who I was. It struck him as a strange thought to have, involuntarily popping into his head. Here was a woman still healthy in body, but perhaps with a mind beginning to atrophy. He wondered if she perceived the atrophy, or if she noticed nothing at all. *Would I know right in this moment if my mind had begun to atrophy?* He thought of himself in his twenties with a growing mind, thought of how far removed he was from that time in his life. He couldn't imagine himself without his mind, or with a shrinking mental capacity. It just didn't seem like him.

Suddenly feeling strange and tall hovering over the two strangers on the bench, he looked down at his coffee, already cold, and walked away.

"Lee!"

He recognized the voice that called his name. Indeed, when he turned, there she was.

"Hi Sonja," he said. It sounded flatter than he had intended, but she didn't seem to notice.

"What are you doing out here?"

Lee wondered why she would ask that question. Why shouldn't he be out here? But he realized then that she was just making small talk. Without the lab, they really had nothing else in common. He didn't know anything about Sonja. He didn't know anything about anyone on his entire team, he realized with dismay, except for Frank. Of course Julie and the rest had been talking about him. They didn't know him either. He was just a strange man with a strange, person-shaped creature in tow.

"I was just getting some coffee."

"Were you at the lab?"

He nodded. She kept her tone light and casual, but Lee caught the seriousness in her voice.

"How is everything going?"

"It's going quite well, thank you," he said looking around. He didn't want to get into a conversation about Elle in such a crowded, open space.

"And you're good?" She didn't wait for him to respond. "How's Elle?"

"Elle is great," Lee replied without elaborating.

"But is she okay, you know, after Walter?"

He sighed. There was no reason for him to not keep Sonja in the loop. She had been a part of the team, after all. She was as deeply invested in Elle as anyone, he supposed.

But he didn't want to let on that there were any problems. He felt like he needed to maintain the image that all was well. But then he remembered that Sonja had taken Elle for the night when Walter died. Had she seen something?

"Well, actually, we've run into a few problems since then."

Sonja nodded, listening intently. She didn't look surprised.

"To be expected. I mean, it's the first one. But you know, I wanted to tell you," Sonja started. She spoke sincerely, and placed her hand on Lee's arm. He felt an uncharacteristic urge to move it away and fought it back. "When I saw Elle that night, it really hit me what an accomplishment she is. I mean, technologically we were all aware of that, but after stepping away from the lab for a while, and then seeing her, I almost forgot that she isn't real."

Lee froze. His face clouded over. He looked at Sonja, with her hair like a poodle and her wide hips and her piggish face, and hated her at once.

"She is real."

"Well of course she's real, but you know what I mean. Human."

Lee nodded, finished with the conversation.

"Well. Thank you Sonja."

He walked away, ignoring her perplexed face. The familiar guilt crept up again as he left. He certainly wasn't the type of person to be rude to a woman, especially when that woman had attempted to pay him a compliment. And certainly at a time when he needed a compliment, which Sonja might have known.

He didn't recognize himself. He would stop by Sonja's for a cup of tea and apologize for his behavior. Explain that she had caught him at a bad time, that he was coming from a difficult day at the lab, and that his mind was elsewhere.

But he wouldn't. He knew. He couldn't even fool himself anymore. It was too exhausting to try.

....

THIRTY-FIVE

Back at his house, Lee walked up to his study feeling like no time had passed since that morning when he had seen Elle on Frank's front steps. He kept the door slightly ajar, not wanting to close himself in. He left his computer off and sat behind his desk. Thinking. Opened no books, wrote on no papers, typed on no keys.

He felt a new urgency layer his desire to solidify Elle in the world. Repeating Sonja's words in his head had become an unstoppable compulsion. All the way home, on the other side of town, past Elle's unlit house, behind his desk.

The "L" necklace poked at the skin beneath his pocket. He pulled it out, feeling the gold hot on his fingertips, then put it back. He looked at the clock, waiting, waiting for three o'clock, watching outside. Hours passed. He stared.

Finally, when the sun hung low in the sky, he saw Elle walking up his front steps. As she disappeared from view he heard a knock. He sat for a moment, the inertia from the previous few hours of sitting in silence and stillness telling his muscles to stay put. But he walked downstairs and let her inside. He kept the lights off. It felt more casual that way. She smiled politely, carefree. There was no physical sign—there never was—that she had undergone any type of procedure that morning. But she was carrying an umbrella, not a drop in the sky.

"Hi," she said.

Lee motioned to her umbrella. "It's raining?"

"It's supposed to. I brought it just in case."

"How do you feel after this morning?"

"I feel good! It's like nothing happened. So what did you want to show me?"

Nothing happening is indeed something happening. A something of absence. Or in this case, creating an absence. Ha! To create an absence. What a confused task!

Lee squeezed the charm of the necklace flat between his fingers, the edges reaching precisely to the sides of his thumb. He pulled it from his pocket, the long chain uncoiling below.

"I wanted to give you this."

Though he kept his eyes lowered, he felt a burst of unexpected pride and excitement as he held the necklace out to her, the gold "L" hanging from the chain dangling lightly in the air. It reminded him of the day he had given the "A" to Allie. But back then he hadn't felt the strange sense of heaviness that was rooted inside him now. Elle stared at the necklace in surprise, looking confused.

"It's an 'L.' For Lee," she said.

It was.

"It's an 'L' for Elle," Lee said lightly with a sheepish smile. "Allie used to wear hers every day. I think that's what's missing."

Elle made no motion to accept the necklace. It hung between them in the air.

"Why don't you wear it?"

"It's just—not me." *Anymore.* His own words landed within him, how much he had changed since he last wore the necklace.

Elle held her hand up to the charm and let the chain sink into her palm. She considered for many breaths, weighing the necklace in her hands.

"I can't take this from you. I think you should keep this. Really. I don't feel right."

She handed the necklace back to Lee, the weight of it visibly returning to his body. It sat backward in his hand.

"I'm sorry—I don't mean to be rude."

"No, no—I'm sorry. I didn't think—you're right. You should have an 'E.'"

Elle knew that Lee was aware of it being more than just a matter of lettering. And she knew that he had downplayed it on purpose. She followed his cue and changed the subject.

"Did you want something to eat? I was just on my way—"

"No, no, thanks. I actually have a call with Frank in a few minutes."

"Oh? Talking about me?" Elle joked. Lee didn't return the smile. She stood awkwardly in his doorway. "Okay, I'll see you later then." Elle opened the door for herself and left, leaving her umbrella on the floor in the entryway.

Lee looked at the necklace in his hand, seeing it upside down like a hangman's knot. He sank into the floor. It wasn't that his knees went first. It was a slow collapse, a simultaneous melting of all the muscles in his body, pouring him like molasses onto the floor against the back of his couch. A wide, desolate home surrounded him. The sun had fallen in the sky to a point just before disappearing completely, painting the walls, the floor, the furniture, grey. He tilted his body, lay down on the cold floor, and stayed there until well after the sun went down.

....

THIRTY-SIX

Hours later, he peeled himself off the floor. First he sat up, adjusting his mind to the sitting position for another twenty minutes. Then he stood, the back of the couch holding on to him to support his boneless legs. He finally walked over to the coffee machine to find it completely empty. The beans in the canister in the cabinet gone. He looked out the window, both mustering strength and wondering why he had to be out of coffee at that moment. After hours in his study followed by hours on the floor, he willed his muscles and his mind to carry him once more to his front door, to maneuver his coat onto his back, and walk outside.

The trip back toward town had never before seemed so tedious. The same path that he had taken day and night, to the lab, to the market, to the café.

His feet knew the route so well they became anxious, displeased with the sameness. This time, as he came upon the café where he usually purchased his coffee beans, he bypassed it. Where he was going, he did not know. But as soon as he passed it and tossed his destination, he grew anxious. It was unlike him to not have a plan. It made him uncomfortable. What was the point of being out, of walking in the cold, if he had nowhere to go? He walked more quickly to appear as if he were heading somewhere, and kept his eyes down to avoid the faces of those around him who were actually going places.

Thankfully, he came upon another coffee shop not too far away. He went inside and stood in line for a to-go cup. He had intended to sit at his usual café after purchasing his beans so that he wouldn't have to go back home. But this was a new café. He looked around, spotting open seats, listening to the volume of the music, eyeing the setup. Someone took one of the open seats, throwing him into a small panic. Once he planned to stay, he would start to feel the anxiety of watching the seats around him fill up before he could even order his coffee. No, he couldn't stay. Another time he could stay. But it was his first time there. It would be too overwhelming to stay, especially being there alone. He realized how silly he was. A brilliant, accomplished scientist, a designer, a tall, confident man who didn't like to order coffee from new places. He wondered how far from reality that tall, confident, brilliant man had become over the years. It felt like a fiction, a façade. Someone else entirely.

Looking around again at the layout of the shop, he spotted a woman staring at him intensely. She looked ghostly, yet seductive. He was startled to see that she resembled Allie, but her features were sharper, her hair blacker, her skin milkier. The dark-haired woman from Walter's funeral, whom Lee had not then seen.

Lee stepped slightly out of line to get a better look at her, intrigued. But her face never fully came into focus, no matter how he shifted. He couldn't get a clear look at her through the crowd, but he knew that her eyes were set on him, as if the crowd didn't exist between them.

She smiled coyly, and slinked out of the coffee shop. No one else seemed to notice her despite her striking appearance. Lee paid for his coffee and left, looking around subtly for the woman. She was nowhere. He tried to picture her face, piece it together from what little of it he had glimpsed. Why the coy smile, he could not fathom. His mood lightened without him realizing, and he began to walk back home with his coffee and no beans, not thinking anything more of it.

The night sky looked particularly dark and starless. He kicked a cigarette butt, still slightly burning, and became mesmerized by the flame. How it sparked as it skittered across the pavement, and how it smoldered while it rested. A low, brilliant shade of orange, such heat packed into such a tiny surface. It grew, surrounded him. The heat pulling him deeper into its white rings. *The white again*, he thought as it engulfed him, making it impossible to maintain perspective. He thought of Elle in the white Procedures room, her complete lack of perception in the depths of her slumber. At the thought of Elle the white dissipated, dropping him back into the gritty reality of the crushed cigarette at his feet. He shoved it aside gruffly and brushed the ash, dispersing it into invisibility against the blacktop. The ash marking a chemical change that occurred that could never go back to what it once was. The cigarette sat smoldering on the ground and eventually died out, only leaving behind the crushed butt to witness the permanent change in what it once was. Before the fire—just heat and light—introduced the ash.

Having been so aware of his footsteps only just before on his way into town, Lee found himself back inside his house without a thought as to how to get there. He couldn't get the face of the woman out of his head, nor could he get it fully into his head. He knew that it wasn't just that he didn't recall it. His mind hadn't filled in completely what she looked like. Even if he had looked directly at her, he had a suspicion that he wouldn't remember her face, though he couldn't come up with a reason for thinking so. His logic looked back at him in disappointment for believing such a thing regardless of what his sensory experience had been. He recognized the dueling parts of his thought processes and shoved them both aside.

Upstairs, while hanging his clothes alongside Allie's, he spotted the ones that Elle had worn. They stood out, looking freshly used. It made the rest appear forgotten, which they had never before looked. The hairs on his neck stood up defensively. Reaching toward the shelves in the back of the closet, he pulled out a bottle of perfume and lightly spritzed Allie's clothes with it. As he pressed, he pictured Frank clicking the key to delete a memory. The fragrance that was released from the bottle was still profoundly floral. Inside the bottle were preserved, liquid memories of Allie and Lee. Each spritz held an environment, a time, a feeling, transforming the bedroom into a season, a walk in the park under the blooming branches of cherry blossom trees, an embrace in the rain as jazz musicians played on under their tarp. The scent of the past came to rest on the clothes, reminding them of the sinewy arms they once covered, the slender legs they protected, the slight frame they clutched. Exhausted, Lee slept, the scent of Allie's perfume filling his head with dreams of places and times he had not remembered in years.

....

THIRTY-SEVEN

Marigold walked up behind Frank in her nightclothes. He had come home from the lab in a mood and began working at the small desk in the living room, wasting no time walking up the stairs. He was concentrating on the screen and didn't notice Marigold watching over his shoulder. He clicked on a memory and saved it to the "Replacement Memories" file, then opened the memory and started deleting and rearranging strings of data within it. Side by side on his screen he compared the old memory to the new memory, making sure that they looked identical. Still hovering behind his chair, Marigold put her arms around him, causing him to cloud with guilt. She knew what he was doing without needing to understand what was on the screen just by looking at his sunken face.

"Do you think she'll tell him?" Marigold asked.

Through his silence he conveyed suspicion that she would, but hope that she wouldn't.

"You did the right thing," Marigold tried to reassure him. Frank caught her uncertainty. He had been so sure that morning that Lee wouldn't be able to handle it if Elle revealed it to him. But he remembered seeing it uncovered once before. He had thought that it was an accident, a slip, and buried it then. But as he buried the memory over again that morning, he realized that it hadn't been a slip. Elle was finding it and uncovering it.

He decided then to uncover as much as was uncovered before he had reburied it. If he didn't meddle, he couldn't be responsible. It would come out eventually.

"I had no choice. I tried to bury the memory, but— she just kept digging it up. This morning, when she came over, she asked me about it. I thought that might be the case, but I had to be sure. And then when I looked back more—she had been digging it up for months. And I missed it. It was so slight. When she would talk to Lee, he would trigger things in her that would cause her to unearth some of it. There was even a visual stimulus at one time, but I didn't catch what it was then. A picture. How could there have been a picture?" He paused. "I didn't see it, but I do now. It was hand-drawn. Lee must have drawn a picture.

"The problem is," Frank continued. "Allie died, but if she hadn't died, she would have told him. And with Elle—that part of Allie exists still in Elle. It's there to be told. It's one of Allie's last memories."

"Maybe you should tell him first."

"I made a promise. Allie can tell Lee through Elle. It should come from Allie."

Marigold listened silently, supportive. "Well. I'm going to bed."

"I'll be in soon. Hey, Lee hasn't said anything to you, right?"

"About what?"

"I don't know, anything."

"No, he hasn't said anything about anything to me," Marigold laughed. "Why?"

"He asked about you. Said something about you not getting out much."

"Ha! Nice. Well I don't. But neither did you two when you were in school. Come to bed."

"Yeah."

Marigold left the room and turned out the light, plunging Frank into darkness.

"Marigold, turn on the light. Marigold? Marigold!" He gave up, his face lit brightly by the only light coming from his screen.

Days later, Elle poked her head through Lee's front door without stepping inside. Outside, it threatened to rain.

"Lee?"

Lee appeared at the top of the stairs. He looked disheveled, undone.

"Elle, what are you doing here?"

"I don't mean to intrude. I left my umbrella here the other day and I wanted to go for a quick walk. I didn't know you were home—the lights were all off."

"It's okay. I didn't see your umbrella though."

Elle smiled, glancing down at the umbrella right beside the front door. She picked it up and showed it to Lee.

"I got it. Thanks."

There was a moment of silence. Lee stared down at Elle from the top of the stairs, keeping a safe distance. Why he needed that distance he didn't know.

Elle noticed him staring at her, not responding to her like he usually did. He didn't rush to her side, he didn't try to fill the silence. She wondered what he was thinking that kept him so quiet.

"Do you want to come with me?" Elle smiled again and closed the front door behind her, expecting Lee to agree. She stood inside waiting for him. She felt comfortable in his home in a way that she couldn't recall feeling comfortable in her own. His house seemed more familiar to her, more like home despite its frigidity.

Lee descended the stairs promptly, as Elle had expected he would. For a moment she worried that he had heard her tone, which she knew sounded more like a request than a question. She didn't want him to feel like she was taking advantage of him, always available when she needed him. But then again, she was technically his job, so it was natural that she had gotten used to his attention.

Their conversation was somewhat forced, a shift nearly imperceptible to an outsider. But they both felt it. This time, Elle filled the silence.

"Why don't you have any pets?"

"Pets! I don't have time for pets. It wouldn't be fair to them." Lee looked at her face but not into her eyes. She looked so much younger than he felt. But he had designed her as Allie had looked over a decade ago. She still had the youthful visage of a woman in her thirties, and wouldn't begin to age for many years. He wondered for a moment if he should have aged her when he designed her so that there would be no gap in their apparent years. After all, Lee had changed in that time. Allie would have changed too, if she'd had the opportunity. But then he wouldn't have recreated Allie. He would have created someone new, someone who resembled Allie, but was older, wiser, more lived. He wanted the Allie he had known, the Allie he remembered rather than a created, false, assumed version of Allie. But he knew that he wasn't the same, and suddenly wondered if Allie had been alive at that moment, in her thirties standing across from Lee in his fifties, whether they would have been together at all. They had wanted to grow together, not separately, not one before the other. As he looked at her young face, her energy, he finally acknowledged the fact that he was unsure if, after his precise designs and careful creation and then recreation of her memories, the simple passage of time could come between them.

"What about a plant?" Elle was still looking around his lifeless home, spotting places she could put a plant.

"What do I need a plant for?"

"It's just—I love your home—but it's so large just for you. It's so empty."

"Yours is the same way."

Elle thought for a minute, and became confused, as if this were a revelation.

"I guess you're right," she said. "But I have plants."

Lee took his coat off the rack next to the front door. Without responding, he motioned for her to head outside, and she obliged.

Side by side they walked along the street. It was drizzling, but Elle's umbrella was dangling at her feet, closed.

"So, how far along are you into erasing all of my memories?"

"It's not all of your memories." Lee tried instinctively to protect her from information that would be painful for her to comprehend. Elle waited for an answer. "We're pretty far along."

"Will they let me keep my memories of you erasing my memories?"

"Probably not," Lee said, unaffected.

"Well, then, since I'm aware of it now, I guess I won't remember this for very long." Elle motioned around her as she spoke, indicating that the moment would soon be forgotten. She was saddened by the futility of their present. But wasn't it just a small-scale version of their very existence? Soon to be forgotten, not mattering what had actually been true.

"You have to stay in the present. You can't think about anything but the present, or it will be snapped up and erased."

"But when I try not to think about it, I'm thinking about it. I can't control it. I can't remind myself to forget."

"It's worse knowing that you've forgotten than never having known at all. It's the awareness that's the hard part. It might be better for you if they do erase those memories."

"But then this would be gone too. This memory, right here of us, will never have existed to me."

"That's right."

Elle stopped walking and looked at Lee seriously, no longer skirting around the point. She couldn't believe that he didn't see it.

"You don't think me not remembering will affect your memory? Don't you think that whatever connection you might feel to me now, you will never feel, because you know that I won't remember? You can't build a one-sided connection. You can't just take pieces of me and replace them and think it'll be the same. I don't know how you've ever felt that I could truly take the place of your wife."

She spat her words more harshly than she intended, but she knew that the memory replacement would not only change her, but Lee too. She couldn't understand how he, the scientist behind her walking legs and breathing lungs, could overlook that. It pained her not only to feel like she was losing herself, but to feel like she was losing the protection of the Lee that she had known, who would objectively make the best decisions for her, who was in complete control of her every movement and thought process, whom she had looked up to for his reasoning skills, without which she knew her own reasoning skills would be flawed.

Lee felt the weight of Elle's words but was unwilling to listen to them. He walked in silence alongside her. Her voice stopped forming sounds as she waited for him to respond. After some time, she continued. "What are you thinking?"

Lee shook his head. He had to make her understand. He knew that she was capable. He knew that understanding was the one thing she wanted above all, and the very thing that had brought them to the present moment. It surprised him to hear Elle speak of Allie as she had, separating them so completely and finally, and seeming so removed. It hit him that she didn't know Allie at all, had never actually known Allie, and would never know Allie, but would continue to be the very essence of Allie.

"I know, in my mind, that you are not Allie. Just like you know, in your mind, that there is something you are missing, but you can't tell what it is or sense that anything should be different. I know that there is something I am missing, but only because I *know* it."

Elle led Lee to the bridge that he had shown her many weeks before.

"Remember this? Remember when you first took me here?"

Lee nodded, the last few minutes with Elle falling away as he recalled. Elle looked away from him, out, just as she had done that first day. But, Lee noticed, there was no spark to her. She looked flat, unlike how he had ever seen her before.

"I don't. I remember being here—with you—and that's it."

"Are you sure?" Lee looked troubled. She wasn't supposed to have forgotten that. He looked around, trying to spot something that might jog her memory, but he didn't have much faith. He covered his concern with a small, hopeful smile. If she had loved it so much the first time, she could experience that awe all over again. "Well, what do you think of it?"

Elle smiled kindly, but unenthusiastically.

"It's a bridge."

Lee was devastated. It was more than just a bridge. Elle didn't remember how important the bridge was to him. If she didn't remember something like that, how was she going to remember the empathy she had developed for him after experiencing her own loss? It was that very connection that the goal was to preserve. But he had been so careful! *How could this have slipped?*

It started to rain harder, louder. The umbrella stayed closed by Elle's side. Lee let the subject drop as he reached out to her. He opened the umbrella over her, and she instinctively moved closer to him so that it covered them both.

"Let's not stand under the trees."

"Why does it always rain?" Her frustration was unhidden in her voice.

They started to walk back in silence, Lee looking torn, and Elle harboring distant thoughts, far from their present.

It occurred again to Lee that their entire conversation, the walk to the bridge and back, would have to be erased. It shouldn't have mattered, then, whether Elle in that moment remembered the bridge, because it was going to be stripped from her anyway. It wasn't cruel of her to not remember, or to not know that it was cruel when she spoke of it so dismissively. But it did matter.

It wasn't enough that he recalled how she had been so excited when he had first taken her to the bridge, how she marveled at the view and at him. It didn't feel real. She didn't feel that same excitement and didn't marvel in the same way in the present, and that was what mattered to Lee. No matter how she felt in the past, it couldn't stand up to what she had begun to display in the present. The past was lost.

"Why did you want to go for a walk?" It struck Lee that if Elle had been alone, she probably wouldn't have gone to the bridge at all. "What would you be thinking if I weren't here?"

"I don't know. I just didn't want to be in my house anymore. You know how sometimes you just can't stand the thought of being home?"

Lee helped Elle over a large tree root. He interpreted her comment as more of a comment about being with oneself rather than being in a house. She took his hand limply, as if obligated, and dropped it, not rudely, as soon as she was over the root. Lee felt the emptiness in his fingers more than he had felt her hand in his. He allowed her to walk ahead of him. Her shoulders were dropped, and though she still looked poised, it was clear that inside her complicated head was a great weight. He watched her, pensive, wondering how much of that weight was her own, and how much was his.

THIRTY-NINE

It was no surprise when well after midnight Lee still couldn't sleep. He sat behind the desk in his study looking through Elle's data on his screen. He knew that time was passing quickly by the sandy feel of his face, which would reach the final point of acceptable natural growth by morning. Half-empty coffee cups left a trail of where he had been. At the bookcase, at his desk, at the window. He worked furiously, desperately, trying to figure out what was wrong. But he didn't quite know what he was trying to figure out. He was looking for something to see rather than looking for something specific, which put him at a disadvantage. There would be something to see, he was sure, and when he saw it he would know. He kept looking, with the broad and narrow goal of seeing. He dialed Frank, hoping that a second pair of eyes would make the seeing a little easier, a little wider, a little more focused.

"Lee—"

Lee heard the sleep dripping from Frank's voice and glanced at the clock not long enough to formulate an apology for calling so late.

"Are you sure there is nothing we're missing?" Lee asked.

"I'm sure. Why? Did something happen?"

"I don't know. Something's off. I keep going through the replacements and it all looks fine, but something's not right. She's losing things along the way. Things—that make her Elle."

"Well she's not going to remember everything. A very small percentage of the population really does remember *everything*."

Lee tensed at the apathetic tone of Frank's voice. Blood rushed to his neck, where he caught it before it reached his face, and calmed himself before speaking again. He was frustrated that he couldn't articulate what he was sensing, but knew that frustration would only make formulating words to describe what he sensed that much more clouded.

"It's not just remembering—something is *wrong*."

"Okay," Frank sat up. "When did you start to notice it?"

"I don't know. Just, something shifted."

"Can you remember anything specific? When you noticed the shift?"

"No," said Lee, irritated by his own lack of awareness.

"The numbers look good, Lee. I think you may be seeing things that aren't there."

Lee shook his head, unable to speak. His mind perceived it. Why couldn't he comprehend it and boil it down to letters, make up words to explain it? He was convinced that something had changed. How could the data not show it? A year ago he would have believed the data and convinced himself that there was no shift. An inexplicable sense was far from a trustworthy source. But the data were wrong. He knew. They weren't picking up the shift. It was an invisible shift even to the most advanced technology. Because it wasn't a physical shift, or even a mental shift. It was a shift of being. A shift that occurred in an undetectable part of a living being.

"Lee?"

He became aware that he had been breathing into the phone wordlessly for moments too long. It would be useless to try to get Frank to see something that didn't show up in the data. It was either there or it wasn't. He would have needed to know Elle on the level at which Lee knew her to see it. Lee would just have to wait until there were words to explain what he perceived.

"Yeah?" Lee replied finally.

"It's two o'clock. Get some sleep."

"Yeah."

Lee hung up and put his head down. As they shut out the physical world around him, the mirrors on the backs of his eyelids showed his eyes only what was inside his head. He saw Elle. He saw Allie. He realized that he had never before pictured them as he did in that moment. At the same time, standing side by side, as two separates. And before he could help himself, he had distinguished between the two.

He pictured the second pair of legs in Elle's kitchen and imagined Elle having split, separated, leaving a part of herself to follow just behind her and evaporate. Why he had suspected Marigold that night, suspected that she was hiding something from him, he did not know. He presumed it was for lack of any other logical alternative. The stimuli that he was receiving didn't match up to any point of understanding, and his mind had begun to make things up behind his back, target-ing the thing that was closest to him, and could most effectively harm him. Frank.

It seemed silly when he thought about it. A second presence in Elle's house would have shown up in the data if she had interacted with it or been aware of it at all. But it wasn't in the data. It was just a shadow, a phantom. Another creation of Lee's mind. *At what point does something become real that had been imagined? If something is imagined, is it not real? Is it not real to the mind? Doesn't the very act of imagining a thing make it real, even if only real inside the mind?*

He lifted his head, wishing to shut out his mind by seeing the world around him. It was why, he realized, he hadn't slept. What was in his mind, it seemed, was worse than what was in reality, but only made so because he didn't understand the reality, and his mind tried to compensate. But perhaps sleep was what he needed. Perhaps he could let his mind sort out what he didn't fully understand. Let it come up with something while he slept that would explain what it perceived peripherally. He left his study, shutting down his computer to avoid the temptation of taking one last look. The black screen against the darkness of the room made Lee feel a distorted sense of reality, as though the dark that his eyes perceived were more a feeling, an intuition, than an actual observation.

Lee went into his bedroom and settled in for the night. He left the light on for a moment, the room illuminated, then turned it off. The room was black with the flip of a switch. As he lay in the darkness, he was aware of the fact that he hadn't seen the room dim as the electricity lessened from the switch of the light. He hadn't seen it, but he knew it had happened. And if he had stopped the switch halfway between "on" and "off," he would have seen a dimmer room, a struggling current. Indeed, he would have heard it. It wasn't just that there was "on" and there was "off," but there were points in between that often went unnoticed. Passed through without question, without sensing the change in current, until suddenly there were no points left, and the switch flips from "on" to "off" in an instant. He thought of this as he fell asleep, not aware of when thinking turned to dreaming, of when his consciousness took a back seat to the unreachable corners of his mind.

FORTY

....

Elle sat up suddenly, visions pouring into her head. A child. A slab of grey stone. What was the stone? Despairing screams. Then, suddenly, silence. Clarity. A grassy hill. The grey stone. Lines of grey stone.

She threw the covers off and pulled on her coat. It was clear to her now. She had unearthed the chest full of memories and released them into her mind. They swirled around, then settled, as she tried to make sense of them. Where they came from she didn't know. They couldn't be Allie's. They certainly weren't her own.

She had to see for herself. If she saw it, she knew that her intuition would tell her if it was real, or at least if it made sense. She locked the door behind her and began to walk. Before she knew where her feet were taking her, she was standing in the center of a quiet field before the entrance to a graveyard.

She lifted her hand and placed her fingers on the gritty, steel bars. The gate creaked open. Fear was not a factor, but Elle had a strange feeling that she was being disrespectful by entering the graveyard at night, as if footsteps on the earth after the sun had set would wake those beneath from their eternal slumber, to find themselves trapped in a small box, larger than they remember it being when they first entered it, but not large enough. Her feet barely touched the ground as she walked.

She knew what graveyards looked like. She had seen them before, though not with her own eyes. This one looked different. The headstones marking the possession of a plot of land, like houses for the living, were aligned in neat rows and exceptionally maintained. There were no cracks, no wear, no dead flowers or petals without stems. On the contrary, it seemed like a lovely place. The stale, cold air became a refreshing cool, the rows of death became tiny, private, polished palaces for what resided inside. *Someone must maintain this place as a full-time job, every day, all day.* Elle thought how strange it was to bury something that had been separated from its life—indeed, to become a some*thing* rather than a some*one*—and then to go on maintaining the land under which it was buried. It wasn't for them that the graveyard attendant replaced dead flowers with fresh ones. It was for the living who would see it. As if to say, "Welcome," and to create the illusion of it being a nice place to permanently settle rather than it being the end of all sensory perception and consciousness. Or rather, a return to the state of pre-existence, of no sensory perception or consciousness, neither in a past nor a future that does not exist.

Elle walked along the carefully placed pathways between the graves, reading each light grey stone. Soon the earth would be filled. There would be no more room to preserve the bodies of the dead. A graveyard planet, the only sign of there ever having been life being the surface of the earth, spiked with slabs of death, and the last man to die melting into the soil that had kept him aboveground for so long.

She stopped at the foot of one plot of land, staring at the headstone from feet away. It had only one date on it, no date of death. A child's birth and death so close, holding hands, only moments in between. It was Alma.

Elle knelt down before it and placed her hand on the soil at her feet, a misplaced grief running through her. A thought occurred to her. That Allie had died before knowing that Alma had died. Was it easier for her to die thinking that she had left Alma behind? Would she have tried to cling to life if she had known that Alma had not? Her pain would have only lasted for a moment. Her wishing. Before joining Alma herself.

Elle suddenly felt a wave of responsibility consume her, a heaviness brought on by the knowledge that she possessed. She sat down in front of the grave, crossed her legs like a child, and stared. There it was.

The memory that she had known was buried had fully exhumed itself. She had thought that if it ever happened, she would be in a state of shock, or it would be too much for her, and she would time out again. But she wasn't. She didn't. The memory shook itself free from its stiff restraints and appeared to her clearly. A secret she had kept from Lee, her last thoughts before her death. It was always last words that those left behind seemed to be interested in. But it was the last thoughts that seemed to matter more to Elle. She had the privilege and the burden of being inside Allie's head. She couldn't forget it. She had to tell Lee before it was removed, replaced, buried. Lost.

She sat still before the grave, letting her mind flood. Letting herself fully become the shell that she was designed to be, letting herself fill with thoughts that weren't hers, memories that weren't hers, and storing them safely. She would carry them with her until they were released through the sound waves of her voice, smacking against the eardrums of those nearby, into their heads as well as hers. She thought how strange it was that such a transfer didn't diminish what of it she kept in her own head. It could be endlessly multiplied at no penalty to the original giver.

She stood up, the grief of another falling from her shoulders to her feet. She would tell Lee. Allie would tell Lee. She was prepared to make a vessel of herself through which someone else could speak.

She glanced up and spotted a figure standing in the distance. A woman. But there was something different about the woman. She didn't appear to be leaning over a grave. She stood in the middle of the headstones, not noticing them at all, staring directly at Elle. A cold coursed through Elle when she noticed the woman staring at her. It would be one thing to discover that she was not alone in the graveyard despite the hour of night, but it was another thing entirely to be discovered and looked upon so unapologetically. She felt that the woman could see her clearly, could look upon her face and distinguish her eyes from her nose despite the distance between her and Elle. That she was closer than she appeared.

The woman stood still, her arms hanging limply at her sides. Her stillness frightened Elle more than anything. The anticipation of movement. Movement in unknown directions. At her? What were her intentions? Why was she there, staring at Elle?

And then she walked. Toward Elle, but not directly at her. As she moved closer, Elle could see the white color of her skin pop against the black night sky, nearly a glow. Her hair, long. Elle noticed that she was wearing only a long, white nightgown with short sleeves that matched the glow of her skin. Though it was below freezing underneath the night sky, the woman didn't look cold. She floated on as if not noticing whether it was night or day, warm or cold, a graveyard or a sidewalk.

Elle kept her eyes on her the entire time the woman walked toward her. As she came closer, Elle prepared herself to run. There was something about the woman that seemed off. Unfamiliar, and yet, somehow familiar indeed. Elle strained to see her face through the dark between them, trying to remain as still as possible.

When the woman was finally close enough for Elle to distinguish her face, she recognized her. She saw her every day, looking back at her from every mirror she stared into, every dark window she passed. She hid behind the glasses of the world and appeared when Elle appeared in front of them. Indeed, Elle recognized herself walking toward her.

But she wasn't disturbed. She had seen her before, released from the glass, walking the earth freely. She had seen her at Walter's funeral, but hadn't recognized her then. A specter that flits from death to death. She passed by, mere feet away, and looked at Elle as she had looked at her the day of Walter's funeral. But instead of her eyes telling her that she wasn't supposed to be there, she smiled at Elle approvingly, and walked on.

She knew then that she had made the right choice, that Allie wanted her to tell Lee, that it wasn't a mistake. She watched the woman disappear into the night. Before she followed, she turned to the grave before her.

"I will release you from these secrets," she said quietly, picturing the sketch of the twelve-year-old girl in Lee's notebook rather than the infant that she knew rested below the earth.

FORTY-ONE

....

It was a fitful sleep. The streetlamps outside Lee's window blinked lazily, painting momentary shadows on his walls. Rest did not come naturally to him and he swayed in and out of his slumber. The shapes he saw through the slits in his heavy lids looked more grotesque than he recalled them actually being in the verity of the daylight. He had struggled to get to sleep, and struggled to wake himself up at the sight of the disfigured objects. Whichever part of him was awake, standing guard over the rest of his mind, knew that the sinister shapes that emerged from the darkness of sleep would transform from faces to pillows at the moment of wakefulness. His consciousness bobbed like a buoy just out of reach in a tractionless ocean as his unfocused eyes lied to him in the dark. In his mind he imagined himself to be awake, but in fact he dreamt of his wakefulness, the resistance in his mind against the dead weight of his body exhausting him. On some level he knew that he was asleep, but he questioned it. In his sleep he asked himself, "Am I awake?" He tried to move his arm to test. If he moved his arm, he was awake.

His arm moved indeed, a heavy, sloppy lift and drop, which woke him momentarily. His unconscious mind had commanded his body to move as his conscious mind often did. But indeed, it had required more effort. A conscious command to "move" that he never had to think when he was awake and wanted his arm to move. When he realized that he had been asleep, he felt tired.

At that moment, when he unconsciously gave up trying to wake to focus on the dysmorphic objects around him, he fell into a deep sleep. Only minutes into his repose was he awakened by a knock on his front door. It came quietly at first. He looked at the clock, but couldn't find the hands through his bleary eyes. Another knock from downstairs, loud and forthright. He put on a robe and listened again, more fully awake. A feeling of entrapment came over him, and he wished that the knocking would go away, that it had never happened. Another knock. Should he answer? Could he pretend he wasn't home?

He walked downstairs and approached the door, his ears perked and his feet light and ready to flee. Another knock, loud, hard, in line with his face from the other side of the door. He felt seen. The knocking stopped, but he knew that its originator stood on the other side. Seen indeed. He wished to call out, "Who is it?" but his throat caught. It seemed safer somehow to stay silent. His ears were still at attention, and he feared that the sound of his own voice would distract them. His eyes begged to see so they could complete his understanding. The handle twisted in his fingers, the steel lock retreating into its echoing chambers within the thick, flat, wooden side. Preparing for the worst, he stood with his bare feet apart, and opened the door.

"Elle!"

That the heavy, forceful knock had originated from her petite, ethereal hands seemed disjointed. She pushed past into the house without a smile or a word. Lee closed the door behind her, relieved, yet apprehensive about the revelation of her familiar, safe face. Relieved because at that hour, anyone else might have had baleful motives for appearing on his doorstep, apprehensive because something must be wrong for Elle to show up in the middle of the night. When he turned around, he was surprised to see that Elle was standing right behind him. She didn't flinch when he recoiled in surprise at her proximity. She just stared at him, with a smile that he didn't recognize. A mischievous smile that belonged to someone else. His unease built.

"So," she challenged. "Where is it?"

"Where is what?" Lee asked.

"I'm not happy. You've been keeping secrets."

Despite him knowing very intimately which of his own secrets he harbored, her tone made him anxious. What could she possibly be talking about? Was there some secret that he had forgotten about that she uncovered?

"Secrets? I don't have any secrets."

"Oh, yes you do," she said in a singsong voice. "And I found one of them. I found one of them all by myself. So. Where is it?"

He didn't recognize the thing that stood before him, testing him, teasing him. An impostor wearing the skin of Elle. *Something must have gone wrong in the memory replacement. Could the needle have missed? But then why am I not hearing from Frank? No, it's something else. Something is not right.*

"Elle—"

"Elle?" she echoed defiantly. "Oh, I'm not Elle." She twirled around to a slow, unheard song in her own head. He watched her spin through his downstairs, stunned, keeping a careful distance. His body sensed a threat before he did, his feet planted firmly apart, his torso pushed forward.

She laughed at his pathetic fighting stance. There would be no fight.

"You didn't tell me you knew what it was like to lose yourself!" She kept spinning, moved in dance-like motions, closed her eyes as if she moved along a path parted by the air around her. "Well?" The smile disappeared from her face. Her voice became low and metallic. "Where is it?"

"Where is what?"

She stopped and looked at Lee, through Lee, a smile creeping toward her eyes. She had led him effortlessly into a line of questioning that required little explanation from her. He would soon see. He would see the manifestation of what it was to lose oneself. Satisfied with her clever manipulation, she took a moment to appreciate how stupid he was. It was obvious that he knew she wasn't his beloved Elle, and yet, he stood before her like a chained puppy begging for her attention. It didn't matter that she was different. He believed what he wanted to believe. A disgusting excuse for a man. A scientist, no less. *And look at him!* Her nose crinkled upward on her face as if she had smelled something foul when she addressed his pitiful mug.

"Your hand."

Lee looked down reflexively at his hands, not processing what was unfolding before him. Hanging from his wrists were hands indeed, but merely the outline of his hands that had just moments before been so fleshy on the doorknob, so nimble with the tie of his robe. As they faded into translucence, he tried out of habit to grasp at them, but had no hands with which to grasp. He still felt them, phantom limbs reaching for each other, but his eyes told his mind that they were no longer there. He kept grasping, to no avail, the stubs of his arms swinging like wooden bats suspended in a violent wind.

The impostor walked calmly, quietly up the stairs while Lee, panicked and thrashing, continued to fade.

FORTY-TWO

....

His elbow slipped off his desk, jolting him awake. He instinctively looked at his hands in full flesh, and glanced up at the hands of the clock infinitely tracking the invisible march of time. Elle's data were still displayed on his screen.

Anger rose within him as questions filled his mind. It had been a dream, not to be taken too seriously, but an unfinished dream leaving him to wonder how it ended. He couldn't fault himself for wanting a conclusion. It was the way the brain was wired, to seek completion. But it had left him with a distaste for Elle that he knew was irrational, and he resented it. Resented his own mind and its whims. Reluctant to give in to its will, he found himself mentally wandering back down the stairs. Had it just been physical fading? Would he still be conscious of his self after his physical body had faded completely, as he still felt his faded hands reaching for each other at the ends of his wrists? Or would he be suffocated with invisibility and cease to exist altogether, his mind vanished along with all of its storage, its memories, its thoughts? Or was the fading just a fade into invisibility, his conscious-ness preserved, his body solid but unseen?

No, he thought as he recalled grasping at his own hands and moving uninhibited through the space where they should have been. *It was a complete fade of the self.* Somewhere his mind knew this to be fact. Per-haps he had learned it from a part of the dream he could not remember. But he knew that it was true, and he suspected in that moment that Elle had learned it long ago, unrecorded in the data, unbeknownst to her scientific caretakers who, he realized, were advanced beyond the point of considering personhood. And he stood at the helm.

By then he was wide awake, as if it were the middle of a dark afternoon instead of the middle of the night. He gathered his jumbled thoughts and disregarded them as sleep-think, determining his state of function-ing wakefulness to be beginning just then. He turned back to his computer and picked up where he had left off, hoping that his disturbed sleep wouldn't influence his search and make him see something that wasn't there, or disregard something that he shouldn't.

As he scrolled he became aware of the silence. Of the loud buzz from the computer being a part of that supposed silence. It distracted his thoughts, letting in elementary concepts like, "What does silence really sound like?" The same thoughts that he'd had as a young boy but never actually answered. He seemed to grow out of them, finding them unimportant as he aged, but kept wondering. It seemed a common question after a while, and he had lost interest.

He sat in the middle of the silence and tried to keep working, tried to remain unaware of the silence that surrounded him. By that very effort making himself that much more aware. The loudness of the running computer cut into his eardrums the more he tried to hear nothing at all. He saw it there in the darkness, the bright purple light of the hum from the computer. He looked within the halo around the monitor, trying to find the source of the noise. It grew louder at his advances into a shriek like a threatened rodent, but he couldn't pinpoint it. Was it indeed just another nightmare from which he could not escape? A purple halo of noise that he could see and hear, but was just beyond his reach. To touch it, to have something to touch, would be what made it real, what made it physical. The light and the sounds could not be grasped by any solid object such as hands, could be cut by air, and could even pass through solid walls. But it wasn't the sound or the shining purple light that he was after. It was the source. The creator of the nonphysical stimulants that drove him mad.

He crawled under his desk, his long body curling like a scared child. It was what he had become. Having suffered through the loneliness for more than a decade in the house that he had shared with his wife—in the house that had been meant to become the home of his daughter, in the house where he sat night after night, creating and destroying Elle—he had grown inward, receding from what he had once been into a man lying under his desk in the dark. The way she had looked at him in his dream, with such disgust, he felt for himself in that moment.

He paused and considered himself with a clear head. There he sat, a grown man in the middle of the floor searching for a sound that he thought of suddenly in non-scientific terms. *What would Allie think? What would she think of me if she could see me now?* The thought deflated him. She would no doubt be disappointed to see him sitting alone in the dark house for hours, staring at the wall and not remembering his own thoughts. He didn't remember when he started doing it. What would she think if she knew of the anxiety he developed when leaving the house, like when he had impulsively passed by his usual coffee shop to buy beans? The woman with the obscured face floated back into his mind. Would she, a stranger who had never known how he once thrived, see only a widower hiding underneath a block of wood? That wasn't who he was.

The purple light in the room diminished and the buzz from the computer quieted to a whisper. He spotted a set of wires that carried the electricity to the computer and pulled them all out. The silence he desired followed. His computer shut off immediately, leaving him completely in the dark. He sat in the middle of the pile of disconnected wires underneath his desk and became uncomfortably aware of how strange his actions were. A man, alone in his house at the darkest hour of the night diving under his desk and unplugging fistfuls of wires. What was the motivation? There would appear, to an outsider, to be none.

He found the wire to his computer and plugged it back in, leaving everything else unplugged. His shredder, which he hadn't used in years. His pencil sharpener, also a relic from his university life. His external hard drive. All of which had been unnecessarily at the ready. He released them, freed them from their eternal wait. He felt as if his body took over for his mind in his moment of desperation, acting of its own accord. It was strange and foreign to him to be sitting on the floor. He scolded himself for the improper shutdown of his computer, but was only just then regaining power over his own body. He perceived the silence pervading the room.

He lifted himself into the chair behind his desk and reopened the data pages on his screen. Right back to where he had been only minutes before. Before crawling under his desk as if nothing had happened at all. He noticed his mind still taking time to process things that were happening to and around him, and assumed that he had passed the point of functioning properly with such little sleep.

At the very moment when he gave his mind permission to rest, he felt his finger press down on the mouse. A receptor blew up on the screen, containing a single replacement memory, clearly highlighted as such. He felt a heaviness underneath his eyes. His mind, finally at rest, spilled the bucket of exhaustion it had been filling for weeks into him. He gazed at the memory thoughtlessly, staring at the small gap on either side. Before the last drops of fatigue were emptied, he unleashed a final push of concentration aimed at the receptor. But his mind was already far away. He knew that he saw something, but didn't quite process a conclusion.

Just as he was about to give in to sleep, convincing himself to write himself a note about what he had just seen and revisit it with a rested mind, there was a knock on the front door. It came softly, as if the hand it belonged to didn't actually intend to wake the resident inside but wanted to say that it had done its job.

Am I asleep? Lee questioned his state of mind, knowing how ready he had been for slumber.

There was a dream that he had as a young boy, night after night. Before he went to sleep, he would imagine the dream, remember it, kick it off in a way, to help him fall asleep. It was a dream that he loved. He wanted to continue its story, but, night after night, he would have the same dream, starting and stopping at the same place, never offering a conclusion. He couldn't remember having any other dreams at night, but suspected that he did, since he couldn't imagine waking at the same part of the dream every morning despite waking at different times.

It had fascinated him that he was able to guide his mind into dreaming what he wished to dream. As he got older, he remembered the dream, but didn't quite believe that he'd had it more than once. He may have thought that he was manipulating his mind into having a recurring dream, but in fact, it was his mind that was likely manipulating him. He must have recalled the entire dream before actually having fallen asleep, and woke thinking that it had been a dream.

But as Lee heard the knock for the second time that night, he wondered if he was about to experience a recurring dream. Even if he was awake, his mind might be inclined to run through the whole dream again, as it had when he was a boy.

He looked out the window, aware as he brushed past papers on his desk that he was feeling physical objects, something that, no matter how real a dream felt, he could never recall doing in one of them. Standing on his doorstep was Elle.

He retreated from the window. Was the dream about to occur again from another perspective? It was different this time. He had seen her from above, before letting her into his house. Would it give him an advantage? He second-guessed for a moment, then relaxed. His mind was tired and his imagination was running uncontrolled. It was Elle. Not a dream, not whatever had shown up on his doorstep in his dream. He called out the window, his body thawing from the cold fear that had washed over him upon first seeing her there.

"Elle—come on up."

It occurred to him then to start locking his front door. It was strange for a man of such acquired introversion and anxiety brought on by the outside world to keep his front door unlocked. *Perhaps*, he thought, *it is a way of keeping out the loneliness.* Loneliness loves a locked door. It bypasses by nature those who are open, even if there is but a single soul on the other side. A soul with an unlocked door hasn't yet closed itself completely off from the outside. Lee remembered keeping his door open at night when his parents shut theirs, an only child welcoming company. Despite his solitary lifestyle during his school years with his personal science kits, and at university when he studied more effectively alone than in groups, interruptions didn't bother him. He could easily regain his focus, and was never far enough behind on his studies to have no time for a break. Though he had always been quiet, pensive, never the first to start a conversation, he was indeed a social being.

It had been at a party during his first year at university that he had met Allie. Though it wouldn't seem as if she would stand out in a crowd, with her dark hair and dark eyes, and soft features that would have melted into the background if carried by anyone else, he saw her almost as soon as he arrived.

She had been standing on the outside of a large group of girls—he couldn't remember any of their names—listening respectfully but with little interest. She glanced around the room more than once. It seemed odd to Lee that she was there at all, and he suddenly felt silly for being there himself. When she met his gaze her lips didn't smile, but a glimmer in her eyes told Lee that if he approached, she wouldn't walk away. He spoke to only her that night, and she made no move to escape.

He knew that she was different. She had charisma, and was brilliant in a way that couldn't be learned from a book. Lee saw her as his equal. Though she was studying literature rather than science, she understood when Lee discussed his coursework with her. She would listen to him as she had listened to the group of girls the first night they met, but with shining eyes and presence.

Neither Lee nor Allie had particularly wanted to go to the party that night, but both wound up there at the request of their friends. Lee had often wondered if he hadn't met Allie that night, whether he would have met her at a future date. If the circumstances would have been right. If she would have welcomed his conversation. She was pleasant to everyone she met, but didn't go out of her way to talk to people. If he had seen her at a coffee shop, or at the university library, would she have been less open to him, having other things holding her attention, unlike the group of girls?

The memory came back to him unexpectedly and vividly. Elle had that memory now, but the circumstances under which he had actually met Elle were drastically different. By then, he was drastically different.

He heard Elle's footsteps on the other side of the wall coming up the stairs, and gave his desk a surface clean, straightening the piles of papers and books. He looked around at the coffee mugs strewn about the room but didn't bother with them. Elle arrived in his study, slightly breathless.

"I'm sorry—I know it's late."

"It's fine."

"I had to come over."

Elle walked over to the bookshelf and pulled the book with the loose pages. Lee tensed. He realized that his reservations originated from the bad taste that was left in his mouth after the nightmare, and let her flip through the book. She opened it to the picture that he had drawn of Alma, and decisively held it up for him to see. He saw her draw a long breath.

"I've been remembering things that she never told you. About your daughter."

Questions flooded Lee at once, his mind now fully awake and churning.

"What things?" he asked simply, the words jamming in his mind.

She gave him an apologetic look before appearing to assume a neutral resting position. An empty container waiting to be filled with a voice, a stance, a personhood.

"I knew the risks of giving birth to her."

Lee noticed a slight shift in Elle as she began to speak, and he realized that it was how she used to speak to him. How Allie used to speak to him. He hadn't noticed that there had been any change, but now, as she resumed that manner of speaking, it hit him. He had felt that there was some kind of shift the second time they went to the bridge, and there it was again in her speech.

"The doctors told me that I might not make it. But you wanted a daughter so badly. We talked about it so much. A little version of me."

Lee became more wary of her. *What does she mean, the doctors told her that she might not make it?* He stood halfway between thinking that the memory replacement had gone wrong and she was remembering things differently, and fearful that there was something more going on. As he listened, her words became more horrifying. He wanted to not believe them. It made sense that he shouldn't believe them. He never implanted these memories in her. She made them up somehow. But he kept quiet, absorbing Elle's words. His cold veins told him that they were true.

"And then when I got pregnant, you were so happy, I knew I had to try. So I kept it, and the risk grew every day, but I kept it. I wanted to give you a daughter, to see her wrap her hand around your finger."

There was another shift in her demeanor. Lee caught it more fully this time, having seen it only moments before. Before him stood Elle, but a version different from the one that he had created. She was a changed Elle. He couldn't figure out when she had changed. Sometime during the memory replacement. He had been so careful day after day to monitor her, watching for something like this, and had seen nothing. And yet, there she was in front of him, different in the way she held herself, in the way she spoke, in what was inside her head, made apparent by her sudden reversion to the beginning, pre-change.

"I'm not saying this to be cruel," she said in a voice that Lee no longer recognized. The same voice that he had recognized only moments before. His mind was spinning, struggling to understand her words and distrusting the foreign voice she held within her.

"But if this memory is removed, it will be lost forever. Allie would want you to know. I know. You should talk to Frank."

"Frank?"

She hesitated.

"He's the one who gave me these memories."

Before his mind had a chance to process her words, his heart processed. It pumped blood faster through his body. His hands shook, though he couldn't feel them, as if they were rubber prosthetics hanging from his wrists.

He didn't know whether to believe Elle. He wanted not to, but his physical reaction to her revelation told him that he didn't need Frank to verify her words. He stood still for a moment trying to quiet his mind and keep his emotions from overwhelming him. He had to talk to Frank. Without a word to Elle, he grabbed his coat and walked out of his study.

It hadn't occurred to her at any single moment. Elle had felt something unlock in her mind when she first saw the drawing of Alma folded inside the book. It became clearer to her in conversations with Lee about Alma, about Allie, but she hadn't been able to fully retrieve the memory. The box in her mind was still closed, though unlocked. After the last memory replacement, it had come to her clearly and unobstructed. It had flooded her mind, spilling into her consciousness, as if only a recently acquired memory that hadn't been long stored in a corner of her mind.

Indeed, Frank had secured the memory in Elle's mind. When he noticed her mentally clawing at the locked box, he released it, knowing that she would tell Lee, knowing that if she'd had the chance before she died, Allie would have told him herself.

Elle watched Lee from the window, fuming as he walked up to Frank's house and pounded on the door. Through the closed window she heard him call Frank's name. She turned away and went after him, knowing that Frank was unprepared for what was headed his way.

....

FORTY-THREE

Frank bolted upright when he heard his name. He ran downstairs, trying not to wake Marigold, and flung open the front door to find Lee visibly shaking as he restrained himself from lunging. Lee wasn't a fighter, but as Frank looked at him, he felt like Lee was hovering just outside himself. He saw the large, hollow eyes and collapsed face of Lee, and knew that something was horribly wrong.

"Lee—?"

Elle quietly walked up behind Lee and up the steps to stand close to Frank. Her appearance startled Lee, and for a moment his rage sputtered into confusion. And then, if there had been any doubt about the truth of what Elle had told him, seeing her standing next to Frank as if they were comrades, there was none left.

Lee suddenly felt repulsed by her, a vile figure harboring grotesque secrets, slinking around in the early mornings to see Frank. He didn't recognize her. The features of her face that he had once so loved seemed foreign and stolen, a face transplanted but never quite worn with the same natural grace as its original. He felt sick.

"I told him," Elle said to Frank.

Frank looked at her questioningly and she nodded. *So it's happened already. So soon.* He looked at Lee and understood the sunken expression, and it dawned on him that the glint in his eyes was not yet one of pain, but of anger. He backed away involuntarily.

Lee saw Frank's weight shift, and didn't need him to verify Elle's words any further. His subtle movement told Lee what he already knew was true. He stood, looking away from Elle and Frank, a hideous pair, and became a raging mix of betrayal, desperation, and helplessness. His insides were so contradictory that he stood paralyzed, wishing that he could die right there on the front steps.

Nervous to break the silence, Frank spoke quietly, guiltily.

"She came to me early on and told me that there were complications. She asked me to take care of you if anything happened to her, and asked me to help take care of the baby, because she knew you couldn't do it alone. She didn't want me to tell you, because she knew what it would do to you."

Lee heard none of it. His voice shook when he spoke, a low, choked growl.

"She didn't have to die. I have nothing."

Elle saw the desperation in Lee and understood deeply the pain out of which she had been created. She hated that it was her words that were the cause of his pain, but knew that he deserved the truth. That Allie wanted him to know the truth. She knew why Frank had done what he had done, and if nothing else, she had fulfilled an important role for Lee. For Allie.

She moved toward Lee. *He still has me, after all.* But even to herself that thought seemed untrue. She couldn't place why.

Lee recoiled and she backed away, feeling suddenly scared and confused. Frank's voice came between them.

"We all loved Allie, Lee. I couldn't tell you. She only wanted to make sure you would be okay."

Lee looked at him through glassy eyes, overwhelmed, defeated. His body was still paralyzed as he tried to process. *At least Elle has the decency to look away,* he thought as he saw Frank watching him stupidly. Without thinking, without planning, he felt his fist curl into a ball and swing through the air, punching Frank directly in the face. It infuriated him that he felt his own hesitation, that he hadn't taken a full swing, that the impact had barely touched Frank's nose and would only leave a nice bruise on one side of his face.

Frank stumbled, but didn't retaliate. A small, slow stream of blood gathered beneath his nose. He couldn't blame Lee for doing it. He understood. The anger had finally turned to pain. As upsetting as it was, he knew that Lee was hearing what he was saying, understood the rationale. He might not forgive him, but somewhere buried deep, he understood Frank's position. After a moment, he said all he could say.

"I'm sorry."

FORTY-FOUR

....

Marigold was awakened by voices coming from downstairs. She could only hear the tone of Frank's voice, not understanding, but hearing the tension between his words like a stretched rubber band.

She tiptoed down the stairs, listening, and walked up behind Frank, pulling her robe tight around her as the winter air crept in through the open door.

"What's going on?" she asked.

Frank addressed Marigold, his bloody nose already only a tint of gathered red, but kept looking at Lee.

"She told Lee."

The simplicity of those three words, and Marigold's understanding of them without further explanation, jolted Lee back to a state of fury.

"You knew?" said Lee in disbelief. "You all knew?" *Even Marigold.*

He wouldn't have expected Marigold to tell him, but he wouldn't have expected her to know either. He backed away from the three of them looking down at him from the top of the steps. He looked at Elle as he backed away, hopelessly confused. The only person he wanted to talk to was Allie, the very person he wanted to talk about. But as he looked at Elle's face, and Allie's face looked back at him, he knew definitively that they weren't Allie's eyes that he was looking into, no matter how much he had tried to make it so. But he couldn't help himself.

"Why didn't you tell me?" he asked Elle, talking as if she were Allie. "This didn't have to happen."

Lee was overcome. He walked away into the darkness, lost, before Elle tried to respond.

Elle looked at Frank's beaten face, a red mark blooming purple where Lee's fist had made contact, and he looked away.

"It'll be fine," said Frank as he watched his friend retreat into the dark.

Marigold addressed Elle. "You could have told him that you just found out. You weren't keeping it a secret from him—we were."

Elle shook her head. "He already knows that. He wasn't talking to me just now. He was talking to Allie."

FORTY-FIVE

....

Lee felt their conniving eyes on him, and hated their words for being true. He staggered into the night, into the deserted town. Lights assaulted him, seeming brighter than they were. Noises seemed louder, streets more winding, buildings taller.

He desperately wished that Allie were there, as desperately as he had wished it in the hours after her death. He felt just as gutted as he had then, just as raw, as if death itself had scratched away at his insides before deciding that he should live. He lost his daughter, and lost his wife in her attempt to birth that daughter. He wished that he could go back. He wished that he had known. He wished that he hadn't told her how much he wanted a daughter.

It wasn't fair to Allie, killing herself for Alma to be born, and it wasn't fair to Alma, an innocent soul lost forever inside her dead mother's womb. It wasn't fair to him, left without Allie, without Alma. And it could have been prevented. Allie could still be with him. The unborn soul of Alma, not yet pieced together, could have lived on inside them until the time was right, until science figured out how to prevent what had happened. He could still have Allie. And he could still have Alma. A different Alma, but she wouldn't have been brought into the world only to exist eternally in the nothingness that is death after being brought out from the nothingness that exists before birth. It seemed cruel to her to give her a consciousness but no experiences to fill that consciousness. From nothing to nothing.

It could have been prevented. Why didn't she just tell me? Allie, Allie. He called to her in his mind despite knowing that there was no one to hear him. *Why didn't you tell me?*

He followed his feet with only a vague notion of where they were taking him. He wanted to be nowhere, but couldn't stay in his house. He let his body guide him through the town while his mind spun, noticing that his limbs had no feeling unless they moved. As he walked through the dark, his ears perked, compensating for his diminished vision. The usual hum of silence was absent. The wind contorted itself through the empty branches of the trees overhead, licking his face. The familiar whisper of his name entered his ears with each gust, then disappeared as it so often did in his presence.

When he looked up, he was on the opposite side of town along a quiet, tree-lined street. Above his head hung a small sign attached to a quaint, boutique hotel. The Chevalier. It was painted a mossy green and boasted flower beds and brassy, antique decorations.

It was a side of town that he didn't venture into often, a hushed, spacious area that sat in the opposite direction of the lab. There were a few bed-and-breakfasts in the area, but not many cafés, and not much reason to stay there other than to spend the night in a real bed, away from the chaos of the city, while passing through.

The Chevalier was the most expensive hotel in the area, only four floors, but top-notch accommodations. It was simple, elegant, and cozy. Mostly used by businessmen who went into the city from the other side of town for meetings but didn't want to stay in the dirty bustle overnight, and wealthy couples who would stay there to simply relax by the fireplace, sip afternoon tea in the library's lounge, spend time together for a long weekend before going back to work. It wasn't a large hotel, but despite having few reading rooms and only one main bar, it always seemed quiet and private, no matter how fully booked it actually was. It was part of the charm of The Chevalier, to make its guests feel like they were renting it to be their private quarters. It wasn't grand or shiny, but it was comfortable. A no-fuss hotel with a staff that seemed to know just what its guests needed before the guests even knew themselves.

Lee had never before been inside. Despite it being within walking distance to his own home, Lee had wanted to take Allie there for a weekend just to experience it. It wasn't that he never had the chance. He had many chances. He just never did.

He burst into the lobby, which was empty except for a single concierge, and spotted small stairs to the right of the front desk. They led to the second floor. Lee noticed that the lobby was less of a first floor and more of a sunken room on the second floor. The thought bothered him, as if he didn't have a right to have any thoughts but grief at that moment. He flung himself up the steps, landing at the top with only two leaps, and looked for room F. It was only three doors down the hall. He banged on the door and waited, hearing heavy footsteps approach. The door swung open. Eamonn's impressive girth spanned nearly the entire doorway. His face lengthened with a look of surprise as he laid eyes on Lee.

Lee was slightly out of breath and looked pale and clammy, as if he had just run a marathon while fighting the flu. He was trembling. The bags under his eyes looked more purple than usual against his pallid skin. His caved shoulders gave his clothes, though not physically different, a distressed look, as if they hadn't been changed in days. The air around him hung low and heavy, a cloud of anguish.

"What happened to you?"

It took a moment for Lee to answer, not knowing what to say now that he was standing in front of Eamonn. He hadn't planned on going to him, but as he walked away from Frank's house his feet took over, his mind preoccupied and disoriented, and he found himself walking farther away from the cul-de-sac, farther away from the familiar Centre-Ville in the direction of Eamonn's hotel. He would be able to make sense of it all for Lee.

Eamonn had always been a kind of watchman, discreetly looking out for those around him, observing but not participating in their dealings unless they needed help, or were about to find themselves in a difficult situation. It seemed ironic to Lee that just as Eamonn showed up, his life spiraled out of his control, as if Eamonn had sensed it from across the world and swooped in to protect him from his own crumbling walls. But it seemed suspect at the same time. How could he have known that Lee's life was about to fall apart if he hadn't spoken to Frank?

Or Marigold, Lee thought with surprising disgust. The fact that Marigold knew before he did was unbearable. Why wouldn't Eamonn know? And Benny? Didi? How about Sonja? Or Julie? Did everyone know? Was everyone privy to this most personal and terrible secret? Did they regard him with pity behind his back? Watch him with watery eyes as his neighbors watched him in fear and distrust?

But Eamonn—Lee couldn't imagine Eamonn taking part. Frank had his flaws, Lee knew. But Eamonn. He expected different things from Eamonn. Though he wasn't as close with him as he was with Frank, he regarded Eamonn as a loyal friend. A man honest to a fault and unwaveringly trustworthy.

"You never liked Elle," Lee began. "Never liked the idea of her."

Eamonn sighed and stepped back, letting Lee inside. He poured a drink for each of them.

"That's right. But you did a good job with her," Eamonn reassured him.

"Why didn't you like her?"

"It seemed unfair to Allie."

"She's different, you know. Frank told you what we're doing?"

Eamonn nodded.

"It's not working," Lee said flatly. "I'm losing her."

Eamonn looked at Lee, debating whether Lee had come to him seeking ears to talk to or words to listen to.

"What you never accepted, Lee, is that you already lost her," Eamonn said.

Lee soaked in Eamonn's words. "And it's happening again," he replied.

"I think it's not her that's different. It's you. And it's affecting her."

Lee remembered what Elle had said to him when she walked with him back to the bridge. *"You don't think me not remembering will affect your memory?"* Eamonn was right. He suddenly wished that he'd had Eamonn watch over the entire trial, keeping everything—and everyone—in check.

"When Allie was pregnant with Alma, she told Frank that giving birth might kill her. She never told me."

"And Frank never told you."

Lee shook his head. "She asked him not to."

Eamonn nodded in understanding.

"You don't seem surprised," Lee said.

"I'm not."

The blood stood ready to boil in Lee's veins. "Did she tell you too?"

"No. But that sounds very much like Allie. Doing what she can to give you happiness, to protect you." Eamonn spoke softly, but bluntly. "She died for you. Acknowledge her death."

Lee hung his head, completely defeated, overcome by guilt about everything that he had selfishly done and felt since Allie's death. He felt the sudden urge to sink into the floor, to forget all that he knew and all that he was.

"It's late," said Eamonn. "Why don't you get a room here for the night."

It was late. Lee was exhausted. But as much as he wanted to be anywhere but his own house, it was the only place he would feel comfortable. He shook his head, partly because he didn't know what else to do.

"No. I'm going home." He walked away without looking at Eamonn, without looking back, the concierge watching him curiously, the strange man dissolving into the night.

....

FORTY-SIX

Marigold stood in the kitchen with Frank making pancakes. Frank was seated at the table, his head hung low.

"What do you want to do today?" she asked, trying to take his mind off Lee.

Frank shrugged and looked out the window. "I don't know. It's not really nice out today."

Marigold was silent. She flipped the pancakes in the air.

"I never understood how you could do that," Frank said.

She was surprised to hear him playing along with her avoidance of the topic.

"What, this?" She flipped the pancakes twice.

"I mean I get it, but where do you learn something like that?"

"I don't know. I guess I just picked it up," she said, piling them onto a plate for Frank. She sat next to him, waiting for him to take a bite. He stared at them. The usually pleasant aroma nauseated him. He glanced at an expectant Marigold, and picked up his fork.

"Wow," he said with a mouth full of food. "These are really delicious." He was sincere. They were. He just couldn't enjoy them.

He swallowed a few bites, then pushed the plate away. Marigold said nothing, but pushed the plate back in front of him and smiled. Frank smiled back at her, suddenly appreciating her. He thought of how devastated he would be if he lost Marigold, a thought that hadn't occurred to him before. She was always just there. He didn't know what he would do if one day she weren't anymore.

Marigold understood what Frank was thinking as he reached out to grab her hand. She thought of how lucky they were, how simple and easy their lives were, and how quickly that could change.

"I could never replace you, you know," Frank said to Marigold.

"I know," she replied.

And Lee couldn't replace Allie, she thought as Frank cleared the rest of the pancakes. The image amused her. *Life goes on*, she thought with a smirk. No matter the situation, no matter how upset or preoccupied, a body needs to eat. Nothing more to it.

She thought about what complexity minds bring to the physical world, how basic and humane a world it would seem if people only passed through with no consciousness of love, desire, loss, despair. No anxiety about death, which was worse than the nothingness of death itself.

She knew that one day she would lose Frank, no matter which of them died first. That one day she would lose her mind, and that everything in it would be lost, wasted. And yet, they carried on flipping pancakes and holding hands as if it mattered. Because it does. Because as long as they're alive and conscious, they might as well. Because life goes on whether you're flipping pancakes or digging graves. Because there is consciousness of love, desire, loss, despair, whether or not it would be more simple without it.

She thought of Lee, how he had held on so tightly to the past that he lost his footing. How he was being spun as the earth turned, how the combination of love, desire, loss, and despair had produced a piece of his past and placed it in the space right before his eyes, and how that piece of his past changed his perception of time and place. How it had derailed his life, which had followed a trajectory that his consciousness could understand, onto a path that had become thicker with aloneness than he had been prepared to fathom.

How simple it could all be one day, and how complex the next.

She scanned Frank's bruised face, seeing how quickly it had healed, from the inside out. A body will do that without a conscious thought, but a body without a consciousness was likely to be dead. Its presence necessary to the physical, but only apparent after it's gone.

"How does it feel?" Marigold asked, gesturing toward Frank's bruise.

"It feels terrible. But the face is healing fine," Frank responded with irony.

"Have you heard anything?"

Frank shook his head. "Nothing."

Marigold sat silently for a moment. "More pancakes?"

Frank looked up at her. Sometimes he could see her youth spill out at unexpected times, and sometimes she used it to lighten him. He wondered if he would always feel her youth, even in his old age.

"Is Elle all right?" Marigold asked, approaching the topic outright.

"She is for now. But it won't last long."

"I know he needs space, but he isn't going to come to you first. Why don't you give him a call?"

Frank was tired. It had been easier over the previous few days to ignore it, helped by the fact that Lee wouldn't answer his calls. But Marigold was right. He was out of time and had to make a decision.

"Yeah. Yeah, I'll do that."

"But—" Marigold started.

"What?" prompted Frank.

"I think before you call you should decide what's going to happen. He can't make decisions right now. You have a chance to fix it right now and make the decision that's going to be best for everyone, even if he doesn't see it. You didn't want to hurt him before, but it happened anyway. Now is your chance to make it right without causing any more pain."

"Isn't that kind of like kicking him while he's down?"

"No, it's pushing him through the mud so he can get to the other side."

"What if we both get stuck?"

"That's why you should decide before you push. He's already stuck, and he's going to grab on to you in desperation, like a drowning person pushes another underwater to push himself up. If you're prepared, he won't drag you into it, and you can pull him out."

"I'll be pulling him into a world he doesn't want to see."

"But at least he'll see. And if he sees that Elle is better off, I think he'll understand."

He thought about the idea of Elle being better off. It seemed that even Marigold had come to see her as a creature with feelings, a consciousness, who could perceive and feel better and worse just as any other human.

With or without Lee, he had to continue. They were so close to the end of the trial. He was tired, but would finish what he started. It was just a question of how he would go about it.

FORTY-SEVEN

In the cul-de-sac the leaves scuttled in droves across the ground. The wind was strong, whistling. Drops of rain fell from the trees though the skies were dry. The leaves turned and turned over, landing far from where they started when the gusts died down.

Lee sat on the floor of his study, his back against the wall next to the closed door, the blinds drawn. Different shades of dark filled the room as the days and nights passed. He didn't move. He was unshaven, unbathed, sunken. The phone on his desk rang, the pitch sounding strange from his place underneath it. It went to voicemail.

"Lee, it's Frank. I understand that you don't want to hear from me, but we need you—you can't abandon the reboot—Elle won't be able to process your absence—"

Lee reached for the phone and hung it up, cutting off Frank's voice. His legs throbbed, having felt weight for the first time in days. His breath was short, his body protesting the energy used to stand. It depleted him. He sat once more, letting himself melt again into the wall, into the floor, until his legs stopped throbbing and his heart stopped palpitating. Until he could no longer feel his body, as if it didn't exist.

Marigold was standing over Frank's slouched shoulders, waiting for him to fill her in.

"He hung up." It didn't surprise him, but he had hoped that the idea of Elle not processing his absence would spur him back into action, at least until the reboot was finished.

"What are you going to do?"

"I'm going to finish the reboot."

"Is she going to remember this?"

Frank shook his head, feeling regretful. He hadn't realized how he himself had gotten used to Elle being around, being aware, the last true vestige of Allie.

"The biggest mistake we made when we first created her was making her aware of her own creation story. If she remembers this, she'll try to understand why

Lee abandoned her—that's how she'll see it—and will start destroying herself again. She doesn't need to have self-awareness. She needs to function properly, and do her job as a companion. That was the whole first idea. To provide companionship to someone who has no one."

"So then, she's going to forget about Lee?"

Frank let the silence hang in the air, then tried to justify his decision.

"We had a plan. A very specific plan. If he won't help finish the reboot, then yes. I'll have to remove the memories of Lee, too."

Marigold thought for a moment before beginning to speak.

"You know, I have a feeling he knows that. Lee was always logical. You said he was even when Allie died, when nothing made sense. I think he knows what has to happen, but can't face it."

"You think he's just stepping aside?"

Frank looked back at his computer screen, contemplating. Marigold shrugged in response as if to say, "It's only a theory," and left the room.

....

FORTY-NINE

The next morning Frank prepared himself to see Lee. He was nervous, unsure if Lee would have become more angry as time wore on, or if he simply needed space. As he left, he saw Mrs. Thatcher walking toward Lee's house. He waited for a moment to be sure, then ran after her, calling to her quietly.

"Mrs. Thatcher!"

She spun around, her eyes wide in surprise as if she had been shaken from a deep thought.

"Oh!" she said. "Good morning." She turned back toward Lee's front door and made a motion as if about to knock, ignoring Frank.

"Mrs. Thatcher I have to ask you not to disturb Lee," Frank said quickly and carefully.

She looked back at him with searing hatred.

"And why is that?"

"He's not well at the moment."

"Then I should check on him," she replied curtly.

"Mrs. Thatcher I must insist," Frank said, moving closer to her.

"And I must insist as well."

"What is it exactly that you want?" The harshness in his voice was unexpected, even to him. He could feel his face turning red, a mixture of anger and shame at his tone.

Mrs. Thatcher stepped back, surprised.

"He's going to make me immortal!" she blurted, dropping any pretense of politeness.

"Dear God help us all."

Mrs. Thatcher glared at Frank.

"He said he would," she stated.

"I don't think that's what he said," Frank replied.

"How do you know? You weren't there. I want to talk to him. No more green bananas!"

Frank paused, his mind halted. "Green bananas?"

"You know, waiting—never mind," she moved closer to the door to knock. "I need to talk to Lee."

Frank stepped in front of her.

"Okay, but not today. He'll tell you everything you need to know, but not right now." He spoke to her as if she were a restless child.

She stared at him for a moment before spinning on her heel and walking away without a word.

Frank watched her, the breath he had been holding in his lungs released. His chest fell.

"Immortal," he muttered to himself. "Come on now."

As he faced the door he felt his heart pumping thick blood through his body. He took a moment to let his nerves calm and refocus his thoughts before knocking. The first knock he could barely hear himself, and he realized just how tense his body still was. He instinctively touched his face where Lee had hit him, recalling how Lee had walked alone into the dark. He knocked again, more forcefully, hoping that by showing up in person Lee would be more inclined to speak to him.

Upstairs, Lee heard the knock but didn't budge. He felt paralyzed. His eyes stared straight ahead, throbbing with every sideways glance. His arms hung heavily at his sides as if detached. He suddenly felt each vertebra of his spine against the wall. Pictured them flattened. He imagined how they would feel if he sat up away from the wall, the pain no longer blocked, rushing to each bone in his back as they inflated from their flattened state.

The knock replayed quietly in his head, a pattern that repeated incessantly, filling the sensory emptiness that he experienced in the dark on the floor.

Frank hadn't expected Lee to open the door, but he waited for the obligatory few seconds before letting himself in.

When he entered he felt the stale air rush around him as if awakened from a deep sleep. The lights were all off. It smelled of abandoned, uninhabited cold.

"Lee?" Frank called.

Frank looked around the first floor of the house, knowing that the darkness of the downstairs wasn't an indication that Lee wasn't there. He recalled some time ago entering Lee's house and finding him standing in the corner of the living room, pressed against the wall, the whites of his wide eyes the only sign that he was present.

The utter quiet of the house made him feel like an unwelcome presence. He shuffled his feet quietly along the wood floor, each creak disturbing the silent slumber of the four walls around him. His ears were perked, desperate to hear anything aside from the hum of electricity, the only invisible life coursing through the air.

He approached the stairs and suddenly felt his throat tighten. It all felt very familiar to him, a nightmare he had relived over and over again in his sleep since Allie died. That he would walk up those stairs, the very stairs before him, and find Lee in a heap on the floor, drained of life.

Frank climbed the stairs with weighted boots. He saw the closed door of the study, and knew that Lee was inside despite the absence of a telltale strip of light at his feet.

He walked in, turned on the lamp, and saw Lee sitting on the floor right inside the door, staring into the black confines of the room.

"Lee—"

He had seen him like that before. The images rushed back to Frank, and his own sadness revived itself as if it were that very day, over a decade ago, when Lee returned from the hospital as a single member of his family instead of a family of three.

Frank sat down next to him, reliving the tortured months that followed Allie's death. The days of shocked silence. The fear of leaving Lee out of sight. The inability to diminish the pain, wishing time would move faster, mend quicker. He had felt back then that he didn't have a right to mourn Allie's death as he had. He wasn't married to her. Had only really become friends with her because of Lee. He thought of how her death must have affected Lee, and thought himself inappropriate for shedding his own tears when there was someone much closer to her who had lost her. But in her death he was reminded of how much he had admired her, and so he had grieved privately, parallel to the endless days of sorrow that would consume Lee. He recalled the black of those days as he sat next to Lee, as if they had never ended. The desperate, futile wish for her return, the inexplicable pain. A physical pain with an intangible root and an impossible cure.

"Don't do this again, Lee."

There was no response. No glimmer in his eyes that showed that he was aware of Frank next to him, that he was hearing his words. He pushed aside the memories of the days following Allie's death and forced himself to speak.

"I'm sorry. I should have told you about Allie."

The words sounded loud to him. Out of place. Somehow existing in the wrong time.

"No. You were loyal to her."

The sound of Lee's voice startled Frank. Not only had he spoken, but he had spoken determinedly. And he understood the position that Frank had been in. It was a relief for him to see that Lee was not in fact receding into catatonia. It was a relief to hear him confirm that Frank had done the right thing. The lump in his throat dissipated. He had missed it before, but he could now see that Lee was processing. There was a long silence as he tried to figure out what to say that wouldn't put Lee back into a shell. But Lee spoke first.

"I know why Elle changed."

"What?"

"The replacement memories. I know why they're not working."

Frank waited for him to go on. Lee took a breath, as if it would require much effort for him to explain what he meant.

"The replacements stand alone, like islands. Not connected to any other memories. Not intertwined with her personhood like they were the first time we input the entire memory package. Each memory that we remove leaves an unbridgeable gap, cutting the continuity, severing connections. When we input the replacement, we filled the gap, and we fused the new memory with the old strings of memories. But there is a fault line on each side of the new memory where we fused it. And that fault line is where things go wrong. When the reboot is finished, she'll be something completely different."

It was what he had been on the verge of seeing before Elle showed up and told him about Allie. It hit him suddenly, without warning, when he arrived back home after seeing Eamonn, as if it had been waiting for him to fill his mind with something else in order to allow it to reveal itself to him unpressured.

The clock ticked on the wall. Lee and Frank sat together in silence. Lee, resigned. Frank, contemplative. He pictured the receptors in Elle's head very clearly as Lee spoke. It reminded him of something he had known long before ever meeting Lee, and it suddenly made sense to him.

"When I was at university, I had this professor who was just perfect. She had these blue eyes, and freckles all over the place. Legs," he looked at Lee for emphasis. "Her hair was a little bit too long, but she never really wore it down anyway. One day she projected this image. A long strip of red and nothing else. But it was all the different reds. On one end was a red that looked pink, and on the other end was a red so dark that it looked black. She pointed to various points on the strip and asked us what color it was. We said red every time. Then she asked one girl up front to pick the one that looked most red to her. And she did. And the professor pointed to the one she thought was most red, and it wasn't the same red as the student's. And she said to us, 'We have pink on this end, and black on this end. At what point along this line is red no longer red?' And we couldn't agree on a specific point. There was no definitive point at which red became not red. But as we moved along the line, we didn't even realize that we were changing from pink to black."

Frank paused to let Lee digest this. He had spoken just as much to himself as he had to Lee, picturing the change that occurred in Elle along the strip of reds as he explained. Lee listened silently with extinguished eyes, but Frank knew that he understood.

"Kat," Frank reminisced.

Lee frowned, confused. Frank continued.

"Her name was Kat."

Frank stood up and walked toward the door with his hand on the light switch, not waiting for Lee to respond. He paused before turning out the light but stopped himself from saying anything more. He had given Lee enough to absorb. He shut off the light and closed the door.

Lee sat, pondering the reds. He heard Frank leave through the front door and became aware of how tired he was of sitting, of feeling empty. His body made itself known to Lee, his spine hurting at points against the wall, his ankles cracking with stiffness. He became aware of himself in space from the inside, feeling his limbs without moving or touching them. He looked around after a moment, absorbing the sameness of how his books were arranged on the shelf, where the empty coffee mugs sat. The familiarity of his study and its present arrangement struck him, pulling him from deep within his mind and thrusting him back into the present. He had known where he was, but it only then occurred to him. He got up slowly, a frail participant in the world, and sat back down, his heart sprinting. He closed his eyes, trying to calm the thumping in his chest.

The day passed entirely, unseen by Lee, who awoke hours later. The rest of his body didn't move, only his eyes looked around the room, already adjusted to the darkness before him as if it were their natural environment. He awakened fully at once, as though the last hours of his eyes closed were just moments, uninterrupted thoughts. The pain of his spine against the wall had subsided, numb from having not been moved. The clock ticked on. He assumed that it had done so the whole time he had been asleep, but he couldn't be sure since he hadn't witnessed it.

He made his second attempt that day to lift himself off the floor. His legs folding on each other like they were made of old clay, breaking at the joints instead of bending as they should. His body cracked back into motion. The pain returned to the bones of his spine as he peeled away from the wall, sure that he had become so melded with it that the paint would peel along with him. His blood, realizing that he still had limbs, that they were still usable, rushed around on the inside of his body while his pounding heart shortened his breath. He felt high and gangly. Felt the compulsion to slouch and make himself small like the rest of the room.

The desk, from a new top view, looked less protective than it had from the ground below it. He looked at where he had been sitting, where he had sat for days, and regretted the time spent there. He had tried to get up a few times, to move, but it was as if his wish were held in a body outside his own, grabbing at his hands to pull him to his feet, but failing, making him feel as if he were in a deep sleep from which he struggled to wake.

Without turning on any lights, without switching on his computer, without checking the messages on his phone, he strode toward the door and slipped away.

FIFTY

....

There was a small bridge that connected two parts of town separated by a river. It was an old bridge, surrounded on either entrance by thick trees. The steel of the bridge floor was covered with thick slabs of wood rotting from underneath. Lee had always thought that it was too small for the cars that drove on it, likely built before there were cars, or when cars were smaller. A path had been paved on either end, and in the summer, groups of girls could be seen with baskets on the front of their bikes riding back and forth between the two sides of town. The path disappeared at the start of the bridge, and then reappeared on the other side. It was not a long distance, taking merely seconds to pass from one side to the other, but it was enough so that, if timed right, a car could approach the bridge from the bend in the road, and its driver might not see a bike swerving inward off the path to get on the bridge. Or indeed, it would be as easy as a blink for a tire to get caught between two planks of wood, for it to get tossed in an unintended direction, and for a car to have nowhere to go but into the rail on the side.

It had never happened before, but Lee had imagined endless such scenarios occurring on that quiet, quaint bridge. He had worried when Allie took walks along the bike path. From it, looking out through the spring trees, she could see faraway fields of dark soil arranged in perfect rows. She didn't do it often, but Lee distrusted the bridge, thought it unnecessarily dangerous, even if it was small. Despite all of his imaginings of what might occur on the bridge, he hadn't imagined that what would kill her would be inside her, implanted by him. Growing until her body couldn't handle it, another body feeding off hers, killing her, and, having nothing left to give, her empty body killing it. Killing each other.

Lee walked along the small bridge, no undesirable scenarios coming to mind. He didn't appear to be aware of where he was, his head hung low as his feet carried him along. But he was aware indeed. He stopped at the side of the bridge and looked out, leaning on the rail, isolated. Not high enough for him to jump. If he was lucky, he would just break a few bones hitting some rocks that he couldn't see, but it wouldn't kill him. His broken body would float to the surface, presenting him again to the world like a living rag doll.

No bikes would be riding along the path, not in the cold, not at that late hour. Cars would be few, most already having been driven home and tucked away for the night. Small waves tumbled over each other, showing Lee where there were shallow rocks. He imagined his body colliding with them and, as his bones were released of their structure, deflating, having nothing else inside to keep him together.

The water below him was the only sound he heard aside from the muffled tires of the few cars that passed. It was more than he expected to see. He wondered what time it actually was, whether it was indeed late at night or just that the sky had turned early at the request of winter.

The moon reflected in the water. Leaves skittered onto the bridge with the wind, and scuttled past Lee's black-soled shoes. He straightened up and backed away slowly, feeling defeated, not knowing what time it was, what day it was, why he had gone to the bridge. He began walking back, watching the cars pass him by.

There was no divider between them, but for the first time Lee noticed a little dirt sidewalk alongside the steel of the bridge. Indeed, he had been standing on that very dirt looking out into the water below. *Is this a way to distinguish between the bike path and the road? Perhaps something unfortunate did happen,* he thought. *And they had to put this here to prevent it from happening again.* He hovered along the side, the soles of his shoes squishing into the rain-filled dirt, feeling the wind in his face.

Lights came around the bend onto the bridge. Another car. Still too big for the bridge. *How silly it was,* he thought, *to think a bit of dirt on the side of the already narrow bridge would be a sufficient sidewalk.* It was his last thought before he stepped calmly, assuredly, forward into the oncoming car.

FIFTY-ONE

....

Spring was nearly growing into summer. The air was thin, as if a winter-long cloud had dissipated. The blue of the sky made the colors of the blooming trees look richer, fuller. The tiny flecks of pollen floated blissfully to the ground, no breeze to carry them far away from their origins.

Elle was out. She meandered slowly through the crowd, shopping at the local farmers market. Smiling, greeting other folks from the neighborhood whom she recognized. Her hair had grown. Her skin showed a healthy hint of tan. She seemed to have been integrated into the neighborhood without struggle. Seemed perfectly normal. A far cry from how the neighborhood had received her so many months before, with trepidation, with fear, with uncertainty. They seemed to have accepted her as if she were just another young woman who had moved into the neighborhood. How quickly they forget.

Her melancholy expression had been erased from her face. Her movements were less stifled. Her arms seemed to float weightlessly as she lifted sweet corn to her nose and inhaled. She was striking, as always, but appeared to have a glow about her that both allowed her to fit in with the rest of the summer-giddy crowd and stand out among them.

As she hovered over baskets full of bright red tomatoes, she noticed a man walking slowly, uncoordinated, with a cane in the distance. She recognized him. His tall figure was diminished by his hunch over his cane, but distinguishable. Her smile faltered, seeing the man struggle, so dependent on his cane, but returned as she paid for her vegetables. She wondered briefly if his limp could be psychosomatic—she had read about that somewhere before—but no, he looked disfigured indeed. Without seeing his face she could picture the expression on it solely from his gait. Sunken eyes, a permanent frown. Lips lifted upward toward a wrinkled nose. A look of permanent disgust, or pain, or rotten smell. She finished paying for her vegetables, not taking her eyes off him, then stepped away from the market. No one around her noticed him, noticed her watching him. Holding the bag in the crook of her arm, she followed in his direction.

FIFTY-TWO

At the top of the stairs outside Lee's house, Elle stood, taking a breath before knocking. A long moment passed before Frank opened the door. Seeing him, Elle stepped back in confusion. *What house am I at?*

"Oh—I was looking for—" Elle started.

Frank was surprised to see her standing before him.

"Elle!"

"Oh—yes—um—"

"Oh. I know you don't remember me. We used to know each other."

"I'm sorry, I don't—"

"It's okay. You're here to see Lee."

Frank stepped aside to let her in. She walked in and looked around, not recognizing the house. A tiny green cactus sat on the end table next to the couch. It was thriving.

"Let me go get Lee," Frank said.

We used to know each other? The words finally hit Elle, but she couldn't remember ever meeting him.

Frank walked down the hallway just next to the stairs that led to another section of the house. Elle wondered what was back there, not having that hidden section in her own house. She had assumed that they all looked the same on the inside, as they did on the outside. They were identical on the outside.

She continued looking around, feeling familiar in the space and assuming that it was because her house had nearly the same setup. She sat at the kitchen table and waited for Lee, folding and unfolding her hands. She straightened herself in her seat, then realized how unnatural she probably looked, and sank back down to try to look relaxed. She heard a click coming from the hall and looked up, the tension immediately returning to her body.

A crippled Lee emerged with a cane. He looked very lived-in, like someone who was being kept alive, but was not present. He spotted Elle when the hallway opened up into the room and froze. Frank walked over to the kitchen table where Elle was sitting, and pulled out a chair for Lee. He didn't move for a moment, looking at Elle. The decided frown on his face raised slightly, then lowered again. He shuffled over and sat across from her, looking down at the table.

"Lee," said Frank. "I'm going to go ahead and finish up the report from my office. I think I have everything I need."

Frank left Lee and Elle sitting at the kitchen table across from each other. There was a long, tense silence. Elle started to tear up as she looked at Lee, but swallowed it and spoke.

"I heard that you were done with rehab. The doctors told me that I should give you space, but I saw you out by the market—"

Lee dismissed what she was about to say with a wave of his hand. He knew that she was remembering his group of scientists as doctors. It pained him to think that he was part of the lie. That she believed it so earnestly.

Mistaking the expression of disgust for himself as being directed toward her, she wiped away a tear and continued.

"Um."

Lee looked at her. He felt terrible seeing her like that, but he was still harboring a bitterness over her, and remained closed off. She continued to speak, trying to control the shake in her voice.

"After the accident, I didn't even know who I was. I knew my name, but didn't know what it meant. But I remembered you. I didn't know anything about you, but I remembered you—something—I don't know— you were—somebody I used to know. And then when the doctors finally told me what happened—I started to remember. I remember seeing the headlights—I don't know where I was going—and I remember you—someone—pushing me out of the way. I don't know if I am a stranger to you, but you don't feel like a stranger to me."

Lee listened silently, bitterly, as the lies dripped from her mouth. Lies that were planted in her head after his suicide attempt.

It had given him joy at first when Elle kept remembering him. It began as her recalling something about someone. Then she started recalling a connection that she'd had with someone.

"There is someone," she would say, "in the periphery of my mind. I can't place who it is. But I knew him well long ago. Who is that man?"

And the scientists would remove the lurking memory of Lee.

Then she would say, "There is someone—I can't remember who—but there is someone. There is something about him, I just can't remember what."

He had felt agony over being erased from her mind over and over, but at the same time was elated that his presence in her was strong enough to permeate her memories. She was holding on to him somewhere else. Holding on to his essence despite not having an image of him in her mind.

The team saw that removing the memory of him each time wasn't working. She would fill it back in like a cracked dam fills a reservoir. So they used his sticky presence in her mind as part of a story. Created a lie that would explain who the someone was and why she could only remember him vaguely, yet have strong feelings about him. He hated being a part of it, but savored their connection. Despite the false explanation for it, it remained. Her mind had been determined to hold on to Lee, and it was a testament to his efforts to strengthen their connection when her mind had been fully intact.

Elle continued.

"I hope I'm not intruding. I just wanted to say thank you, for giving me another chance to live. And I'm sorry that you suffered for it."

Elle grabbed Lee's hand to show her sincerity. Lee returned the gesture with silence. Not knowing what else to say, she stood up and tried to pull her hand away. Lee stopped her for a second, gripping his fingers tightly around hers and looking into her eyes. He wanted to tell her. He couldn't bear listening to the lie, watching her believe it sincerely and fully. If he told her, she would remember him. He wanted to see it. To see her remember him. To cut through the lie and justify her memory of their connection. But he couldn't. It was too much to tell. Too much to erase and replace all over. It would be futile, like it had never happened. Like he had never told her. Like it was now, again.

The sudden gesture of Lee gripping her hand surprised Elle, but she didn't pull away. She looked back at him, waiting. Waiting for him to say something. Waiting for him to release her. Waiting. His eyes were lit, gazing into hers, pleading. For a moment she felt something shudder in her mind, as if she were uncovering, second by second, pieces of herself that she had long forgotten. The ground felt unsteady to her, rippling under her feet, shifting the walls around her. They bowed. *Behind them*, she thought as she watched the walls, *lay all things forgotten. And they are about to snap.*

Then slowly, subtly, she felt him release her. His palm opened. Her hand slipped out of his. After years of reaching, grasping, holding on, he finally let go.

The walls sprang back and the shake of the floor subsided. Elle paused, holding her gaze long enough to see Lee crumble limply back into his seat and cast his eyes downward once more.

She stepped away, her long hair flowing down her back as she walked toward the door. She vanished.

....

FIFTY-THREE

Sunlight streamed in through the open curtains of Lee's windows, casting its rays on the glistening furniture. His house was neat, but used. The cushions on the couch somewhat flat. The cactus, a deep, healthy green, stretching its spines in the hot sun.

Lee wasn't there. In the river near the field where Walter's funeral had taken place, Lee lay face down. His body floated, holding his head halfway out of the water. It was warm. With every breeze it rippled, bobbing up into his ears and then back down below them.

He opened his eyes in the water and watched the life happening below the surface. Though the water was clean he couldn't see far. Only a small fish passing here and there. When his lungs felt sufficiently imploded he lifted his head, the water running off him slowly, silently.

He noticed a woman floating nearby. Branches hanging low in the water separated her from Lee. He got out of the river and stood behind a tree, not hiding from her catching him watching her, but not wanting her to see him. He watched every movement as she ran her lithe arms up and down the surface of the water. She straightened up, her head and shoulders visible above the water. In the same place she had been floating, she stood, the water coming up to her waist. She was topless. Lee watched, wondering who the woman was. She turned around to look in Lee's direction, her eyes landing on him softly, immediately, as if she had known that he had been watching her. As if she had expected it.

He gasped and recoiled as he recognized her. The water in his eyes blurred his focus, but he knew who she was. The woman from the coffee shop, the same ghostly face. He blinked the water away, wishing to see her face fully. Her dark hair was just like Allie's. Her skin the same milky color. Her face, from what his mind could piece together from the blurred features, identical. As the water cleared from his vision, he squinted to see her. He noticed then how the water around her didn't move. Didn't distort around her body as she walked or ripple behind her. It made no sound. He looked at her, a naked body having no physical effect on another body as it passed through it. It made no sense to him.

As he watched her, not caring that she was looking at him, he became more sure that the face he was looking at was Allie's. *A mirage*, he thought. A mirage that had appeared once before at the coffee shop. He tried to remember the other patrons whom he hadn't noticed that night, and remembered feeling as if no one else had seen her. Remembered how she had vanished as soon as she walked out the door, how he couldn't find her even after following only moments behind her.

Without warning, he recalled the night he had watched Elle in her kitchen, followed by a ghostly pair of legs. He questioned again what he had seen, questioned what his eyes fed to his mind and how his mind had processed it in the midst of his overwhelming fear of loss. He recalled how the legs moved the same way, how they moved at the same time, only one pair slightly delayed. How had the legs first appeared in the window? He couldn't remember.

Nonsense, he thought. *My memory is pandering to my present thoughts.*

Suddenly he thought of Elle's hand in his, how he had held it tightly, and how he had let it go. How, when he released her, she had vanished, his front door clicking shut behind her. It had echoed in his mind for hours, vacuuming the sounds of his surroundings and holding them until the echo faded.

As he replayed it in his mind, the topless woman looked directly into his eyes and smiled coyly. She turned back around, facing away from him, and sank into the water.

She never emerged.

ABOUT THE AUTHOR

Kaitlin Puccio is an author, screenwriter, and founder of Bent Frame Entertainment Media. She holds a BA in philosophy from New York University, a JD from Georgetown Law, and an MS in bioethics from Columbia University.

www.kaitlinpuccio.com

www.ingramcontent.com/pod-product-compliance
Lightning Source LLC
Chambersburg PA
CBHW032112110726

47902CB00003B/556